When Day Breaks

When Day Breaks

Mary Jane Clark

An Imprint of HarperCollinsPublishers

LT
M
Clark

This book is a work of fiction. The characters, incidents, and dialogue are drawn from the author's imagination and are not to be construed as real. Any resemblance to actual events or persons, living or dead, is entirely coincidental.

HarperCollins books may be purchased for educational, business, or sales promotional use. For information please write: Special Markets Department, HarperCollins Publishers, 10 East 53rd Street, New York, NY 10022.

FIRST HARPERLUXE™ EDITION

HarperLuxe is a trademark of HarperCollins Publishers

Library of Congress Cataloging-in-Publication Data is available upon request.

ISBN: 978-0-06-144371-8
ISBN-10: 0-06-144371-9

08 09 10 11   ID/RRD   10 9 8 7 6 5 4 3

FOR MARGARET ANN BEHRENDS,

honor student, homecoming queen, weathergirl,
talk-show host, television producer, animal lover,
communicator, humanitarian.
Happy birthday, dear sister, happy birthday to you!

And for all those who struggle with
Fragile X syndrome,
with the persistent hope that a cure is near.

Acknowledgments

In a world where energy is increasingly precious, it never ceases to amaze me how many people are willing to lend me their power, supplying the current to get the book written and published.

This time around, Jennifer Rudolph Walsh and Joni Evans delivered the voltage to inspire a series with a fresh take on KEY News, conveying the idea to a new publisher and leaving us all revved up at the prospects of the Sunrise Suspense Society. Their verve and excitement is contagious.

At William Morrow, Carrie Feron, my supportive editor, provided her unique electrical charge, generously offering her editorial wisdom and publishing acumen, conducting *When Day Breaks* on the trip from manuscript to bound book. I'm new to the HarperCollins world, but I know that so many others infused their talent, including Tessa Woodward, Lisa Gallagher, Jane Friedman, Michael Morrison, and Liate Stehlik. Many, many thanks to Tavia Kowalchuk, Adrienne DiPietro, and Lynn Grady for their marketing expertise; to Barbara Levine, Richard Aquan, and Ervin Serrano for the "electrifying" jacket; to Josh Marwell, Brian Grogan, Mike Spradlin, and Carla Parker for stimulating sales; and to Sharyn Rosenblum and Debbie Stier for zapping up the all-important publicity buzz.

A special thanks goes to Maureen Sugden, who copyedited this book with such exacting care. Her corrections were actually a pleasure to behold.

Walking the grounds and touring the halls of the Metropolitan Museum of Art's Cloisters jolted my brain and stirred my thinking as I worked on the plot. The Cloisters is a magical place and spending time there stimulates the imagination.

Rob Shafer has helped me in the past. He came through again, this time providing a clear explanation of electrocution and how to make it happen in a home swimming pool.

Beth Tindall and Colleen Kenny provide their resourcefulness and artistic dynamic to www.maryjaneclark.com.

The zest and sensitivity Peggy Gould brings to her job moves me, reassures me, and enables me to write.

There have been many who have bolstered me on, each helping with this story in some particular way: Louise and Joel Albert, Doris and Fred Behrends, Joy Blake, B.J. D'Elia, Elisabeth Demarest, Liz Flock, Roberta Golubock, Cathy Haffler, Katharine and Joe Hayden, Elizabeth Kaledin, Linda Karas, Norma and Norman Nutman, Steve Simring, and Frances Twomey.

From beginning to end, the input of Father Paul Holmes cannot be overestimated. He contributed his creative intensity and burning enthusiasm every step of the way. My continuing gratitude, Paul, for making the journey with me.

As always, the driving forces are Elizabeth and David. Every day that breaks is brighter because of them.

So, if I've left anyone out, I'm truly sorry. Another Sunrise Suspense Society story will be out next year. I'll make it up to you then.

When Day Breaks

Prologue

Thursday, May 17

Here's a real treasure." The animal-shelter attendant pointed at the small, sad-eyed beagle who peered out of the cage. "She's a sweet little thing, but she still doesn't know what hit her. Her elderly owner died, and nobody in the family wanted to take her."

"Actually, I was thinking of something larger."

"Well, we have a nice collie–German shepherd mix over here."

The animal sat on the floor of his pen, his head resting on his outstretched paws. As the attendant approached, the dog rose to his feet, wagged his tail, and eagerly pressed his nose against the metal screen.

"Why is he here?"

"The owner said the dog shed too much. Can you imagine? This dog is highly intelligent, loyal, and dependable. But it wasn't worth brushing every day."

"What about that one?"

The attendant turned to the large pen against the wall.

"Ah, the Great Dane. He's our gentle giant, but he's not going to be an easy one to place. He'll eat somebody out of house and home."

"What do you think he weighs?"

"I can tell you right now."

The attendant opened the cage and led the black dog to the scale at the rear of the room.

"One hundred and twelve pounds," he announced, petting the dog's short, shiny coat.

"How hard is he to handle?"

"He's a sweetheart, very affectionate and playful. He was well trained when he was a puppy. Too bad, his owner had to move across the country, and he couldn't take the dog with him."

The dog licked the attendant's hand.

"What's his name?"

"Marco."

"As in Polo?"

The attendant shrugged and smiled. "What can I tell you?"

"Does he like the water?"

"He should. Danes usually do."

"I think he's the one for me."

"Are you sure?" asked the attendant. "A Dane should really have a large yard and plenty of exercise room. He'll require very long walks regularly."

"I promise. That won't be a problem."

After the nominal adoption fee was paid in cash and the licensing application filled out, the attendant slid a piece of paper across the counter.

"Here's a list of care instructions and suggested dog food."

"Thank you very much."

When Marco was led out onto the city sidewalk, his new owner dropped the instructions into a trash can.

As the vehicle traveled farther and farther away from Manhattan, the trees lining the highway grew more plentiful, covered in the fresh green leaves of spring. An unusually warm, sweet May breeze blew in through the open windows. The dog stuck his nose into the whipping air as the car sped up the Hutchinson River Parkway, while his new owner removed a baseball cap and the thick-lensed eyeglasses that had been purchased at a drugstore.

With no traffic it was only about an hour's drive to Constance Young's country home. There were still several hours until the evening rush hour would begin, when too many cars would funnel into roads and highways that were now too narrow to accommodate an ever-expanding population's travel needs. There should be plenty of time for the practice run and the drive back down to the city.

The car merged onto Interstate 684 before getting off at the exit for Bedford. Passing stone farmhouses and blooming gardens, the vehicle traveled deeper into the countryside. Acres of rolling pastures provided a place for well-groomed horses to graze, exercise, and rest.

Success had many rewards. Having a place up here was definitely one of them. The real estate in this area provided privacy, insulation, and a sense of well-being. Constance must feel quite protected here when she came up on the weekends.

Forced to take a turn at the end of the road, the car crossed over a short bridge and climbed a hill. At the top, an easily opened wooden gate and a gravel driveway led to a multilevel house hidden by trees. As the engine was turned off, the dog pawed excitedly at the window. The driver leaned over and opened the car door. The animal sprang out and headed to a nearby bush to relieve himself.

"Good boy, Marco. Good boy."

The Great Dane wagged his tail, watching as his new owner went to the rear of the car and took out a coil of orange electrical cord and a box from the trunk.

"Come on, boy."

The dog did as he was told, following the path that ran around the side of the house and down to the pool. He watched his new owner enter one of the cabanas that flanked the pool but lost interest as the plug at one end of the orange cord was inserted into the wall socket. While the coil was unwound, Marco chased a gray squirrel that scampered into the trees.

"Marco. Marco. Come back. Come back here right now."

The dog came trotting out of the woods. He was panting and muddy.

"Oh, Marco. Look at you. What have you done?"

The dog sensed the displeasure in his new owner's voice.

"Over here, Marco. Go ahead. Get into that pool and wash off."

The dog stared at the finger pointing to the pool.

"Go ahead. Go into the water, boy."

The rubber ball was tossed toward the shallow end of the pool. Marco went in after it, his head held proudly out of the water as his legs paddled beneath the surface, his paws scraping the bottom. He reached the ball and wrapped his jaws around it, turning to bring it back to his owner. But then Marco saw his owner throw something else toward the pool, something big and shiny and attached to the orange cord.

As the toaster hit the water, the electricity ran through the dog. His lungs struggled to breathe, his heart stopped pumping, and his head slipped below the surface.

The new owner watched closely.

Yeah. That was going to be enough current.

FRIDAY
MAY 18

Chapter 1

The morning rush was on.

Breakfast eaten. Teeth brushed. Hair clipped. Shoes tied. Sweater buttoned.

As she hustled Janie out to the garage, Eliza picked up her daughter's backpack. "Anything in here I should see?" Eliza asked.

Janie's blank expression prompted Eliza to unzip the nylon bag. She pulled out a yellow sheet of paper.

"Oh, yeah. You need to fill that out, Mommy," said Janie. "It's for the picnic."

Eliza scanned the notice. The first-grade family picnic was coming up in a few weeks to celebrate the end of the school year.

"This sounds like fun, sweetheart," said Eliza as she grabbed a pen from the kitchen counter. "Should we ask Kay Kay and Poppy if they want to come?"

Janie shook her head, a solemn expression on her face. "No, Mommy. Mrs. Ansley says no grandparents or friends. It's only for parents and children."

Thanks, Mrs. Ansley, thought Eliza. *Thanks a lot.* "I'm sure if I asked Mrs. Ansley, she'd let us bring Kay Kay and Poppy and even Mrs. Garcia," said Eliza.

Janie shook her head. "Uh-uh. Mrs. Ansley says there's not enough room, and she can't make any 'ceptions."

"Exceptions," Eliza corrected.

"Exceptions," repeated Janie. "Mrs. Ansley says, 'No exceptions.' "

Eliza didn't want to hear any more about what Mrs. Ansley had to say. She took the pen and signed her name to the form, filling in the appropriate information.

One child. One adult.

There were just two in the Blake family eligible to attend the first-grade picnic.

Eliza hurried back to the house after dropping Janie off. She poured a second cup of coffee and positioned herself in front of the kitchen television set just in time. Constance Young was looking straight out of the screen, tears welling in her luminous blue eyes.

"The years I've spent with all of you have meant more than I can possibly express. Each morning we've faced the world together. We've learned new things together, explored possibilities together, had some laughs together, and faced too many harsh realities together."

Listening to the words coming from the television, Eliza found herself admiring Constance's beautifully cut green jacket and the lighting that accented her glowing skin and her ever-blonder hair. Eliza wondered if she should talk to the director about making some adjustments to the lighting on her own *Evening Headlines* set. She was definitely going to talk with Doris about upping the makeup magic to camouflage the darkness that inevitably developed beneath her eyes. In the last tapes Eliza had reviewed, there was no denying she'd appeared tired.

When Eliza went from hosting *KEY to America* to anchoring *The KEY Evening Headlines*, she had been thrilled at the professional achievement and the privilege of becoming one of the select few to whom the national audience turned to deliver the news of the day. But the mother in her had also looked forward to a more civilized schedule. She wouldn't have to get up at 4:00 A.M. anymore. She could have breakfast with Janie and take her to school in the morning before leaving for work. Other mothers might sigh at the daily grind of transporting their kids to and from school, but Eliza—though she could well afford a driver—savored the normalcy of those car rides with her first-grader. As it turned out, the reality of the nightly anchor job was just as much study and homework and travel as she'd done in her previous position, and though Janie and she could share scrambled eggs in the morning, they never had dinner together during the week. Eliza considered it a good day when she was home in time to tuck her daughter into bed at night.

Constance Young had replaced Eliza on *KEY to America*. And now Constance was leaving the highly rated morning program as well, but not for the evening broadcast or even another job at KEY News. Constance was going over to the competition. Next month she would be greeting morning viewers from another network. Today was her last appearance on *KEY to America*, and Eliza wanted to hear every word of the farewell address.

"The news hasn't always been happy or predictable. Far from it. Sometimes the things we've confronted together have been almost impossible to wrap our minds around. But I've always felt that no matter how worrisome the event or how painful the news, gathering together each morning and sharing the issues and problems of the day has somehow lightened the load a bit. There has been reassurance in knowing that there are millions of us, all hearing the same thing at the same time, all digesting the same information. And because knowledge is power, we go out better prepared to face the day, better equipped to take care of our children and parents, abler to be better spouses and friends, more likely to be solid citizens."

Pausing to dab a tear from the corner of her eye, Constance smiled bravely before continuing.

"There are so many people I should thank. There just isn't enough time to name them all. But I do have to express my gratitude to Harry. He has been the best colleague anyone could ask for as we've sat at this desk together every morning, and I'll miss him more than I can say."

The director cut to a two-shot of Constance and Harry Granger sitting beside each other. Constance leaned over and gave her cohost a kiss on the cheek.

"And I wish the very best of luck to my successor, Lauren Adams, who has already been part of our KEY News family as our lifestyle correspondent. I know Lauren will do a wonderful job as host."

Constance stared earnestly from the television.

"The *KEY to America* family is just that—a family. It includes all the people you see on the screen each morning, countless people you don't see as they work so hard behind the scenes to get us on the air, and all of you, the viewers. Without you there would be no

KEY to America. Because of you, *KEY to America* will go on and thrive. My departure is really only a tiny blip on the radar screen."

Eliza smiled as she put her coffee cup down on the counter. If she hadn't known Constance Young and witnessed what had been going on over the last year, she would actually have believed that the popular morning-show personality meant every word.

Chapter 2

I need this job," whispered B.J. D'Elia.

"Me, too," said Annabelle Murphy as she stood with him at the edge of the *KTA* studio. The cameraman and producer waited for their cue.

"So I'm gonna smile until my face hurts," said B.J.

With five minutes till the end of the broadcast, an ornately decorated sheet cake was rolled onto the *KEY to America* set. Executive producer Linus Nazareth came out of the control room and joined the other staff members who moved in and gathered around Constance Young.

Champagne was poured, and Harry Granger raised his glass. "To Constance. Thank you for putting up with me and for making me look better than I am every morning. Good luck at . . . " Harry cleared his throat.

"At your new job. Now that we'll be competitors, I'm not going to tell anyone where to find you."

Everyone on the set laughed, and someone called out, "As if anyone in the free world didn't already know where Constance is going."

At the fringe of the gathering, B.J. muttered under his breath, "Harry must be so relieved to be rid of her. I know *I* sure am."

"I don't know, Beej," Annabelle whispered back. "Be careful what you wish for. Lauren Adams is no bargain either."

"I find it hard to believe that anyone will be worse than Constance," said B.J. "She's a cameraman's worst nightmare, always finding fault with the way she's shot, the way she's lighted. She's a real bitch."

Annabelle winced.

"Sorry, Annabelle. I keep forgetting you two are friends."

"*Used* to be friends, Beej. *Used* to be. Constance isn't the same person anymore."

As soon as the final credits rolled and the television audience could no longer see what was going on in the *KEY to America* studio, the smiles faded and Annabelle and B.J., along with everyone else who had been commanded to celebrate with Constance Young, turned and walked away.

Chapter 3

Stuart Whitaker adjusted his black-framed eye-glasses as he stared with distress at the television set. Constance was wearing green, the color of unfaith-fulness. She undoubtedly knew he would be watching her farewell appearance this morning, and she was rubbing his nose in the fact that she wasn't going to be true to him. Worse, she was wearing the crowned-unicorn amulet, right there for an audience of millions to see.

What was she thinking? Was she trying to destroy him?

Stuart snapped off the set, stalked over to the window, running his hand backward over his bald head. He stared out at the Chrysler Building and the other apartment buildings in his complex. A man of his wealth could well afford to live at a more prestigious address, but Stuart preferred his two-bedroom apartment at Tudor City, a historic district in midtown Manhattan. The "old world" appeal of the place suited him. It was a quiet refuge from hectic city life, its real charm lying in its architectural style, dating back to England's Tudor dynasty.

Gargoyles, dragons, and other mythical creatures peered out from his building's rooftop. Tapestries and stained-glass windows adorned his lobby. Neighboring building exteriors featured detailed stonework and inscriptions. There were private parks where, in nice weather, he could walk, meditate, or sit and read.

Constance hadn't appreciated the charm of the place, though. She'd come to his apartment only once. He'd made dinner for her himself, his version of a medieval meal: pike and carrots and parsnips and baked apple and pear. He'd explained that fish had been favored in medieval times for its purity.

"And God said to Adam, 'Cursed is the ground for thy sake,'" Stuart had said, quoting Genesis. "You see, Constance? The people back then thought fish had escaped Adam's curse."

"Well, thank God I didn't have to live in those days, Stuart." Constance had grimaced as she pushed her plate away. "I'm sorry. I know you went to a lot of trouble, but this just isn't for me."

Stuart remembered taking her hand and raising it to his lips. "There's absolutely nothing to apologize for, my dear one."

Utterly smitten, he could forgive her almost anything. He was attracted to her from the moment she'd first caught his eye as she presided, dressed in queenly blue, as the mistress of ceremonies at a benefit dinner last fall. Then he had worshipped her from afar for a few months, making it a point to get up every morning and watch her on *KEY to America*. Finally he'd gotten up the courage to call her at the office. Getting through had been easier than expected. He'd left his name with her assistant, and within a few hours Constance herself had called him back. It wasn't till later that he had admitted to himself why.

These past few months had been heavenly for Stuart. And even though he would have loved more time with Constance, he was grateful for whatever time they had together. There were some candlelit dinners in some of the city's finest restaurants, a few hours spent holding her hand in the theater and on hansom-cab rides through Central Park. But by far, Stuart's favorite activity had been showing Constance his passion for medieval art and architecture.

The afternoon they'd spent wandering though the museum and gardens of the Cloisters had been his biggest pleasure. He had loved showing Constance the extraordinary collection of artistic treasures and strolling with her in that majestic setting in upper Manhattan overlooking the Hudson River in Fort Tryon Park.

Constance had been an eager student. She was so bright and interested in the story of how the core of the museum was constructed from medieval French monasteries and chapels that had been purchased and shipped, stone by stone, window by stained-glass window, statue by statue, across the Atlantic Ocean. She was fascinated by the seven magnificent Hunt of the Unicorn tapestries that hung in the gallery and hungry to learn about the symbolism of the one-horned creature. She marveled at the plants that were tended in the cloister gardens, some grown for food, some for medicinal purposes, some for their magical powers. She was awed by the stone coffins with carved effigies of knights and noblemen that lay in the Gothic chapel. It was after they'd viewed those tombs together that Stuart had explained the principle of courtly love.

"It was the idea that a nobleman would dedicate his life to the love of a lady. The relationship was intended to flatter the lady and inspire the knight to accomplish bold deeds in order to be worthy of her love."

What could be bolder than procuring the amulet that King Arthur had given to his love, Guinevere?

Stealing the ivory unicorn with the golden crown for Constance *had* been bold, but not enough, apparently. It hadn't ensured her love. He'd risked his reputation with a deed that went against his principles in order to win his lady's favor. But Constance favored him no more.

He'd asked her to wear the amulet only when they were alone together, and she had promised she would. Yet not only had Constance broken her promise to him, she'd broken his heart.

Chapter 4

Traveling down the West Side Highway, Eliza stared out at the Hudson River from the rear window of the dark blue sedan. She tried to focus on the day in front of her, but she found her mind turning to Janie's picnic.

As far as Eliza knew, Janie was the only child in her class without a father. There were already a few divorces among the parents of the six-year-olds, but those fathers were still alive, still part of their children's worlds. Those fathers would be at the picnic. Janie's would not.

For all the good fortune she'd been given, for all the natural gifts she'd been blessed with, for all the accomplishments she'd achieved, Eliza often reminded herself to be grateful. Yet having lost John was something that could never be fixed. She and Janie had a good life, a wonderful life, but there was a gaping hole in it. Eliza had lost the man she loved, and Janie had never had the benefit of knowing her father at all.

Eliza was determined to raise Janie as normally as possible, and so far things seemed to be working out pretty well. Still, now that Janie was in school, there were going to be more and more recitals, plays, and ball games, where parents would be clapping in the audience and rooting from the sidelines. Inevitably Janie was going to become more acutely aware that her daddy wasn't there.

The sedan turned onto Fifty-seventh Street. Eliza's attention was diverted by the camera crews and a crowd of reporters gathered on the sidewalk in front of KEY News headquarters.

"What's going on today?" asked the driver as the car pulled up to the curb. "The president coming or something?"

"It's something all right," answered Eliza from the backseat. "It's Constance Young's last day."

"Oh, yeah. I heard them talking about it on the radio this morning. They said she's going to make twenty million dollars a year in her new job. Is that right?"

"That might be a little on the high side," said Eliza. "But you can bet she sure is making a lot of money."

"I knew I picked the wrong line of work." The driver shrugged, getting out and walking around to open the door.

As Eliza extended her long legs from the car, the newspeople swarmed toward her.

"Are you going to miss Constance Young?" asked one reporter, sticking his microphone in Eliza's face.

"Constance has been a major presence here at KEY News. We're all going to feel her absence."

Eliza made her way to the Broadcast Center entrance.

"Constance Young has jumped ship!" shouted another reporter. "Do you think her audience will jump with her?"

"That's the multimillion-dollar question, isn't it?" Eliza answered before she pushed through the revolving door.

Taking the elevator up to her office, Eliza glanced at her watch. She had fifteen minutes until the *Evening Headlines* editorial meeting. That would give her just enough time to check in with her assistant, pick out something to wear, and go over any last-minute details about today's luncheon.

Paige Tintle was on the phone when Eliza walked into the small office that adjoined the anchorwoman's large one.

"No. Yellow." Paige frowned. "There are supposed to be yellow tulips on the tables. Yellow tulips are Ms. Young's favorite."

Eliza watched as her assistant shook her head and rolled her eyes in consternation. Paige let out a deep sigh as she listened to an answer she did not want to hear.

"I know that people will be arriving in just over an hour," she said. "All right, we'll have to go with the pink ones." Paige hung up the phone.

Eliza flipped through the tiny pile of messages that sat on the corner of the desk. "Don't worry, Paige. I'm sure everything will be beautiful."

"It just frustrates me," the other woman said. "I so want today to go well."

"It will, Paige. It will," Eliza reassured her. "Barbetta has been around for more than a century. It's the perfect spot for the farewell lunch. I'm hoping it will be hard for anybody to be nasty in such glorious surroundings."

In the dressing room next to her office, Eliza flipped through the racks of dresses, skirts, and slacks before selecting the pink Chanel suit. It was her favorite, but she rarely wore it on the air at night. She gravitated to navy blues and blacks, browns, grays, and beiges for the *Evening Headlines* set.

Eliza slipped off the well-cut trousers and crisp blouse she had worn for the ride in to work and put on the designer suit. As she appraised herself in the mirror, she noted that the pink fabric made her skin glow. Her shoulder-length brown hair seemed richer and more lustrous, too. Even her eyes seemed bluer. The garment was a real miracle worker.

She finished changing and then went downstairs.

Walking toward the Fishbowl, Eliza could see through the transparent walls that the *Evening Headlines* producers and writers had already assembled to discuss the dozens of stories developing around the world that had the potential of being reported that night. But as she entered the glass room in which the decisions were made on what the nation would see and hear, the topic of conversation was Constance Young's final appearance on *KEY to America* that morning.

"I almost believed she truly was upset about leaving. I think those tears looked real," said Range Bullock, the executive producer of the evening broadcast.

"Are you kidding? She's crying with joy at the thought of all that money she's going to be making," said one of the news writers. "And you can't tell me she didn't time her departure to make sure it occurred smack dab in the middle of sweeps. Constance knows that the ratings are scrutinized more than usual now.

She wants KEY News to take note of how powerful she is and to realize how much money in advertising dollars she could be taking with her."

"If you ask me, good riddance. They can have her over there."

"Easy for you to say. You don't run the network news division. *KEY to America* brings in five hundred million dollars a year. Any audience that Constance takes with her costs KEY News big time."

"But think of the pressure she's under. What if she doesn't bring up the ratings on the other show?"

"Don't cry for me, Argentina. It might hurt her pride, but she's set for the rest of her life."

Chapter 5

Faith stuffed the sheets into the washing machine, added detergent, and turned the water temperature dial to hot. Mother had soiled the bed again.

Closing the lid, Faith felt herself growing tense. Though she had packed the kids' lunches and set out their clothes the night before and gotten up early to wash her own hair, Mother had needed a bath, and it had taken her even longer than usual to nibble down her tiny breakfast. Now Faith was going to have to rush to get dressed in time to catch the train into New York.

Climbing the stairs from the basement, she heard the doorbell ring. She glanced into the hallway mirror, running her hands through her still-damp hair and wishing she'd made the time to get it colored. She pulled the belt of her bathrobe tighter around her thick waist before opening the front door.

"Hi, Mrs. Hansen." The young woman was standing on the front porch. Her eyes swept Faith. "Am I too early?"

"No, Karen. You're right on time. It's me who's running behind. Come on in."

Faith held open the door as the sitter entered. Karen was carrying several large books.

"I hope you don't mind, Mrs. Hansen, but finals are coming up, and sometimes your mom just sleeps the whole time I'm here."

"Sure, Karen. That's fine."

"Oh, and, Mrs. Hansen, I have to leave by three o'clock. Is that okay?"

Nice of you to have waited till now to tell me, thought Faith. *It has to be okay. I have no time to line up somebody else.* "Gee, Karen," said Faith, "I'm going to this fancy lunch in the city for my sister today. It'll be a real push to be back here by three."

The sitter smiled apologetically and shrugged. "I'm sorry, Mrs. Hansen, but I have an appointment with my adviser about my courses for next semester. I have to leave here by three to make it in time."

Faith tried to manage a smile. *What choice do I have?* she asked herself. Though playdates had been arranged for the kids after school, Mother couldn't be left on her own. Faith knew she was going to have to leave the luncheon by two o'clock, whether it was over or not, whether she wanted to or not.

It never seemed to matter to anyone what she wanted. Todd and the kids took her for granted, but so many of her friends were in the same boat. While they stood waiting for their children to come streaming out of the building at the end of the school day or bumped into one another in the supermarket or got together for coffee once in a while, they frequently commiserated about spouses who had no clue about how hard they worked at home every day and children who took for granted the clean clothes in the drawers and the hot meals on the table.

Yet Faith had almost come to accept things. While she craved a husband who was more concerned about her and their children than with the weekend weather reports signaling what golf conditions would be, Faith had chosen to be a stay-at-home mom, and she liked to believe that her children were the better for it. But she hadn't bargained on being responsible for her mother as well. She'd always thought, when she thought about it all, that when the time came, Constance and she would jointly shoulder the burden of taking care of their mother. After their father died, Mother had managed for several years in their childhood home outside

Washington, D.C., but eighteen months ago it became apparent that Mother couldn't live alone anymore. The house had gone on the market, and Mother had moved up to New Jersey.

In fairness to Constance, Faith had to admit that her sister had agreed to letting the proceeds from the sale of the house go toward any nursing care that Mother required. But all that money had actually gone to something else—bailing Todd out of a cockamamie business investment. When Faith finally went to Constance with the news that the money was gone, Constance hadn't offered more.

Faith knew that it made sense for Mother to stay with her family. Their Colonial-style home had a fourth bedroom with its own bath right off the kitchen. A maid's room, the real estate agent had called it when she showed them the place. But in the six years they'd lived in the house, no maid ever slept in that room. Faith was the maid in the Hansen household.

"Mother is in her room, probably asleep, Karen. Just tiptoe down there once in a while and check on her."

"Will do, Mrs. Hansen."

Faith began climbing the stairs to her bedroom, calculating how much time she had to get dressed, knowing she was going to have to rush to put on her makeup, when she heard her mother calling.

"Faith? Faith, come here."

"I'll be right there, Mother." With resignation, Faith went back down the stairs. She thought about her sister. Constance surely had plenty of time to dress today in one of the dozens of designer outfits in her closet. She would have her makeup expertly applied, her hair tinted by a professional colorist and arranged by her personal hairstylist. She would look happy and glamorous and rested, every inch the famous personality the magazines, newspapers, and television shows had been reporting on. While Faith would look and feel like a frump.

Constance didn't have to plan every move she made based on figuring out who was going to stay with Mother. Constance didn't take their mother for her doctors' appointments or make sure she had fresh bedclothes or enough to eat. Constance didn't have to help their mother bathe or clean up after her accidents. Constance didn't have a husband who got fed up sometimes at the intrusion on their lives and who, no matter how many times Faith pleaded with him to pay attention to her, was more worried about his poker games with his buddies than he was about the state of their marriage.

Constance had never married, though Faith knew that her sister had been linked to a variety of successful and interesting men. Faith knew this not because Constance had confided in her but because she had read the articles and seen the photos in magazines and on the society page. Constance had an exciting life, admired by millions and financially compensated on a mammoth scale. How Faith's life would change if *she* had that money.

Faith hated herself for being jealous, but she couldn't help it. Every week that passed, their mother deteriorated further, Todd paid less attention, and Faith gained weight, feeling more trapped and angry with her lot in life.

Chapter 6

G ive Boyd a call, will you please, Paige?" Eliza asked as she returned from the morning editorial meeting. "See if Constance wants to ride over to lunch with me."

Going into her office, Eliza walked to the large windows and looked down on the *Evening Headlines* studio below. She never tired of the view. All those people situated at all those desks, connected by phone and Internet and satellite to hundreds of other KEY News staffers around the globe, all of them assigned some specific part in getting the news on the air.

"Eliza?"

Roused from her thoughts, Eliza turned toward Paige's voice. Her assistant stood in the doorway.

"Boyd says Constance was very grateful, but she'll have to meet you there."

"Okay. Thanks, Paige." Eliza took a seat at her desk.

"You know what I think?" Paige didn't wait for a response from her boss. "I think Constance wants to make her own grand entrance—alone. She doesn't want to share the spotlight with you."

"It doesn't matter, Paige. It's her day, not mine."

As Paige shrugged and left, Eliza glanced at the picture of Janie that sat in a silver frame on her desk. It was the kindergarten picture, and, like so many school pictures, it wasn't perfect, and Eliza loved it more for that. Though the collar on Janie's shirt was wrinkled and errant strands of hair had escaped her headband, the then five-year-old's blue eyes sparkled and her crooked smile revealed shiny white baby teeth, marred only by the gap where one of the front two had fallen out. The expression on Janie's face reminded Eliza so much of John.

It was over six years now since John's death, and sometimes Eliza still couldn't believe she had survived losing him, bearing their baby without him, and raising their daughter by herself. John had been cheated, never getting to know his child. And Janie, the little girl who had her father's smile, lived on, without experiencing the love her daddy would undoubtedly have showered on her.

In the grand scheme of things, Constance Young's desire for the spotlight didn't matter worth a damn.

Chapter 7

Why was it, Boyd Irons wondered, that whenever Constance bossed him around, it always sounded like she was calling him "boy"?

"Get me Linus on the phone, Boy."

"Boy, would you go out and get me an iced coffee?"

"I have a prescription to be filled, Boy. Run over to the pharmacy, would you?"

As he watched Constance stand by his desk flipping through the avalanche of messages he'd taken this morning, Boyd was convinced she thought of him as her hack, her lackey, her slave. And just like a callous overseer, Constance had no regard for the human being who worked for her. As long as a warm body showed up to labor at her beck and call, she didn't care a whit about the servant's name, workload, or personal life.

Boyd had heard that Constance hadn't always been like this. People who'd been at KEY News for years said that she had actually once been a nice person. But Boyd found that hard to imagine, because in the entire thirteen months he'd worked as her assistant, Constance had been a shrew.

"Boy, I think you should go ahead of me to the restaurant and make sure everything is all right."

"There's a *d* on the end of that," Boyd muttered.

"What did you say?" Constance asked sharply.

"Nothing."

Constance looked down again and continued reading through her messages. "Once everyone has arrived, call me and I'll come over."

"Do you think it might be a better idea for you to be there from the beginning to welcome your guests?" Boyd asked, trying to be helpful.

"If I thought that was a better idea, I'd be doing it." Dismissing her minion, Constance turned and walked into her office.

She wants to make her grand entrance, thought Boyd, *have the spotlight all to herself.* It didn't matter to Constance that everyone was going to the luncheon to honor her. If she came late, she wouldn't have to make polite small talk with the guests, wouldn't have to extend herself too much. She could envelop herself in that protective cocoon of hers and still be the center of attention.

Boyd knew he should be glad that Constance wasn't taking him with her to *Daybreak*. He should be relieved. He hated coming to work each day. Constance could be so thoughtless and insensitive about the hurtful things she said. She was utterly self-absorbed, wanting what she wanted when she wanted it and never considering how her demands affected him. Still, Boyd had done the best he could to please her.

At first, knowing that she didn't think enough of him to invite him to go with her to *Daybreak* hurt. Lately her rejection angered him.

He had worked twelve-hour days and had given up weekends and vacation time. Sick and tired of last-minute disappointments and canceled plans, his lover had broken up with him. Boyd hadn't had a good night's sleep in over a year, waking in the middle of the night and lying there till dawn, his mind and stomach churning over another one of Constance's belittling remarks or unreasonable demands. His doctor said he had the beginning of an ulcer, and the mirror told him he had less hair on his head than the year before.

The phone sounded. Boyd answered politely, put the caller on hold, and buzzed his boss.

"Stuart Whitaker is on line two, Constance."

Boyd heard an exasperated sigh.

"What's the matter with *him*?" Constance snapped. "Hasn't he gotten it yet? Oh, well, just tell him I'll get back to him as soon as I can."

What the hell, thought Boyd. *She's leaving, and I won't be working for her anymore.* "He's called a dozen times, Constance. I'm not going to lie to the poor guy again."

He hung up and watched the phone pad. The light for line two stopped blinking, signaling that Constance had taken the call. Boyd got up from his desk and walked down the hallway. When he entered the men's room, B.J. D'Elia was standing at the sink washing his hands.

"So it's her last day, huh?" B.J. grinned. "I bet you're gonna miss her."

"Yeah, right. She's busting my chops to the bitter end." Boyd looked at his reflection in the mirror and shook his head in wonderment. "I've picked up her dry cleaning, made her doctors' appointments, cleaned her cat's damned litter box and fed it every weekend she goes out of town. I don't even know why she has the cat. She pays so little attention to it. It might as well be mine." Boyd turned to look at B.J. "I've booked her social engagements and lied for her when she's wanted to get out of them. I've listened to her complain about the people she works with, the men she dates, her relatives, and her so-called friends. I'm always thinking of her and trying to protect her. For God's sake, I didn't even tell her that the pool-service guy called here this morning to say he found a dead dog in the woods at her country house. I wanted to spare her that ugliness on her last day."

"That's nasty," B.J. said.

"Yeah, I just told the pool man to get rid of the dog right away. I've worked my ass off for Constance Young, and what do I get for it? A slap in the face and another bitch just like her coming my way as a new boss."

"Steady there, brother."

"You have no idea what it's like working for Constance day in and day out."

B.J. pulled a paper towel from the wall dispenser. "You're right, and I count myself lucky," he said. "But I get your drift. I've had to work with her on too many stories. She can be a nightmare. She found fault with every video I shot and every interview I set up. Constance is never satisfied." He tossed the crumpled paper into the trash can.

"And I've heard that Lauren Adams can be a prima donna, too, and now I'm going to be *her* whipping boy." Boyd groaned. "Another former beauty queen–turned–TV star. She finally stopped chain-smoking, but now she snaps her gum incessantly. She'll drive me out of my mind. What did I do in a former life to deserve this?"

"Why don't you quit?" B.J. asked.

"When I find something else, I will, believe me," answered Boyd. "But until then I'm stickin'. I have rent to pay, and besides, it's KEY News. Since I was a kid, I wanted to work in network-television news."

"And you were a kid about . . . uh, ten minutes ago?"

"I'm not as young as you think," said Boyd.

"Twenty-three?"

"Twenty-seven. It took me a while to even get a page job here."

"You're right, Boyd. You're an old man," B.J. said as he walked out the door. "And at thirty-four I must be ancient."

Constance held the phone to her ear, leaned her head against the back of her ergonomically designed office chair, and looked up at the ceiling.

"How *could* you, Constance?"

"How could I *what*?"

"You promised me that you would never wear the unicorn in public. You promised you would only wear it when we were alone together."

"Oh, Stuart, don't be ridiculous. We're never going to be alone together anymore, so if I kept the promise you say I made, I'd never get to wear the unicorn amulet at all, would I?"

"Please, my dear, I would like to have it back."

"I never took you for an Indian giver, Stuart."

"It really was not mine to give, Constance."

"Meaning what?"

"When you admired it in the display case at the Cloisters, I was determined that you should have it."

"Yes, and you told me you had a copy made for me."

Silence.

Constance sat upright. "Didn't you, Stuart?"

No answer.

"Don't tell me it's the real thing—the ivory unicorn that Arthur gave Guinevere. Don't tell me you *stole* it!"

"I prefer to think I procured it for my lady love. It was a heroic deed of valor to win my lady's heart."

"Are you insane, Stuart? This unicorn is supposed to be at the center of that upcoming exhibit at the Cloisters. It's priceless!"

"Yes, my dear, I fear I *am* insane. I am crazy *about you.* I am fifty-two years old, but I am like a teenager in love when it comes to you. I wake up thinking about you, go to bed at night thinking of you, and just about every minute during the day is spent wondering about you.

With all the furor in the press over you right now, it has been fairly easy to track what you have been doing."

"You're scaring me, Stuart. You sound like a stalker."

"Oh, Constance, forgive me. The last thing I would ever want to do is frighten you. You are my lady, and I only want you to feel safe and secure."

"If you truly mean that, Stuart, you'll stop calling me all the time," said Constance in exasperation. "Let's just remember the good times we had and be friends."

"Of course I want to be your friend, Constance. This gentle knight pledges his total allegiance to you, forever."

"Look, Stuart, I have to go now. I've got an appointment, and I have some things to take care of first."

"I know where you are going, Constance. There is that big luncheon for you today. I read about it in the newspaper."

"Yes, that's right."

"I was hoping I might get an invitation."

Constance shifted in her chair. "It's really just a business lunch, Stuart. Mostly people in the industry, not my friends."

"All right, Constance. I have to believe that you would never lie to me. But let me ask you, again. Please, give me back the amulet."

Constance felt the small carved ivory figurine that hung from a black silk cord around her neck. "Oh, Stuart, I hate to part with it. The unicorn is my talisman. I wore it all through my negotiations for my new job, and look at the good luck it brought me."

Stuart's voice rose an octave. "You are telling me you wore it in public more than just this morning?"

"Don't worry. Nobody would dream where it actually came from."

"I am afraid you are being naïve, my dear. Somebody, someone who either saw you in person or saw you on television this morning, will surely recognize that amulet."

"You worry too much, Stuart," said Constance, her mind racing ahead. If somebody did recognize the purloined unicorn, she would be able to say she had no idea it was stolen and point the person in Stuart's direction. But if she gave it back to Stuart and somebody came looking for it after seeing her wearing it, Stuart would doubtless go into his pathetic diatribe about how he'd taken it for her because she'd admired it and he wanted to make her happy and that she'd given it back to him once he told her it was stolen. The cops would think she should have alerted them, and there would be hell to pay in the press. The adverse publicity would anger her new bosses. For the kind of money they were paying her, they expected her to be scandal-free.

But some publicity, if it cast Constance in a positive light, could be a good thing. As she thought about it, she came up with a plan. She didn't want the amulet sitting in her jewelry case, a quietly ticking bomb ready to go off anytime the police got around to knocking. She would orchestrate things, continue to wear it in public, and force the authorities to come to her. Then she would explain how wealthy Stuart Whitaker had given the unicorn to her, that she'd had absolutely no idea it was stolen and had of course assumed he'd a copy made for her. She could imagine the headlines now: CONSTANCE YOUNG'S SMITTEN SUITOR STEALS IN THE NAME OF LOVE.

That kind of publicity would get even more viewers to tune in during the crucial first weeks of her new gig. She was definitely going to wear the unicorn amulet to the luncheon and try to bring things to a head, sooner rather than later.

"Constance? Are you there?"

"Yes, Stuart. But I really have to go now. I'll give you a call later. I promise."

Chapter 8

Eliza made sure to give herself enough time to get to Barbetta before the first guest arrived. As she and Paige entered the open-air garden at the rear of the old brownstones that housed the restaurant, Eliza inhaled the scent of magnolia. Flowering bushes and century-old trees edged the courtyard. In the center of the garden, stone cherubs sprayed water as they frolicked in a beautiful fountain. Arrangements of pink tulips graced the white table linens on a dozen round tables, each set for four people. It was all more reminiscent of a grand country estate than a city garden.

"Everything looks so pretty, Paige. You did a wonderful job arranging this," said Eliza. "And I'm so glad we have such a beautifully warm day. It would have been a shame to have had to move the party inside."

KTA producer Annabelle Murphy and cameraman B.J. D'Elia were the first arrivals. Eliza walked over to greet them. As they chatted, Eliza's gaze kept shifting from the entrance to the garden. She was growing concerned that guests were only trickling through the French doors.

"God, where is everybody?" Eliza checked her watch. "I hope that everyone is coming."

"I wouldn't worry," said Annabelle. "They'll be here, but they're not in a hurry. I'm afraid everyone is coming to this luncheon more because you're hosting it, Eliza, than to honor Constance."

B.J. swiped a flute of prosecco from a waiter's tray. "It's Friday, and I don't have to go back to the Broadcast Center, so I can really celebrate." He held up his stemmed glass. "And man, do we have something to celebrate."

"Cut it out, B.J.," said Annabelle, nudging him, as Eliza went to welcome the woman who stood uncertainly in the doorway.

Eliza was struck by the family resemblance, though Constance's sibling looked considerably older and heavier than her sister. When they shook hands, Eliza felt the rough skin of someone who did her own housework, or at least didn't take care of herself enough to apply hand cream. As they made small talk, Eliza found herself sympathizing with Faith Hansen and speculating on how hard it could be for her to be the sister of the glamorous and famous Constance Young. Probably very hard.

"How many years are there between you and Constance?" asked Eliza.

"She's three years older than I am," Faith answered quietly. "I know I don't look younger, but I am."

Casting about for a tactful response, Eliza wished she hadn't asked.

"We all look older than Constance," she said. "She never seems to age." Changing the subject, Eliza asked Faith about herself.

"I'm a stay-at-home mom." Faith smiled. "I have two boys, seven and eight. They keep me pretty busy."

"I'll bet," said Eliza. "I have a six-year-old daughter."

"I know. I read that article about you in *Good Housekeeping*. How do you do it all?" Faith asked. "I guess you must have lots of help."

"Yes, fortunately, I do. I have a wonderful housekeeper, some great baby-sitters and neighbors, and my daughter's grandparents live close by and spend a lot of time with her. Janie loves them, and they adore her."

"I wish my kids had that," said Faith. "But they only have my mother, and she's in pretty bad shape. Some days she doesn't even know who they are."

"That must be tough," said Eliza. "Where does your mother live now?"

"With me."

"So you really do have your hands full, don't you?"

Faith nodded, and her eyes welled up.

"I'm so sorry," said Eliza, reaching out and touching Faith's arm. "I didn't mean to upset you. I know how hard it is to watch as someone you love slips away."

"Don't mind me," said Faith as she dabbed at the corner of her eye. "I'm being ridiculous."

"No you aren't. You aren't ridiculous at all," said Eliza, smiling at the worried-looking woman and wondering how much her sister was doing to help her.

Slowly but surely, the garden filled with people. Most of the guests were KEY News staffers. Eliza went from group to group, making a point of introducing Faith around. Constance was aware that Faith wouldn't know people, thought Eliza. The least she could have done was be here to make her sister feel at ease.

Eventually the executive producer and the new cohost of *KEY to America* arrived. Linus Nazareth's arm was around Lauren Adams's waist as they walked though the French doors.

"God, they aren't even trying to hide it anymore," whispered Annabelle to B.J.

"It paid off for her big-time, didn't it?" B.J. sneered.

"Well, you can't really blame Linus for going for her," said Annabelle. "With her hair swept up like that, she looks just like Audrey Hepburn."

"Everybody says that," B.J. acknowledged. "But I don't see it."

Annabelle watched Lauren take a glass from a waiter's tray. "What I wouldn't give to have a figure like that!" she said.

"I like my women thin," said B.J., "but she's *too* skinny. There's nothing to hold on to."

"Linus doesn't seem to think so." Annabelle nodded in the direction of the executive producer and his new star. Lauren was staring adoringly at her boss-cum-boyfriend, and Linus was basking in the glow of her attention. "That's the happiest I've ever seen him."

Inside the brownstone Stuart Whitaker sat at the long wooden bar nursing a glass of wine and waiting for his lady love to arrive. It wounded him to think that Constance had not respected his wishes by wearing the amulet. Even more, it worried him. If anyone at the Cloisters recognized the ivory unicorn, Stuart knew that its disappearance from the museum case could eventually be tracked down to him. He had to get the amulet back from Constance and somehow return it to where it belonged. Since Constance gave him no satisfaction on the phone, Stuart hoped a face-to-face appeal would work.

A young man took a seat three places down and pulled out a cell phone. "Okay, Constance. Everybody's here. You can come on over."

The young man flipped the phone closed and gestured to get the bartender's attention. "I'll have another Bloody Mary, please."

Stuart watched the fellow stir his drink with a celery stalk. "Excuse me."

"Yes?" The young man didn't look up from his drink. His brusque answer left little doubt he didn't really want to be bothered.

"Are you Boyd?"

The young man lifted his head and stared at Stuart. "Do I know you?" he asked warily.

"I am Stuart Whitaker. I overheard you speaking just now to someone named Constance, and I know there is a luncheon here this afternoon for Constance Young. And I also know she has a male assistant named Boyd, with whom I have spoken many times on the telephone. I was wondering if that would be you."

The expression on the young man's face softened. He smiled as he leaned over the intervening barstools to shake Stuart's hand. "Ah, Mr. Whitaker. It's nice to meet you."

"Good to meet you, too, Boyd," said Stuart.

Boyd moved to the stool next to Stuart, sat down, and crossed his legs. "Yes, Mr. Whitaker. She is on her way over, but I know you realize she's coming here for a party in her honor."

"Don't worry, son. I am not going to make a scene. I just want to talk to her for a moment."

"I don't think this would really be a good time, Mr. Whitaker."

Stuart looked at the young man and managed a weak smile. "There is never a good time, is there, Boyd? Constance does not want to have anything to do with me, does she?"

Boyd was silent.

"I did not think so," Stuart said quietly.

"Maybe I could help you, Mr. Whitaker," Boyd offered.

Stuart took a swallow of wine. "You have always been very kind to me on the telephone, Boyd. I appreciate that."

"Of course, Mr. Whitaker."

"You would be surprised at the bad manners some people have, Boyd."

"No, I wouldn't. Unfortunately, I wouldn't be surprised at all. I encounter bad manners every day."

"Terrible, is it not?"

"It sure is."

"People have so little consideration for other people's feelings, Boyd."

"You can say that again."

"I don't want to be part of that, Boyd. The last thing I would want to do is ruin this special day for Constance. I do not want to hurt her feelings."

"Of course you don't."

There was an earnest expression on Stuart's face. "Maybe you *could* help me, Boyd."

"If I can. How?"

"This is a delicate situation, Boyd."

"What is it?"

"I gave Constance something, and I need to get it back."

Boyd stared at Stuart and waited for him to continue.

"I need to get back the unicorn amulet she has been wearing."

"Why don't you just ask her for it?"

"I have."

Boyd let out a low whistle. "And she doesn't want to, right?"

Stuart nodded. He put his elbows on the bar, folded his arms, and rested his head on top of them. "But if you get the unicorn amulet back for me, Boyd, I will certainly make it worth your while."

Thirty seconds passed. Boyd looked nervously at the restaurant entrance, expecting Constance to walk in at any moment. "I'll help you out, Mr. Whitaker."

Stuart lifted his head and turned to Boyd. "You would do that for me?"

"Yes, sir. I know what it's like to have Constance give you a hard time."

On the sidewalk in front of Barbetta, a gaggle of reporters and paparazzi awaited the arrival of Constance Young. As she alighted from the car, cameras whirred and clicked as reporters shouted out questions.

"Are you going to miss KEY News, Constance?"

"Do you think Lauren Adams will be able to fill your shoes?"

"Will you finally confirm how much you'll be making in your new job?"

"How does it feel to ruin people's lives, Constance?"

Constance looked in the direction of the last questioner. The man who stood near the steps that led to the restaurant looked vaguely familiar. His face was long and thin, his hair dark and tousled. He wore a corduroy sport jacket, an open-necked shirt, and a pair of wrinkled chinos. Unlike the other reporters gathered around her, he held no microphone or notebook.

"I asked you a question, Constance. How does it feel to ruin another person's life?"

Constance glared at the man, then passed by him.

After she had disappeared into the brownstone, one of the reporters pulled the man aside.

"You're Jason Vaughan, aren't you?"

"I was," answered the man before he skulked away.

Chapter 9

As soon as the guests took their seats at the tables in the garden, Eliza stood and offered the first toast.

"To Constance," she said warmly, holding up her glass. "Today we celebrate your accomplishments at KEY News and look forward to your future success, though we are all too well aware that you will be a fierce competitor. You are talented and beautiful, and you have had an impact on the life of everyone assembled here. Your absence will be keenly felt."

"That was tactful," Annabelle leaned over and whispered to B.J. as all the guests raised their glasses.

B.J. nodded as he took a drink and put his glass back down on the table. "Yeah, true enough, but Eliza chose her words carefully, didn't she? Constance sure did affect everyone's life. She made just about all of us miserable."

After the saltimbocca was served, Linus Nazareth raised his hefty form from his chair and gave his own toast, making sure that Lauren Adams stood beside him.

"I can't say I'm happy that you're going over to the competition, Constance. I liked what having you on our team did for our ratings, and I still haven't gotten over the gall you have to leave me."

The guests laughed—some heartily, some nervously.

Linus continued. "But, in all fairness, I also can't say I have ever known anyone, with the exception of me, of course, who works harder than you do." He arched one eyebrow and grinned devilishly. "So I do wish you the best of luck. It was great having you on the team, but now Lauren and I look forward to whipping your ass."

Lauren Adams added, "You can say that again!"

More laughter.

"Now, Constance, I have some lovely parting gifts for you," said Linus.

Constance opened a large blue box and seemed genuinely pleased with the silver tray engraved with her name, KEY NEWS, and the dates she had worked at the network.

"Okay," said Linus as he presented a bigger box, this one orange. "The tray is ceremonial, but these are practical, something you can use every day."

The package contained a luxurious robe with KEY NEWS monogrammed over the breast pocket, along with a half dozen Hermès beach towels.

"One of those towels could pay for my twins' school lunches for a month," marveled Annabelle as she watched Constance hold up the robe.

"Nothing but the best for Constance, baby." B.J. laughed. "Everybody knows she swims every day. Would you expect Constance to wrap herself in anything less?"

Though she was hosting the luncheon, Eliza couldn't stay until the very end. She had to get back to the Broadcast Center, but before she left, she stopped at Constance's table.

"Well, Constance, I'm not going to say good-bye, because I'm sure we'll be seeing each other around often," Eliza said.

Constance rose from her chair and kissed her on the cheek. "Thank you so much, Eliza. It really was so kind of you to have this for me."

"My pleasure," said Eliza. "And what are you going to do between now and when you start at *Daybreak* next month?"

"I'm heading up to the country later this afternoon. I'm not sure how long I'll stay, but I'm going to take the next few days at least to relax."

"That sounds great," said Eliza. She leaned closer, looking at some long, angry pink scratches on Constance's neck. "What happened there?" she asked. "Did your cat do that?"

Constance felt gingerly at her throat. "No," she said. "I pulled my top off, forgetting I was wearing the unicorn. The prongs of the crown scratched deep into my neck. I've been covering it with makeup, but the powder must have worn off."

Eliza looked more closely. The eight-pointed crown had left only four scratches, with four of the points only retracing the scratches left by the points opposite them. In between the scratches was a deeper red gash caused by the horn of the unicorn.

Eliza winced. "Maybe you shouldn't put any more makeup on it, Constance," she said. "Let it heal cleanly."

"I intend to," said Constance. "I'm going makeup-free for a while. Upstate I can do that."

Eliza turned and leaned down to shake hands with Constance's sister. "It was very nice to meet you, Faith," she said sincerely.

"Yes, I really enjoyed meeting you, too," Faith answered as she rose to her feet. "Thank you for inviting me."

As the sisters watched Eliza head for the door, Faith commented on how impressed she had been with meeting the *Evening Headlines* anchorwoman. "I can't get over what a nice human being she is," said Faith. "Not stuck up at all. It was so lovely of her to give this farewell party for you, Constance."

Constance looked at her sister with scorn. "Don't kid yourself, Faith. Eliza gave this lunch because it was in *her* best interest. Hosting it made *her* look good."

"I can't believe you're saying that, Constance. That's pretty ungrateful of you, don't you think?"

"I'm just being honest."

"Just being honest." Faith repeated the phrase, feeling her body stiffen. "How's this for being honest, Constance? Some people actually do nice things for other people without having an agenda. They do those things out of love or friendship or just plain decency. Did that ever occur to you?"

Constance smiled for the benefit of any lunch guest who could be looking her way. "Grow up, will you, Faith?" she said, barely moving her lips. "When are you going to stop being Little Mary Sunshine?"

"I stopped being Little Mary Sunshine a long time ago, Constance. Funny how nursing our sick mother has wiped just about all the optimism out of me."

"Oh, no. Here we go again," Constance groaned. "What do you want me to do about it, Faith? If you'd done what I wanted to do and put Mother in a lovely nursing home, we wouldn't be having this conversation."

"After all Mother did for us, Constance, she should live out her days taken care of by her family, surrounded by people who love her. I can't put her in one of those places."

"Well, that's *your* choice, Faith, not mine."

"Still, some help would be nice. I know you don't think you have any more financial responsibility since Todd made that bad business investment and lost Mother's house money, but how about making a little trip across the river to visit with her? Actually, Constance, just about anything you did would be an improvement over nothing." Faith decided to let Constance really have it. "Look at you. You've got everything. Do you think I have anything like that necklace you're wearing? I'm excited when I get a new pair of rubber gloves to wipe Mother's behind."

"You *would* have to try and spoil today for me, wouldn't you, Faith?"

Faith was silent.

"Well, I'm not going to let you do it," said Constance.

"I don't want to fight. But why can't you just invite Mom to your country place? After all these years, you've only had us there once."

Constance sighed. "You just don't get it, Faith, but then I guess I shouldn't expect that you could. You live in your insulated housewife's world, without any conception of what real pressure is."

"At least I graduated college," Faith blurted out.

Constance stared coldly at her sister. "I'll ignore that, Faith, because I know how upset you are. But these past few months have been difficult for me, and I need my rest before I start my new gig."

Faith picked up her purse. "How do you live with yourself, Constance?"

"Don't worry about me, Faith. I sleep very well at night." Constance turned and walked away.

While Faith stood watching her sister's back, she heard the faint ring coming from her purse. She dug inside and pulled out her cell phone.

"Mrs. Hansen? It's me. Karen."

"What is it, Karen? Is my mother all right?" Faith asked fearfully.

"Yes. She's fine, Mrs. Hansen. She's still taking her nap. But I just wanted to let you know that my adviser called and canceled our appointment. You don't have to rush home now."

Faith put the cell phone back in her purse as she decided what she was going to do with her newly found free time.

Chapter 10

Constance arrived at her country house as the sun was beginning to set. As she turned in to the gravel driveway, she shifted the car into park and got out to open the wooden gate that blocked the entry. The gate wasn't designed as a hindrance to any would-be intruder. All it took was simply sliding up the iron latch, and it swung open easily. The real safeguard for Constance and her property was the sophisticated electronic alarm system that armed the place.

She looked at the house, thinking, as she always did, how much she loved owning it. The architect had done a skillful job in designing a modern structure that was framed by the beauty of nature. There were lots of windows that let in the light from the outside and provided soothing views from the inside. Downstairs there was ample, flowing space for living with ease and entertaining graciously. Upstairs there were only two bedrooms, one for guests and another, larger room for Constance.

She went directly upstairs, carrying the orange box containing her gifts. She took off her green suit and changed into a black one-piece swimsuit and donned the robe she'd just gotten as a going-away present. She grabbed one of the new towels and went downstairs to pour herself a scotch and soda.

Out on the deck at the rear of the house, Constance sat for a while, sipping her drink and watching the sky darken. One by one, lights clicked on inside the house. She waited for the timers to go off down the hill around the pool, but the lights there never came on. Constance went back inside the house and checked the central circuit-breaker panel. Sure enough, the switch that controlled the pool lights had tripped. Constance popped it back into position.

When she came outside again, the air was noticeably cooler. Constance wondered if the pool heater had been affected by the interrupted electrical circuit. She hoped not, because one way or another, warm water or not, she was determined to get in her exercise.

At the edge of the pool, Constance stopped and dipped her toe in the water. It was a bit cooler than she would have liked, but not too bad. Even if the heater was off, the sun had been beating down on the pool for the past few days now. Constance knew that once she got in and started swimming, she would be fine.

She took off her robe and threw it, along with the towel, on one of the lounge chairs. As she started to pin her hair up, her hand brushed the silk cord around her neck, and she realized she'd neglected to take off the amulet when she changed into her swimsuit. Constance unfastened the unicorn and placed it on the table. Then she walked to the side of the pool and eased herself down the ladder, inhaling as her body slipped into the cool water. Slowly and methodically, Constance began swimming her laps, pulling the water behind her in long, even strokes, totally unaware of the eyes watching her from inside the cabana.

Back and forth, back and forth, Constance's sleek body sliced through the water. Her toned arms reached out, hands slightly cupped. Her legs fluttered rapidly, propelling her forward. At every other stroke, she turned her head to the right, her mouth breaking above the waterline, able to take deep breaths to keep going.

When Constance finished her laps, she flipped over onto her back. Her blond hair fanned out on top of the water, and she stared up into the night sky as she neared the shallow end of the pool. Her ears were beneath the water, and she heard nothing except the silence.

She began to shiver, and, rubbing her fingertips together, she could feel that they had puckered. Constance stood up, her feet touching the pool floor.

As she neared the steps, she sensed she was not alone. She turned to look just in time to see the object flying through the air. The light around the pool revealed the orange electrical cord as well. In that terrifying instant, Constance knew what was going to happen to her.

The toaster hit the water, and Constance felt the current begin to run through her at the same moment she saw her killer's face.

Chapter 11

*T*he pool lights flickered and then went off, but there was no time to look around for the electrical box and try to reset them. Just enough illumination filtered down from the spotlights over the deck at the rear of the house to light the way. The three-pronged plug, which had been reduced to two when the grounding prong had been purposefully cut off, was pulled from the outlet on the cabana wall. The thick orange electrical cord was efficiently wound up, the toaster at the end of the cord was pulled out of the pool.

All the while, Constance lay motionless, facedown in the water.

When the Great Dane had been electrocuted yesterday, it had been essential to get the dog out of the pool, leaving no trace of the poor creature's fate. What a job that was, hoisting the massive and soaking-wet animal and dragging it into the woods. But Constance could be left right where she was, ready to be discovered.

The early-evening stillness was marred by a sound coming from the deck above, but a visual sweep of the area revealed nothing. Something glimmered, however, from the table at the side of the pool. Curiosity revealed the source of the faint gleam. The light was hitting the bright green gem in just the right way. It was the reflection from the emerald eye of the carved ivory unicorn.

Constance's good-luck charm, her talisman, her gold-crowned unicorn, was slipped into a pocket with hopes that it would bring its new owner the best of fortune.

SATURDAY
MAY 19

Chapter 12

Saturdays were busy at the Cloisters. On a hill over-looking the Hudson River, this place might have been the closest approximation of a monastic setting in an American city, and people flocked there in the spring. Children and adults streamed in for gallery talks and family workshops on subjects ranging from medieval motherhood to magic and medicine in the Middle Ages. Visitors listened to audio guides as they wandered through the chapels and halls of the museum, immersing themselves in the world of monks, kings, knights, tapestries, stained glass, and carved stone. Outside, picnickers and sunbathers spread their blankets on the lawn, enjoying nature and serenity.

Today Rowena Quincy was scheduled to give a special lecture on the Unicorn tapestries. As she headed to work, Rowena wasn't nervous. She knew her subject so well that notes were unnecessary. Sitting on the uptown bus, she relaxed and read the *New York Times*. She dutifully flipped through the first section before turning to her favorite part, the Arts.

There, below the fold, was a picture of Constance Young. Rowena read the caption: "Constance Young trading one morning show for another."

The story went on to chronicle Young's last day on *KEY to America* on Friday and the luncheon held in her honor at a restaurant in the theater district.

Rowena finished reading the article and then studied the picture. Constance Young was photogenic, but even more attractive in person. Rowena had realized as much the day Stuart Whitaker had requested a private tour for himself and the *KEY to America* host. Rowena had greeted the couple when they'd arrived, and she'd been impressed with how pretty Constance was.

Even in this newspaper picture, Constance's hair shone and her eyes sparkled as she walked into the restaurant. That green suit she was wearing was beautifully tailored. Rowena looked harder at the picture, trying to make out what Constance Young was wearing around her neck.

No. It couldn't be.

Chapter 13

The little girls in red-and-white uniforms were gathered at the side of the field waiting for their turns at bat. Eliza watched as Janie broke from the group and made her way to home plate.

"Remember, Janie, don't throw the bat!" Eliza called. At last weekend's game, Janie had carelessly tossed her bat after smacking the ball off the tee. The bat had hit her teammate Hannah in the leg.

Janie glanced over at her mother, and for an instant Eliza wished she had cheered her daughter on to a good swing rather than calling out a warning. But Janie looked unperturbed. She positioned herself behind the raised tee, holding her bat back as she'd been coached to do.

"She's looking good."

Eliza turned toward the voice, smiling when she recognized her neighbor standing beside her. Michele Hvizdak was holding her four-year-old son's hand.

"Good morning. How's it going, Michele? Is Hannah's leg all right?"

"Eliza, yes. Her leg's fine. And it has been fine every one of the half dozen times you've asked since last weekend. Stop worrying, will you?" Michele nodded to the young players. "Look at her over there. Does she look hurt to you?"

Hannah Hvizdak's chestnut-colored hair flew through the air as she executed a perfect cartwheel.

Satisfied, Eliza leaned down to Michele's son. "Hi, Hudson. How are you today?"

The little boy's face lit up, but he said nothing.

"What I'd give for those eyelashes," said Eliza as she stood upright again. She noticed that Hudson was wearing the same sweatshirt and shoes that he'd worn at last weekend's game, and at the game the weekend before that and at the one before that, too. Eliza knew it was a pretty good bet that Hudson had been sporting that sweatshirt on many of the weekdays as well. His mother had explained his penchant for wearing the same jacket and sneakers over and over and his insistence on donning his favorite Power Ranger sweatshirt, even in the heat. Obviously, Michele had to do laundry almost every night so Hudson's attire would be clean.

Cheers erupted from the sidelines and Eliza looked over just in time to see Janie rounding first base. Novice fielding ensured that Janie scored a home run. Eliza was grinning and giving the thumbs-up sign to her daughter when she felt the BlackBerry vibrating in her pocket. With a sinking heart, she read the text message: URGENT. CALL RANGE BULLOCK ASAP.

Eliza strode from the ball field and found a relatively quiet spot from which to make the call to Range. Urgent? That couldn't be good. Eliza had never gotten a weekend call from the executive producer of *The KEY Evening Headlines* just to chat about the weather—unless, of course, there was a hurricane brewing.

"Range. It's me. What's up?"

"There's no way to break this easily, Eliza."

Eliza braced herself. This must be personal. Range would normally just blurt out headlines. "What is it?"

"Constance Young is dead."

"Oh, my God," Eliza gasped as she bent at the waist to absorb the blow. "That can't be, Range."

"I'm afraid it is."

"What happened?" she asked, closing her eyes, bracing herself for his answer.

"Not sure. Her housekeeper found the body this morning. In the swimming pool."

"Constance drowned?"

"It looks that way. I assume there will be an autopsy to determine the cause of death. But here's the deal. We want you to anchor tonight. Everybody at KEY News is going to be involved in covering this."

Eliza recognized the pragmatism their profession required. A plane could crash, a bomb could blow up a bus on its way to school, a friend and colleague could die—and there was limited time to feel, or mourn. Always the immediate concern was how the story was going to be covered. Tears and sadness were luxuries that had to wait. "Of course," Eliza managed to say, collecting her wits. "But I don't love bigfooting the regular Saturday-evening anchor."

"You won't be. He's on vacation. We were just having Mack McBride do a tryout as a fill in tonight."

Eliza felt her chest tighten. She hadn't seen Mack since they'd broken up months before, but the sound of his name made her pulse race.

"I didn't know Mack was interested in anchoring." Eliza restrained herself from asking when Mack had gotten in from London, how long he would be in New York, and where he was staying.

"They're *all* interested in anchoring," said Range. "Anyway, where are you now?"

"At Janie's T-ball game."

"All right. I'll see you when you get in."

"Fine, I'll be there as soon as I can. But you know what, Range? Constance Young was a fabulous swimmer, and I'd bet my life that she didn't drown."

Chapter 14

The sound of the hooves as they pounded the soft earth was music to Lauren's ears. Urging her horse on, she was exhilarated by the spring wind in her hair, the morning sun on her face, and the fact that she, Lauren Adams, was now the cohost of *KEY to America*. Monday morning she would take her place alongside Harry Granger and welcome millions of Americans into the *KTA* living room. She hoped those millions would reciprocate by inviting her to stay in theirs in the weeks, months, and years to come.

Linus had been right to insist she come up here for a nice long ride this morning. The ride was relaxing. It had been such a tense month. All the attention and media interviews and photo sessions and Botox injections and hair and makeup experiments. There was another rehearsal scheduled in the studio at the Broad-cast Center this afternoon. Lauren still hadn't made a final decision about the outfits her stylist had brought for her to choose from to wear on the first morning. She'd narrowed it down to two: a marine blue jacket and a red one. Either one she intended to team with a cream-colored skirt she knew cut her legs at the most favorable spot.

Lauren dismounted, stopping to pat the horse's neck before handing the reins over to the stable hand. She took off her riding helmet as she walked toward her car. Opening the door, she reached for her canvas bag, pulled out a bottle of water and a pack of gum, and checked her BlackBerry. Five messages from Linus. She took a deep breath and called him.

"Lauren, I've been trying to reach you." Linus sounded angry.

"I know, Linus, that's why I'm calling you back." Lauren slipped a stick of Juicy Fruit into her mouth.

"Nice answer. Do I need to remind you that now you need to be available for breaking news? You're not doing lifestyle stories anymore."

"Okay, Linus. You've made your point." Lauren rolled her eyes as she checked her reflection in the visor mirror. "What's up?"

"Tell me you're still upstate."

"Yes. I just finished my ride. I can be at the Broadcast Center in an hour if you need me."

"No. I want you to go to Constance's country house. You can't be too far from it."

"I'm not. I think I remember how to get there from that party she had last summer. Why?"

Linus voice softened. "Lauren, honey, this is a helluva way for you to start your new job, but I'm just going to tell you. Constance is dead."

"What?"

"She was found at the bottom of her swimming pool this morning."

Lauren let out a nervous laugh. "Very funny, Linus. Dead bodies don't sink."

"They do until the gases build up inside," said Linus. "I'm serious, baby. Constance is dead."

"Don't call me 'baby.' I hate it when you call me 'baby,' " Lauren snapped.

Though he was tempted to correct Lauren, letting her know that it was never all right to talk to him in that tone when they were communicating professionally, he decided to let it pass. Not because he knew that he himself had been unprofessional in calling her "baby," but because he didn't want to upset her. He needed her to be at the top of her game, focusing only on her job. He didn't want her to waste a bit of energy being angry with him or resentful of his pulling rank with her.

"All right, I won't call you 'baby.' But the sad fact of the matter is, what I'm telling you is true, Lauren. Constance Young is dead, and you need to drive over to her place right away."

Flashing lights emanated from the tops of the police cars parked on the road in front of Constance Young's country house. When Lauren arrived, the police had already cordoned off the driveway. She pulled the yellow tape up and slid beneath it, striding with confidence up the gravel trail.

"Ma'am, this is a crime scene. You'll have to leave."

Lauren looked at the tall young police officer who blocked her path. Her mouth formed a tight smile.

"I'm Lauren Adams with KEY News." She showed him her press pass.

"Glad to hear it," said the cop. "But the fact remains, you have to get off the property."

"Surely you know that this is Constance Young's home. Constance, until just yesterday, was with KEY News as well. I'm sure she would want us to have access."

"No dice."

"I want to speak to your superior."

"Be my guest. But the chief isn't going to tell you any different. In the meantime, please get off the property, ma'am."

Lauren turned and stomped down the driveway. She saw a CBS van pulling up and a CNN truck behind it. Newspeople were setting up all over the place, staking their claims to the best live-shot locations. Lauren was the only KEY News presence to have arrived so far, and she felt outnumbered and outmatched. When she returned to her car, she called Linus and told him what was happening.

"Look, Lauren," said Linus, "Annabelle Murphy and B.J. D'Elia's crew are on their way up. They should get there any minute. Just stay put until they arrive."

Lauren rifled through the glove box hoping to find a forgotten pack of cigarettes, but she had to settle for another stick of gum. She was snapping away impatiently when her KEY News backup team arrived.

"It took you guys long enough," she greeted her colleagues.

"We got here as fast as we could, Lauren," said Annabelle.

"Well, what do you propose we do now?" Lauren asked. "The police won't let us on the property to shoot."

Annabelle was about to answer when a middle-aged woman emerged from the driveway and walked into the street. Her face was ashen, her eyes swollen, her hair in disarray. Correspondent, producer, and camera crew converged on the stricken woman.

"We'd like to ask you a few questions."

The woman looked at Lauren with fear in her eyes. "Well, I don't want to get involved. Witnesses always end up getting the short end of the stick." Her voice trembled.

"We're with KEY News, too. We're friends of Constance's," Lauren reassured the woman.

"You are?"

Lauren held up her KEY News card. "Yes, all of us worked with Constance on *KEY to America* every day."

The woman blew her nose with the balled-up tissue that was in her hand. "I really don't want to talk to you," she said.

B.J. balanced his camera on his shoulder and reached into his pocket. "Here. Take this," he said, holding out a snowy handkerchief.

With a shaking hand, the woman reached for the folded linen. "That's very kind of you. Thank you," she said.

"Just a few questions, please," Annabelle urged. "I promise we'll be brief, and then we won't bother you anymore."

The woman's eyes darted around, and she looked as if she wanted to run away. Finally she swallowed and sighed, clearly just wanting to get it over with. "All right, then," she said, bracing herself. "Go ahead."

B.J. clipped a small microphone to the collar of her blouse.

"How do you know Constance?" Lauren asked as B.J. started recording with his camera.

"I help her with the house," said the woman.

"What's your name?" asked Lauren.

"Ursula. Ursula Bales."

"So, Ursula, what happened?"

"I came in this morning, just like I always do, trying to be quiet. I thought Miss Young was still asleep. So I started some coffee and cut up some fruit and mixed up a batch of the low-fat blueberry muffins she likes so much."

Lauren listened, a concerned expression arranged on her face.

"Then I went out on the deck," Ursula continued. "I could tell that Miss Young had had a drink the night before. She'd left a glass out there. So I brought it inside and put it in the dishwasher." The woman's eyes filled with tears again.

"Then what happened?" urged Lauren.

Ursula's hand trembled as it wiped her cheek. "I went back out on the deck, and I looked down to the pool. I could see a towel on one of the lounge chairs, so

I went down to straighten up. But as I got closer, I saw something dark under the water. At first I didn't recognize it. And then I realized what it was. It was Miss Young, in her black bathing suit, at the bottom of the pool." Ursula lowered her head and cried.

Annabelle made a notation in her notebook, marking the time of Ursula Bales's statement.

"And then what happened?" asked Lauren.

"I called the police," said Ursula, her voice quivering.

"You didn't try to get Constance out of the pool?" asked Lauren.

"There wasn't much point in that." Ursula looked hurt. "There was no saving Miss Young."

"Why were you so sure?"

"Sure of what?"

"Sure that she was dead," said Lauren.

Ursula stopped, unable to continue.

Lauren repeated the question. "How did you know for sure Constance Young was dead?"

"I've told you everything I know," said Ursula, finding her voice. "I have nothing else to say. I have to go now." She pulled the microphone off and hurried away.

Chapter 15

As soon as she arrived at the Broadcast Center, Eliza went directly to the Fishbowl, where Range Bullock and the other producers were going over coverage plans.

"You'll, of course, anchor from here, Eliza. For the lead piece, Lauren Adams will do a live-to-tape report from Constance's house."

"Who's producing?"

"Linus sent up Annabelle Murphy. She and Lauren already have an interview with the housekeeper who found the body." Range paused and shook his head slowly. "I can't believe she's dead," he said.

"Neither can I," said Eliza.

Range took a deep breath and shifted back into "coverage" mode. "Anyway, Lauren and Annabelle are sniffing around to see what other elements they can gather."

"Good," said Eliza. "What else?"

"We're trying to get police authorities to speak to us, maybe get a doctor to describe what happens when someone drowns."

"Are you sure we want to go with the doctor?" asked Eliza. "We don't know for sure that Constance drowned."

"No, we don't."

"I'm still reeling," said Eliza, incredulous. "I can't believe that this has happened. I was just with her. Yesterday she was on top of the world, and today . . . "

Range took a Tums tablet from the bottle he kept on the desk and popped it into his mouth. "No. You never know, do you?" he said. "I'm thinking I better get that will of mine together." He bit into the antacid tablet. "Do you think Constance had a will? She was only thirty-six."

"Probably," said Eliza. "Constance has a sizable estate, and she wasn't the sort of person who left much to chance."

"I wonder who inherits," Range mused.

"She has a younger sister," said Eliza. "I met her yesterday. Faith seemed very different from Constance."

"Well, now she stands to become a very wealthy woman."

"That can be cold comfort when you've lost your sister," said Eliza. "But getting back to tonight's broadcast, we don't know how Constance died—only that she was found in her pool. Maybe we should do a piece toward the end of the broadcast on water safety. Summer is about to start, and it might be a good idea to go over the hazards at the pool and at the beach. Get some statistics on the number of drownings and other water-related accidents and what can be done to prevent them."

"Yeah. A cautionary piece. News they can use," said Range. "All right with you if I get Mack McBride to do that story?"

Eliza nodded.

"Fine," said Range. "At least he'll be part of the show. He was pretty bummed out to hear he wasn't anchoring tonight."

"I don't blame him," said Eliza. "I'd be disappointed, too, if I came all the way from London thinking I was going to get the chance to anchor and then found out I was being pushed aside."

Range shrugged. "That's the breaks," he said. "You're the top dog. Mack's not." He turned his attention back to planning the evening news. "We'll want to do an obituary, tribute-style piece on Constance. I think you should voice that, don't you, Eliza?"

"Yes."

"And I thought it might be interesting to do something on how anchorpeople affect the lives of their audience. How, in Constance's case, millions of Americans started their day with her every morning. Viewers felt they knew her. We'll get reaction from around the country. I was also thinking of calling in Margo Gonzalez to get a psychiatrist to talk about how Constance's death might be affecting our viewers."

"Getting reaction from people on the street sounds like a good idea," agreed Eliza, "but isn't calling in a psychiatrist a bit much? Won't we be overstating the influence of an anchor? Come on, Range, will viewers really be psychologically affected by Constance Young's death?"

"Don't kid yourself. Of course they will be. That's why the networks pay you guys the salaries they do. Because people tune in to see *you*, not just the news. They can get their news from many different sources. But they're loyal to the anchor they trust and love. That's the person they invite into their kitchens, their living rooms, and their bedrooms. When one of them dies, it's personal."

The door to the makeup room was open. Eliza peered inside, hoping that only Doris Brice would be there. The tall, erect woman, wearing a leopard-print tunic, black leggings, and a gold-sequined baseball cap, stood with her back to the door. She was alone and arranging bottles, containers of powders, and brushes on the top of the makeup table.

"Do you have any?"

Doris looked up at the light-rimmed mirror and saw the reflection of Eliza standing behind her. She smiled, knowing exactly what Eliza meant. She drew open the top drawer and pulled out a Butterfinger.

Eliza tore open the orange wrapper and bit into the candy bar. "I needed this," she said. "What a day."

Doris looked sympathetically at Eliza. "Yeah, it's absolutely horrible about Constance. Just horrible."

Eliza nodded.

"Do they know what happened yet?"

"Not exactly," said Eliza. "They don't know if she drowned, had a heart attack, or even if she's been murdered or committed suicide. Nobody's sure. It's just so unexpected and terrible."

Eliza climbed into the makeup chair and looked into the mirror. Wide-set blue eyes crowned by perfectly arched brows stared back. The lipstick had worn off, but the natural color of her full lips still provided contrast to her pale skin. Eliza rested her elbow on the arm of the chair and fingered the scar on her chin, the vestige of an eleven-year-old's miscalculation and diving too deep in a Newport, Rhode Island, swimming pool. The scar was just out of camera range, but Eliza often absentmindedly rubbed it when she was deep in thought.

"Quit picking at that scar," Doris commanded.

Eliza put her hand down and laid her head back against the headrest. "And to top things off, Mack's here," she said, closing her eyes.

Doris tightened the cap on a bottle of moisturizer. "Yeah, good news travels fast. I heard the skunk was in town."

"You know everything before I do, Doris."

"A lot of people come through this door, Eliza. And I've been here a long time. People tell me stuff."

"I know they do," said Eliza. "You knew Mack had slept with that woman in London way before I did. In fact, let's remember, you were the one who told me."

Doris's big brown eyes moistened. "I hated telling you about that, honey, but I figured it would be better coming from me. I didn't want someone catching you off guard and then gossiping to everyone about how you took the news. You know how everybody talks around here."

"You did the right thing, Doris. It was better to hear it from you." Eliza bit off more of the Butterfinger.

"How do you feel about Mack being back?" asked Doris.

"Glad that he's just here for a few days," answered Eliza. "But as much as I dread seeing him, I want to see him, if that makes any sense. I want to hate him, but I don't."

"You better watch out, Eliza. My mama always told me once a cheater, always a cheater."

Eliza found herself defending him. "Mack and I had a good thing going. I enjoyed being with him. He's smart and sensitive and fun to be with."

"And he couldn't keep it in his pants," Doris continued for Eliza.

"I know," said Eliza. "I know. But is a drunken one-night stand, when one of you is in a foreign country feeling alone and sad, enough to negate an entire relationship? Is one mistake enough to sink everything that we had together, everything we could have together?" asked Eliza.

"I guess you have to answer that for yourself," said Doris. "But be careful and quit frowning, will you? It's not good for your face."

Chapter 16

By two o'clock scores of visitors had gathered in the large hall at the Cloisters, listening to the explanation of the giant woven masterpieces on the walls.

"These hangings are a mystery," explained Rowena to the people who stared up at the seven enormous tapestries depicting the hunt of the fabled unicorn. "We aren't certain who commissioned these weavings, nor do we know why this extraordinary set was produced. What we are fairly certain about is that these rich hangings, shining with brilliant silks, wools, gold, and silver, were woven in the Netherlands and the costumes of the men and women featured in the tapestries establish the time of the design to be around the year 1500."

Rowena paused and cleared her throat.

"In no other work of art has the symbolic pursuit and killing of the unicorn been presented in such astonishing detail," she continued. "The history of the unicorn is complex and varied. The idea of a creature with a single horn growing from the center of its head is an ancient one; sculpted figures of such beasts have survived from as early as the eighth century B.C. The unicorn continued its mythical evolution through the Holy Roman Empire, coming to be considered a representation of Christ and the implied twin virtues of strength and purity—might and right. But even as the unicorn came to symbolize earthly and heavenly love, it also came to signify death and violence."

Slowly Rowena traveled, in her thick-soled walking shoes, from tapestry to tapestry, pointing out the vulnerable unicorn in various stages of the hunt. Found, fleeing, fighting to stay free, and then killed and brought to the castle. She pointed out the individualized faces of the hunters and the naturally and accurately depicted flora and fauna that formed a dominant part of the setting of each piece.

"What about the unicorn's horn?" a man asked. "Wasn't that supposed to have mystical powers?"

"Yes," said Rowena. "The unicorn was believed to have many practical applications for humanity, most of which revolved around its magical horn. Legends arose about the unicorn's ability to purify poisoned water, to cure impotent men and barren women of their afflictions, and to prevent plague, epilepsy, and a host of other diseases."

Rowena gave the visitors an opportunity to study each of the tapestries before concluding her talk. Having taken the time to answer a few individuals who came up to her afterward to ask questions, Rowena left the hall and made her way through a labyrinth of corridors until she got to the large back storeroom where the most important items were housed for the special exhibition devoted entirely to the Camelot legend. It had been years in the planning and was set to open next week.

All the items in the room sat in their respective cases or crates, awaiting their final placement in the exhibit hall. Every artifact would have its own distinctive placard describing what it was and giving a short explanatory history of its provenance.

The ivory unicorn with the golden crown that King Arthur was thought to have given Lady Guinevere was to be the highlight of the exhibit. Its image was the focus of all the brochures and banners that heralded the show. Unicorn-inspired stationery, scarves, jewelry, books, and games were being stocked in the museum gift shop. But, more important, the love story—the legendary love *triangle* involving Arthur, Guinevere, and Lancelot—had intrigued and fascinated countless people over the centuries, and the Cloisters was counting on that magic to attract throngs through its doors.

With just a few days to go until the debut of the exhibit, Rowena opened the box. She searched intently, then desperately, through the special batting. The unicorn wasn't there.

As she walked to her small office, Rowena tried to stay calm. She was uncertain about what she should do first. Should she call security or the police and alert them that the amulet was missing? If she did that, the story would be out of her hands. There could be a lot of negative publicity, and Rowena very much wanted to avoid that. Scandal wouldn't be good for the museum.

Stuart Whitaker was one of their largest donors. Rowena herself had arranged the private tour for him and Constance Young while the exhibit was being constructed. Maybe there was some misunderstanding that could be cleared up and rectified without bringing law enforcement into it. That would be better for everyone involved.

Rowena made up her mind. She went to her small office, closed the door, and found Stuart's number in her Rolodex. The phone rang half a dozen times, and Rowena was about to hang up when Stuart answered.

"Hello?" his voice sounded raspy.

"Yes. This is Rowena Quincy from the Cloisters. Is this Mr. Whitaker?"

"Yes, it is." There was no note of recognition in his voice.

"I don't know if you remember me, Mr. Whitaker. You asked me to set up a private tour for you a few months ago."

There was an uncomfortable silence before Stuart replied. "Oh, yes, I remember you, Ms. Quincy. Thank you. We had a lovely tour."

"I'm so glad, Mr. Whitaker. I wish you had allowed me to escort you around myself."

"That is very kind of you, Ms. Quincy, but as you know, I did not need a docent, because I know a fair amount about the Cloisters myself."

"Of course you do," said Rowena.

"Providing a guard to take us to the areas closed to the public was more than enough. You were very gracious."

"Again, it was my pleasure, Mr. Whitaker."

Stuart waited for her to continue.

"This is very awkward, Mr. Whitaker. I'm not quite sure how to bring this up."

"Why not just say whatever it is you have to say?" Stuart suggested quietly.

"Well, I remember that Constance Young was with you then, Mr. Whitaker. In fact, after that, Miss Young agreed to be the mistress of ceremonies for our Camelot Exhibit preview and reception Wednesday night. But in the newspaper this morning, I saw a picture of her taken yesterday, and she was wearing what appeared to be a carved ivory unicorn that we had procured for our upcoming exhibition."

"Yes?"

"I checked, and the ivory unicorn is no longer in its case here, Mr. Whitaker."

"And your point is . . . ?"

"My point is, I thought I would confer with you before I did anything else."

"What are you suggesting, Ms. Quincy?"

"I'm not suggesting anything, Mr. Whitaker. I was just letting you know, in case . . . " Her voice trailed off.

"In case what?"

"In case you might know what happened to it."

"Why would I know that?" asked Stuart.

"It's just that I didn't want to go to the authorities . . . in case there was a reasonable explanation," said Rowena.

"How can you be sure the unicorn you saw Constance wearing in the picture came from the Cloisters?"

"I'm *not* sure, Mr. Whitaker. But I do know the unicorn that should be here is missing."

"Don't tell me you think Constance Young obtained the unicorn illegally."

"I don't want to think that, Mr. Whitaker. Believe me."

Stuart's voice rose in anger. "To suggest that Constance Young would steal something is an outrage."

Rowena ran her free hand through her mousy brown hair. "No, no, no, Mr. Whitaker. I'm not suggesting that she stole it. Of course not."

"You had better not be, Ms. Quincy." Stuart warned. "It is wrong to speak ill of the dead."

Rowena recoiled. "What do you mean?"

"You have not heard?"

"Heard what?" asked Rowena.

"Turn on the radio or CNN. Constance Young is no longer with us, and you will have to find someone else to host your reception Wednesday night."

Chapter 17

What's worse? Faith wondered. Would it be worse to have Mother lucid and heartbroken when she heard the news of her daughter's death? Or would it be worse to break the news to a childlike, uncomprehending shell of a woman and watch her show no reaction at all?

Faith sat with her hands tightly clasped in her lap at the kitchen table. Her husband slid a mug of tea in front of her.

"I'm not sure how she'll take it," Faith said. "I could use some moral support, Todd, when I go in there to tell her."

Todd glanced at his watch.

"Please don't tell me that you're still thinking you can get your golf game in, Todd. Not today."

"Your mother is sleeping, Faith. What should we do? Wake her up to tell her the bad news?"

"No, but when she wakes up on her own, I think we have to tell her then." Faith took a cautious sip of the scalding tea.

Todd leaned against the Formica counter and crossed his arms in front of his chest. "I don't see where a couple of hours one way or the other makes any difference. When we tell her is not going to change anything."

"My sister is dead, Todd, and I don't think it's too much to ask that you skip your Saturday golf game."

"It relaxes me, Faith. And let's be honest here, shall we? There was no love lost between you and Constance."

Faith looked at her husband. "That was a cruel thing to say."

Todd shrugged. "I'm only calling a spade a spade, Faith."

"Don't kid yourself, Todd. You're only trying to justify leaving to play golf." Picking up her mug, Faith rose and walked down the small corridor that led to her mother's room. As she stood in the doorway, watching her mother sleep, Faith heard the door to the garage open and close. She fumed as she listened to the sound of the car engine turning over.

Faith walked back to the kitchen and opened a bag of cookies. With tears of frustration in her eyes, she found herself speculating about Constance's will. Her sister's estate had to be quite substantial. On so many levels, having all that money would be so freeing.

Chapter 18

Jason Vaughan sat on his couch staring at the television set, waiting for any scrap of new information about the death of Constance Young. The CNN anchor was recycling the same information over and over, just telling it in different ways. An employee had found Constance's body in the swimming pool of her weekend home in Westchester County. There was no obvious sign of foul play, yet there was already speculation that the death might not have been an accident. An autopsy would be performed.

Footage of Constance in her farewell appearance on *KEY to America* was shown. Then, in what must have been a hastily assembled video package, an obituary included family pictures of Constance as a young girl and as a high school cheerleader. Later there were shots of her taken in college, followed by video of Constance after she won the Miss Virginia title. Next came shots from her early days as a reporter in small-market local television. As the footage continued, viewers watched the progression of hair and clothing styles that led up to the sassy blond hair and smart green suit Jason had seen Constance wearing just yesterday in front of the restaurant.

There were clips of Constance interviewing the president of the United States and the First Lady as well as Elmo, Miss Piggy, and Oscar the Grouch. Constance was shown stirring up cake batters in cooking segments and trying to keep her balance as a teenage champion attempted to teach her how to skateboard. She was shown laughing with lottery winners and crying with people who had lost their homes in New Orleans after Hurricane Katrina. Whether she was kissing a monkey or wiping away an orphan's tears, the scope of her job was as wide as human experience and a constant source of continuing education.

But nowhere in the television profile of Constance Young was there any mention of the havoc she had wrought in his life, Jason thought. In the list of professional accomplishments, wrecking him hadn't even been worth listing. He had gone from man of the hour to persona non grata, and Constance had pounded the final nail into his coffin.

The phone rang. Jason leaned over the pile of un-opened bills to reach the receiver.

"Hey, Jason. It's Larry."

Larry Sargent? Jason was baffled. When was the last time his agent had called him on a Saturday? In fact, when was the last time Larry had called him at all?

"Hiya, Larry. What's up?"

"I guess you've heard the news."

"You mean about the witch?"

"It's not nice to speak ill of the dead, Jason."

"You're right."

"But now that she's dead, the timing of this couldn't be better, could it? The book comes out on Tuesday."

Jason chuckled bitterly. "Yeah, what are the chances of that? Too bad we sold it for such a crappy advance. The publisher isn't doing a thing to push it."

"*Wasn't* doing a thing to push it," the agent corrected. "Past tense. Young's death changes everything. She's given us a big fat gift. We'll earn out that miser-able advance in the first week."

"I don't know about that, Larry." Jason was afraid to get his hopes up.

"Are you kidding me? Before today your book was just the ranting and grumbling of some bitter loser."

"Thanks, Larry. I really appreciate that."

"You know what I mean, buddy. We couldn't get any of the big boys interested in the book, and we had to settle for this second-rate house. But if we play our cards right, we have the most mouthwatering public-relations and marketing opportunity. Constance Young is dead, and your book tells the world why."

"Not exactly, Larry."

"Not exactly *what*?"

"I don't explain why Constance Young is dead. I only explain how she screwed me, how she ruined my life."

"Yeah, and you give a couple of other nice examples of what a viper she could be. Believe me, the media—and the public—are going to eat this up. We just need to get you booked on the morning shows."

Nobody should rejoice in the misfortune of another, but in this case, Jason thought as he hung up the phone, he was entitled to a bit of gloating. Constance Young had ruined his life, and now, not only had she gotten what she deserved, her death was going to reinstate him into respectability and fiscal security.

Chapter 19

Engrossed in thoughts about what had happened to Constance, Eliza was walking toward her office when she spotted Mack McBride coming down the hall. She could feel her heart start to beat faster and only hoped the heat she was immediately beginning to feel in her cheeks wouldn't show. For a moment Eliza wondered if she could slip into her office and just pretend she hadn't seen him, when the deep voice called out.

"Eliza."

Too late to escape, she thought, arranging her face in a pleasant expression. As Mack drew closer, Eliza could tell that London was agreeing with him. He looked fit and as handsome as ever. Eliza braced herself as Mack reached her and kissed her on the cheek. Instantly she recognized the smell of his aftershave.

"Mack." Eliza smiled. "How *are* you?"

"Can't complain, I guess, except the KEY News anchor bigfooted me. I came all the way across the pond thinking I was going to get to sit in the big chair, and now I'm doing a story on water safety instead." Laugh lines crinkled at the corner of Mack's eyes. "I'm off to New Jersey now to shoot my stand-up at some suburban pool."

"Sorry about that," said Eliza.

"Not as sorry as I am," he said. The smile on Mack's face masked any real disappointment.

"Unbelievable about Constance, isn't it?" Eliza shook her head and shivered involuntarily. "It's so terrible, so sad."

"Honestly?" Mack asked. "I was never really a fan, but it's always tragic when someone so young dies. Constance was in her prime. But you want to hear something really sick that occurred to me?"

Eliza nodded.

"I bet Linus Nazareth isn't sad she's dead. I bet he's glad."

"That's a little cold, isn't it?" asked Eliza.

"Maybe," said Mack. "But nobody leaves *KEY to America* unless Linus wants them to leave. And Linus didn't want Constance to go over to the competition."

Eliza looked at Mack with skepticism. "I don't know about that," she said. "Linus laid on a little guilt, but generally he was pretty supportive when I left *KTA* for the *Evening Headlines.*"

"That's because you weren't going to compete with him on another network," said Mack. "He liked the idea that 'his girl' was talented enough to take over the *Evening Headlines* after Bill Kendall committed suicide. After that whole thing, this news division was rocked to the core. I heard that Linus took plenty of credit for grooming you for the evening anchor chair."

"I heard the same thing." Eliza smiled. "I don't know what I would have done without him, do you?"

"Joke if you want to, Eliza," said Mack. "But I'm telling you, Linus only wants what's good for Linus. And even though he's been able to install his girlfriend as the new *KTA* host, Constance Young was still his first pick. He was infuriated that not only did she have the audacity to leave, she was going to compete with him."

"Well," Eliza observed, "now at least he doesn't have to deal with coming up against her every morning. Life was going to be jolly hell for the *KTA* staff."

Mack shrugged. "It still will be," he said.

Eliza looked up into Mack's face and tried to read what was in his eyes. Discontent? Cynicism? Sadness?

"How's everything else with you, Mack?"

"Okay, I guess."

"Are you enjoying living in London?"

"Yeah. It's great. But I can tell I'll be ready to come back home when my overseas stint is finished."

"Have any idea when that will be?" she asked.

"I still have another six months on my contract," he answered. "Then we'll see where I go and what I do."

Eliza looked at him quizzically. "You aren't thinking of leaving KEY News, are you?" she asked.

Mack looked down at his shoes. "I've had a lot of time to think over there, Eliza. I've been thinking about life and what I want from it. Professionally I'm not totally certain about what I want." He raised his head and looked directly into her eyes. "But personally there is one thing that I'm always sure of."

Eliza felt her pulse quicken. She wasn't ready for this conversation. Not now. Part of her wanted to put her arms around him and hold on to him. The other part of her wanted to run away from him. She chose the flight response.

Looking at her tank watch, she made an excuse about having to attend to something for the broadcast. She left Mack standing in the hallway watching after her as she fled into her office.

Chapter 20

As the Saturday-afternoon visitors were milling through the halls of the Cloisters, Rowena sat in her office. She listened intently as the head of security questioned the man who had stood guard while Stuart Whitaker and Constance Young took their private tour.

"Were you with them every moment?" the security chief asked.

"Yes."

"You never left their sides?"

"No, sir."

"You know, Jerry, sooner or later the truth always comes out. There are pictures of a national news anchorwoman wearing what looks to be a piece that we're depending on for our new exhibit. Now that woman is dead. Don't you think that when the police are told that the unicorn amulet is missing from the Cloisters and they look at the images of Constance Young wearing just such a piece right before she died—don't you think the police will be up here to investigate?"

"Probably."

"Well?"

"There aren't any video cameras in the area where the unicorn was kept," said Jerry.

"And that means you think no one will be able to figure out who took it?" asked the security chief. "Don't kid yourself, Jerry. Something will give it away, and if you know anything, it'll be a helluva lot better if you share it now."

Jerry squirmed in his chair.

"If I find out you know something, Jerry, not only will you be fired, I'll see to it that you never get another security job."

Jerry's shoulders sagged. "Okay, okay. Mr. Whitaker pressed a hundred-dollar bill into my hand and told me to go outside for a smoke. I just thought he wanted to be alone with her in there for a little while. Who wouldn't want to be alone with a babe like that, especially a nerdy guy like him? I thought, what the heck? Whitaker has given millions to this place. Why would he take something from it?"

Rowena interrupted. "We don't know that Stuart Whitaker took the amulet, Chief. Maybe someone else did."

"What? You think Constance Young took the amulet?" the head of security asked.

"I don't know what to think," said Rowena. "But even though I hate to have the museum exposed to negative publicity, I do know it's time to call the police. There's no other choice."

Chapter 21

A string of vans, cars, and satellite trucks with New York press plates lined the road in front of Constance Young's country house. With each addition of a rival news organization, Lauren Adams grew more tense.

"We don't have enough," she complained, snapping her gum. "We should have the very best access, but we're stuck out here just like every other network or station. We don't have anything that will separate our coverage at Constance Young's house from our competition's, and that's just crap. What are we going to do about it, Annabelle?"

You mean, what am I going to do about it? thought Annabelle, refusing to get flustered. "I'm not sure, Lauren," she said aloud. "Our hands are pretty well tied. If the cops won't let us in, they won't let us in."

"Exactly the kind of defeatist attitude I love to hear from my producer," Lauren answered. "If that's the best you can come up with, we're in even more trouble than I thought."

B.J. stood within earshot, listening to the exchange. He glanced at Annabelle, who subtly shook her head from side to side, warning him not to say anything. He knew that Annabelle could take care of herself. She had one of the best reputations at KEY News. Correspondents were constantly asking that Annabelle be assigned to produce their stories. Yet B.J. ached to put Lauren in her place. Experience, though, had taught him that there was a price to be paid for contradicting or even speaking up to the on-air talent. He had tried that when he'd worked as a producer-cameraman with Constance—and when his contract was up, he wasn't renewed as a producer. Only his union membership had saved the cameraman portion of his job. B.J. was certain that Constance had been instrumental in cutting him down. He suspected that Lauren might also be capable of destroying anyone who got in her way.

He'd been debating whether to mention to Lauren what Boyd Irons had told him when they were in the men's room. Just the day before, a dead dog had been found in the woods that surrounded the country house. B.J. didn't know if that would turn out to be a coincidence, but screw Lauren and her bad attitude. He wasn't going to share any editorial information with her at all. He was going to concentrate solely on the video he recorded. He would still do his utmost to get the best pictures he could, though—since that was what he was going to be judged on.

He approached Lauren and Annabelle. "I'm going to cut through these trees and see if I can get in there and get some pictures of the pool," he said, softly so that none of the other newspeople could hear.

Lauren nodded approval. "Finally somebody's doing something," she said.

Making sure nobody was looking in his direction, B.J. made his way through the high grass at the side of the road and slipped between the trees. His shoes sank into the soft, muddy ground, and he cursed himself for not wearing his work boots. He'd thought he'd be shooting at Constance Young's luxurious country house, not traipsing through the woods.

As he went deeper, B.J. began to hear voices, which he assumed to be the police searching the property. He followed the sound, coming to a high fence. Tall evergreens on the other side blocked the view to the pool, but the bushes also shielded B.J. from sight.

If he wanted pictures of the pool, he was going to have to climb the fence. Getting the camera over would be no small feat.

Taking off his belt, B.J. threaded it through the handle of the camera and fastened it, creating a long leather circle, which he pulled over his head. Then he carefully slid the camera around to his back. With his hands free, B.J. reached upward and boosted himself off the ground, managing to grab onto the top of the fence. He tried to hoist himself up, but he couldn't make it over, and the leather strap, weighed down by the camera, nearly strangled him.

Standing on the ground again, B.J. could hear the voices coming from the other side of the evergreens.

"Something new has been added."

"What is it now?"

"We're supposed to be looking for a unicorn."

"A what?"

"A unicorn. You know. Those horses with the long horn coming out of the middle of their heads? Well, we're supposed to look for a little ivory one."

"What's the deal?"

"It's some sort of antique, and it's missing from a museum, and Constance Young was seen wearing it around her neck. We're supposed to see if we can find it out here."

"How did she get it?"

"What do I look like? The *Jeopardy!* champ? How do I know? Maybe someone gave it to her, maybe she stole it, maybe she was killed for it."

Lauren watched for B.J. while she paced up and down at the side of the KEY News satellite truck. Finally she spotted him coming out the woods and rushed toward him.

"Did you get the pictures?" she asked with an expectant look on her face.

"I couldn't. The fence was too high," B.J. explained, out of breath. "But—"

Lauren cut him off. "What do you mean, you didn't get them?"

Her tone irked B.J. "Just what I said," he answered. "I wasn't able to climb over the fence with my camera. But—"

"No buts, B.J. You didn't get the pictures, and that's that. I don't have time to listen to any excuses. I have a script to finish writing." Lauren spun around and stalked back to the satellite truck.

B.J. watched her go and struggled to keep his face expressionless. If anyone asked him later, he could truthfully say that he had tried to tell her.

Stupid, stupid woman.

Chapter 22

Getting increasingly closer to deadline, Lauren found fault with every single script suggestion Annabelle made and complained bitterly that she wasn't getting the support she needed. Though Annabelle attempted to reassure Lauren and do everything she could think of to provide the most editorial and material assistance possible, she was relieved when her cell phone rang. It was an opportunity to escape the truck and get away from Lauren.

"Hi, Annabelle. It's Eliza. How's it coming out there?"

"It's coming." Annabelle's voice was flat.

"That good, huh?"

"Don't worry. We'll be able to make a piece. We have exteriors of the property, an interview with the housekeeper and some neighbors."

"Any of them see anything?" asked Eliza.

"Well, the housekeeper, as you know, is the one who found the body. We have only reaction to Constance's death from a couple of the neighbors. Nobody can see anybody else's house out here. So far we haven't had anyone come forward to say they heard or saw anything suspicious."

"Police?" asked Eliza.

"They say they'll send someone out to talk in a half hour. I really wish we could get pictures of the pool, but the police still aren't letting anyone on the grounds. I called Boyd Irons and asked him to call Constance's sister and see if we could arrange access through her."

"That's kind of a long shot, isn't it?" asked Eliza. "If the cops want the crime scene cordoned off, they aren't going to open it just because Constance's sister asks them to."

Annabelle heaved a deep sigh. "You know that, and I know that, but Lauren wanted to try anyway."

"I get the picture," said Eliza. "Not the easiest assignment you've ever had, huh?"

"Let me put it this way," said Annabelle. "Lauren is a challenge. I know she's under a lot of pressure, so I'm trying to make allowances."

"All right," said Eliza. "Get back to it . . . but, Annabelle?"

"Yes?"

"I just wanted to tell you that I'm very sorry about Constance. I know you two were very close."

"Thank you, Eliza. I appreciate your saying that. Our friendship disintegrated quite a while ago, but at one time we were really tight. We started out at KEY together, and over the years she was a good friend to me. But, unfortunately, the relationship changed." Annabelle paused as she reflected. "I always hoped that Constance and I might patch things up someday. I always thought there would be plenty of time for that."

Chapter 23

The five o'clock news blared from the radio in the taxi Boyd took uptown from his place to Central Park South. He listened carefully to the announcer's words. Constance had been found dead in the pool at her home in Westchester County. Police weren't sure yet what the cause of death was. It was the same information Boyd had gotten from Linus Nazareth when the executive producer had called for Constance's sister's phone number this morning. Boyd was glad he hadn't had to break the news to Faith Hansen.

The cab pulled to the curb, and Boyd paid the fare. The doorman standing beneath the awning nodded in recognition. He wondered if the doorman had heard the news yet.

Taking the elevator to the fifteenth floor, Boyd dug into his pocket and pulled out the key. He let himself inside and stood listening in the entry hall. He heard nothing but the clock ticking from its case on the fireplace mantel.

"Kimba. Where are you?" he called, and waited. But the cat didn't appear.

How many times had he resented having to come up here to feed Constance's cat? How many times had he come into her apartment and wished it were his, instead of that tiny downtown studio he could barely afford? How many times had he looked out the huge window at the sweeping view of Central Park and pretended he lived here? How many times had he told himself that Constance didn't deserve this place? She could afford it, yes. But she didn't *deserve* it.

Boyd went into the kitchen and put out fresh food and changed the water in the cat's bowl. Then he went down the hallway and cleaned out the litter box. He was in no hurry to complete the unpleasant chore, because the next one he had to undertake would be much more difficult.

After he washed his hands, Boyd went into the master bedroom and stretched out on the tufted chaise longue positioned in the corner. He opened his cell phone and, finding the number, pressed the button to call Constance's sister. Faith Hansen answered on the third ring.

"Hello. This is Boyd Irons, Constance's assistant." His voice trailed up at the end, in a question.

"Of course, Boyd."

"Thank you. I wasn't sure if you would remember me." He'd programmed Faith's number into his cell phone so that he would be able to reach Constance's next of kin in case of an emergency, but Constance hardly ever asked him to get her sister on the phone for her. Boyd was glad now that he'd made it a point to speak to Faith at the luncheon yesterday. The poor woman had looked so ill at ease that he felt sorry for her.

"God," said Faith. "Was the luncheon only yesterday? It seems like a hundred years ago."

"I'm so sorry about your sister, Mrs. Hansen. I really, really am."

"Thank you, Boyd. I appreciate that."

"I wanted to ask you what I could do to help."

There was a momentary pause as Faith considered the offer.

"You know, there is something you could do to help," she said. "Would you go to Constance's apartment? I would really appreciate it if I didn't have to drive in and pick something out for her to wear. You know, something to send over to the funeral parlor. You probably know what her favorite things were more than I do."

"I'd be happy to do that," said Boyd. "Well, not happy exactly, but . . . "

"I know what you meant, Boyd."

Boyd thought of the fabulous garments hanging in the closets and wondered what he would pick for a last outfit for Constance. The blue Oscar de la Renta? The pale yellow Ralph Lauren? The black Armani? And who was going to get all the gorgeous dresses and suits and handbags? He had friends in the Village who would kill for that wardrobe.

"I'm actually at Constance's apartment now," he said, pulling himself from his reverie. "I'm feeding her cat."

"Oh, no. I hadn't realized Constance had a cat."

Real close sisters, Boyd thought.

"Yes. Kimba." Boyd hesitated before continuing. "I was thinking maybe I should take the cat home with me—or I could bring it out to *you* if you'd like."

"Uh-uh. I've never been a big animal fan," said Faith. "I can't even think about having a cat. I already have enough poop to clean up around here. I'd appreciate it if you would take care of it, Boyd."

"All right, Mrs. Hansen."

"Thank you, Boyd."

"People will be asking me, Mrs. Hansen. Do you have any idea what the arrangements will be?"

"We can't plan anything firm until the autopsy is completed, but I understand that the police are fast-tracking that," said Faith. "I do know that we'll have a private funeral and burial as soon as possible. No sense in prolonging things." Faith paused, trying to focus on the essentials. "I guess that's something else you could help me with, Boyd. Would you prepare a list of people you think should be invited to attend the funeral? I really don't know who Constance was close to."

"All right," Boyd agreed. "But are you just interested in having good friends of Constance's, or do you want to include some of her professional colleagues as well?"

"What do you think about that?" asked Faith.

If you only ask people who felt affection for Constance, the pews will be pretty empty, thought Boyd. "I think it's respectful to include the people she worked with," he said. "Her professional life meant so much to her."

"It was just about everything," said Faith.

"Okay. I'll get the list together and check on the clothes," Boyd said. "Anything else?"

"Actually, Boyd, there *is* something else," answered Faith. "I'll need Constance's attorney's phone number. Please don't think terribly of me, but I really need to know what's in her will."

"Of course," said Boyd. "Hold on. I'll look up the number on my cell phone."

From his many "reconnaissance missions" through the drawers and closets of Constance's apartment, Boyd knew exactly where the will was—and what was in it. *God,* he thought. *When she finds out what Constance actually left her, she's going to lose her mind!* Revealing that information wasn't Boyd's job, he felt, so he dutifully gave Faith the attorney's telephone number.

"I have one more thing to ask you, Mrs. Hansen. I hate to bother you with it."

"What is it?"

"Our newspeople are out at Constance's country place, and the police aren't letting them on the property. They wanted me to ask you if you could pull any strings. You know, as next of kin and all."

"You know what, Boyd? I don't really want to get in the middle of that. I hope you understand."

"Certainly. But I had to ask."

"I get it," said Faith. "No problem."

As Boyd snapped his cell phone closed, Kimba jumped up on the chaise and into his lap. A tear trickled down Boyd's cheek as he stroked the cat's soft gray fur. He was surprised that he actually felt as bad as he did about Constance's death. Yesterday Boyd had been relieved that he no longer would have to work for her. Now, sitting in her bedroom, he felt conflicted at the thought that he would never see Constance again.

Chapter 24

B.J. waited until Lauren's piece had been fed from the satellite truck to the Broadcast Center before he walked down the road and found a secluded spot.

"B.J. D'Elia for Eliza Blake," he said into his cell phone, momentarily wondering if he was going to be put off onto an assistant. But Eliza took the cameraman's call herself.

"Hi, B.J. What's up?"

He recounted the conversation about the missing ivory unicorn he'd overheard as he crouched behind the fence near the pool, and he told her about the dead dog that Boyd said had been found on Constance's property the morning before.

"Interesting," said Eliza. "Very interesting. We'll make some calls here and see what we can find out."

"Should we tell the police about the dog?" asked B.J.

"No, let's hold off on that," answered Eliza. "If we can confirm it, the police will hear about it on the broadcast tonight, along with everybody else."

The police would neither confirm nor deny that an ivory unicorn, or any other jewelry, was missing, but Boyd Irons provided the phone number for the young man who had spotted a dead, full-grown Great Dane on Constance Young's property when he went to empty the contents of the pool's skimmer baskets in the woods.

"I was told to dispose of the dog, so I did," the pool man said. "But let me tell you, it was a pretty hard job getting that thing off the property and out to the dump."

After Eliza introduced *The KEY Evening Headlines* from the Broadcast Center, Lauren Adams's piece from Westchester County led the show. Lauren's narration explained what had been happening, the housekeeper described what she'd found when she came to work that morning, well-heeled neighbors expressed their shock, and a police spokesperson said only that it was too soon to determine the cause of death and that the investigation was continuing. There were pictures of the media frenzy that had been created as every news organization wanted to have a story on their airwaves about the death of Constance Young, but there were no pictures from inside the fencing that surrounded the property.

At the end of the preedited package, Lauren appeared live, on-screen, standing at the head of Constance's driveway.

"Eliza, there are still many unanswered questions tonight. Police sources tell us that they hope to have the results of Constance Young's autopsy as early as Monday."

The camera shot was switched to the Broadcast Center studio, where Eliza sat at the anchor desk.

"Let me ask you, Lauren, about this report that a dead dog was found on the property yesterday. What do you know about that?"

Lauren stared into the camera, a blank expression on her face. There was an awkward pause before Eliza realized that Lauren had no idea what she was referring to.

"A workman says he found a dog, a Great Dane, lying dead in the woods out near the pool yesterday," Eliza jumped in. "It could be just a coincidence, of course, but the police will certainly be checking into that, won't they?"

Lauren's discomfort was apparent. "They certainly will be, Eliza."

"Thank you, Lauren."

The second she was sure she was off the air, Lauren pulled out her earpiece, disconnected her microphone, called the Broadcast Center, and asked to be put through to Range Bullock in the control room.

"What was that all about, Range?" Lauren fumed. "I looked like an idiot."

"I don't know, Lauren," the *Evening Headlines* executive producer answered, keeping his voice low. "You tell me."

"Why didn't anybody talk to me about that dead-dog story?" Lauren demanded.

"We assumed you knew about it. You're out there. You should have known. Don't you talk to your own people?"

"What do you mean?" Lauren's voice rose in suspicion.

"B.J. D'Elia is the one who told Eliza about the dog, and we confirmed it with Boyd Irons and the pool guy," said Range.

"So my cameraman and my assistant are both screwing me," Lauren pondered aloud. "Nice. Very nice."

Chapter 25

At 6:57 P.M., during the commercial break, a medium-height, red-haired woman mounted the platform and took the seat beside Eliza at the anchor desk.

"Ten seconds." The voice of the stage manager boomed though the studio.

The woman waited while a microphone was clipped to her jacket.

"Five, four, three, two, one." The stage manager cued Eliza to begin.

Eliza looked directly into the camera. "Tonight we've told you what we know so far about the untimely death of Constance Young. In the days to come, we will learn more about what actually happened, the hows and whys that we don't understand yet. We here at KEY

News have lost a colleague, someone we've known over the years to be a gifted and dedicated newswoman. But tonight people across America are feeling the loss of Constance Young as well."

Eliza turned to the woman sitting beside her. "KEY News psychological expert Dr. Margo Gonzalez is here to tell us why. Dr. Gonzalez?"

The director cut to a head-on shot of the woman.

"Thank you, Eliza. On the surface Constance Young led a very glamorous life. Professionally, viewers saw her interviewing presidents and kings and sports heroes and rock stars. Her access to and association with these celebrities made her a celebrity as well. On the flip side, the morning-television audience saw her talking with children or petting camels and elephants or dressing in Halloween costumes. That made her very human, very approachable. So on the one hand Constance was up there on a pedestal, and, on the other, people felt they knew her."

"They felt they knew her even though they'd never met her?" Eliza asked.

Margo nodded. "Yes, because they learned so much about her. People were intrigued by her personal life, whom she dated, where she went, what she wore. There were countless articles about her, discussing her family, her friends, where she grew up, where she went to school, where she lived, what she did for fun. How many times have you seen a picture of Constance in a magazine, Eliza?"

Eliza smiled. "Too many to count."

"Exactly," said Margo. "All that exposure—on the air, in the print media, in ad campaigns—made Constance a public figure, but in addition to that, her coming into our homes on a daily basis, so we started our day with her, morning after morning, bred a real familiarity. When the day broke, there was Constance Young, just like the sun. We came to feel we actually knew her, that she was a part of our lives. Of course we're going to feel upset and sad that she's gone."

Chapter 26

As soon as the broadcast was over, Lauren tore down the country road in her BMW. Annabelle and B.J. drove back to Manhattan together, dreading what was waiting for them at the Broadcast Center. The executive producer had instructed them to meet him in his office before they went home for the night.

"We're in it deep, Beej," said Annabelle, resting her head back and closing her eyes.

"I might be in it, but you're not," B.J. said calmly. "You didn't know a thing about the dead dog or the cops talking about the missing unicorn, and you certainly didn't know that I was going to tell Eliza instead of Lauren."

"I was the producer, B.J. It's my responsibility to know."

"Don't worry. I'm gonna take all the heat, but there isn't really that much Linus can do about it." B.J. shrugged. "The worst that will happen is he'll drop me from the show, but he won't be able to fire me from KEY News. The union will protect me."

Annabelle stared straight ahead at the highway. B.J. was single, and while he still had his rent and bills to pay, it somehow seemed that he would be all right no matter what. But Annabelle was the main breadwinner in her house. Her family couldn't continue the life they had without her salary. A family of four, living in New York City, wouldn't be able to cut it on the money Mike made as a firefighter. She couldn't afford to lose her job.

Though she sometimes daydreamed about quitting her job at *KEY to America* and escaping the grinding pressure Linus inflicted on his staff, Annabelle didn't delude herself that things would necessarily be any better at another network. Plus, she felt a loyalty to KEY News and didn't want to leave. Now she prayed Linus wasn't going to force her to go.

The office door was open.

"Well, well, if it isn't the dynamic duo." Linus sat behind his massive, cluttered desk. He was leaning back in his chair, a football palmed in his thick hand. "Come in. Close the door and take a seat."

Annabelle and B.J. obeyed as Linus tossed the ball in the air and caught it.

"You know, I've been in this business for over thirty years, and I've seen a lot of things, unbelievable things." Linus spoke calmly. "But I don't ever recall seeing such a blatant screwing of a network correspondent by her colleagues as I witnessed tonight."

"First of all, Annabelle had nothing to do with it," B.J. spoke up. "I tried to tell Lauren what I'd heard, and she wouldn't listen to me."

The executive producer leaned forward and slammed the football down on the desk. "That's not the way Lauren remembers it!" he yelled.

"Well, that's the way it happened," B.J. said, quietly but firmly.

"Are you telling me Lauren is lying?" Linus pressed.

"I'm saying I made an attempt to talk to Lauren and she dismissed me," said B.J.

Linus turned to Annabelle. "And you. What part did you play in all this?"

Before Annabelle could answer, B.J. spoke up again. "I *told* you, Linus. Annabelle had nothing to do with it. She didn't know that I was going to *call* Eliza, and she didn't know anything about what I was going to *tell* Eliza."

"Well, damn it, she should have known." Linus's face was flushed now. "That's her job." He turned to Annabelle. "What do you have to say for yourself?"

Annabelle looked Linus straight in the eye. She swallowed, knowing that she was about to commit professional suicide.

"Here's what I have to say for myself, Linus. You are a bully and a tyrant and a nightmare to work for. But I have never given anything less than my all for this show. Yeah, I need my job, but I'm sick and tired of the crap you dish out."

Annabelle rose from her chair, turned, and walked out, leaving Linus and B.J. staring after her.

Chapter 27

The report on the Evening Headlines meant that it was probably just a matter of time before the police started calling around trying to figure out where the big dog had come from. If the Dane hadn't been so damned heavy to move, he could have been stashed in the trunk of the car and dumped in some remote and nameless location. That had been the plan. But that hadn't been possible. As it was, dragging the heavy, soaking-wet dog a few yards into the woods had been messy, and a lot of work.

But that guy from the shelter might have seen, or he would see in the days to come, the report of the dead Great Dane at Constance's house and volunteer the information to the police. Even though great care had been taken to find a shelter that didn't require personal references and picture identification, even though a fake address had been given for the license and a disguise of sorts had been worn, one could never be too careful. There might be some incriminating loose end. And that wouldn't be good.

Chapter 28

The kids were already fed, bathed, and in their pajamas when Annabelle arrived home at her Greenwich Village apartment. Thomas met her at the door and threw his arms around his mother's waist.

"Mom's home!" he called out to his sister.

Tara ran over, brown hair flying, her round, blue eyes sparkling and a satisfied smile on her face. "I'm glad you're home, Mommy."

"I missed you guys," said Annabelle, hugging and kissing them. "Where's Daddy?"

"He's in the shower," said Tara.

"How was the day with Mrs. Nuzzo?" Annabelle asked. "Did you have a good time?"

"Yes," Thomas answered. "We had pancakes for lunch."

"Pancakes? For lunch? Wow, that's neat," said Annabelle.

There were many things for which Annabelle was grateful, and one of them was the fact that, at seven years old, her children didn't hold grudges. Today they'd been looking forward to their riding lesson at the Claremont Riding Academy. Annabelle's parents had given the twins a series of lessons for their birthday gifts. The children learned how to walk, trot, and canter their quiet mounts. The horseback program stressed patience and concentration along with physical coordination, strength, and agility. Students also developed a sense of responsibility in caring for their animals. Annabelle enjoyed the lessons, because the kids had fun.

But when the twins were told this morning that there was a change in plans—their mother had to go to work, and they'd be spending much of the day with Mrs. Nuzzo while their father got some sleep after working the night shift—they took the news in stride. Annabelle wondered how much they remembered about the period of Mike's terrible depression and if they were just so glad to have him back, going to work at the firehouse, reading stories to them at bedtime, and being the loving father they remembered, that they didn't want to complain about the missed riding lessons lest they rock the family boat.

"I brought you something," said Annabelle, holding out a white cardboard box.

"Magnolia Bakery!" Thomas screeched, recognizing it immediately.

The kids hopped from one foot to the other as Annabelle opened the box, revealing the three-inch-wide cupcakes, top-heavy from all the pastel-colored vanilla frosting.

"I want a green cupcake," said Thomas.

"I want a pink one," Tara chimed in.

"Eat them at the table, please," said Annabelle.

While the twins sat in the kitchen, Annabelle went into the bedroom. Mike was standing by the bed with a towel around his waist. He was rubbing his hair dry with another one.

"Hey, good-lookin'." He grinned. "Did I hear Thomas yelling about Magnolia Bakery?"

"Don't worry," said Annabelle. "I bought some of the chocolate drop cookies you like."

"God, I knew there was a reason I married you." He kissed her on the neck.

"I thought it would be a good idea to soften you up before I give you the big news."

"What?"

"I quit my job."

Mike sat down on the edge of the bed. "You wanna give that to me again?"

Annabelle sat down next to him. "I just couldn't take Linus Nazareth anymore, Mike. He's insulting and obnoxious, and I can't work for him. I've had it with him, and I quit. But now that I've done it, I don't know how we're going to pay the bills." She leaned forward and put her head in her hands.

"Wait a minute, Annabelle." Mike pulled her up and put his arm around her shoulders. "I'm not getting something, honey. Linus is obnoxious and insulting every day. Why was today so bad that you felt you had to quit?"

Annabelle recounted what had happened at Constance's place, how B.J. had given his information about the stolen unicorn and the dead dog to Eliza rather than Lauren, the uproar that caused, and the general unpleasantness of working with Lauren Adams.

"I know she's under a lot of pressure, Mike, but come on. It's so unprofessional to beat up on the people who are working for you. And then to have to come back to the Broadcast Center only to be abused by Linus—it was just too much."

Mike pulled her closer and kissed the top of her head. "You know what I think?" he asked.

"What?"

"It's not Lauren Adams or Linus Nazareth that's bothering you. You deal with their stuff all the time, and you usually just let it slide right off your back. No, I think what's really bothering you is what's happened to Constance Young."

Annabelle looked up at her husband and nodded. "Maybe you're right, Mike. I'm just so shocked that it's come to this. How could this have happened to Constance?" Annabelle felt a tear escape from the corner of her eye and trickle down her cheek.

At one time Annabelle had been so proud of the friend she'd made in her early years at KEY News. They'd both been rookies on the network television news scene, Annabelle as a first-time researcher and Constance as a young reporter, fresh to KEY News after stints at local stations around the country. Constance had kept her nose to the grindstone, while Annabelle devoted herself to getting, and staying, pregnant until the twins arrived. After two miscarriages Annabelle finally had the family she craved, while Constance remained almost monomaniacal in her drive to succeed. Eventually Constance had made it to the anchor chair, and for a long while she managed to remain a genuinely nice person, the one who'd been such a good friend and trusted colleague. But eventually the pressure and competition had changed her.

Yet Annabelle realized that if not for Constance she'd never have gotten her job back at KEY News. Upon hearing that after 9/11 Mike was on disability from the fire department and suffering from post-traumatic stress disorder, Constance put in a good word to executive producer Linus Nazareth. Annabelle knew that Nazareth had little patience for women on the mommy track, and she was sure that he kept her on the payroll just to make his popular star happy. With Constance Young as her champion, Annabelle was in.

"She was really good to us when we needed help, Mike."

"I never said she wasn't," said Mike. "But I didn't like those stories you've brought home over the last year or so. She was ignoring you, and when she wasn't ignoring you, she was finding fault with your work. She had gotten much too big for those silk britches of hers."

Annabelle managed a smile. "How do you know they're silk?" she asked.

"I don't," Mike admitted. "But I know they're expensive britches, whatever they're made of."

"Well, I still feel awful about this, Mike. Constance used to be my best friend, and it's terrible."

"I know it is, honey." Mike gave her a final hug and stood up from the bed. He walked to the dresser, took a white cotton T-shirt from the drawer, and pulled it over his head. He felt Annabelle watching him.

"What?" he asked, trying not to smile. "One of us has to go to work."

Annabelle threw a pillow at him. "It's not funny, Mike. What are we going to do without my salary?"

Chapter 29

When the phone was answered, the sound of dogs barking and whimpering could be heard in the background.

"Hi. I'm the one who came in on Thursday and adopted the Great Dane."

"Marco?" asked Vinny, a smile spreading across his face. "How's he doing?"

"That's the problem. Marco isn't eating. He won't run after a ball like he used to. He just lies there."

"Have you called a vet?"

"Yes, and the vet said there's nothing physically wrong with him. I think he's lonely. I want to come in and get another dog to keep him company."

"Great. We have plenty of 'em," said Vinny. "I'm closing up now, but if you can come in Monday morning . . . "

"Are you open tomorrow, by any chance?"

"No. But you come on in on Monday," the young man suggested. "We'll find you another great dog."

"I was hoping to come in tomorrow. I can't make it any day next week, and I don't want poor Marco to wait and suffer."

Vinny looked down the aisle of caged dogs, knowing that if homes weren't found for them, they faced euthanasia.

"All right. I'll meet you here tomorrow morning," he volunteered. "Nine o'clock."

SUNDAY
MAY 20

Chapter 30

Eliza was still asleep when Janie came cautiously into the master bedroom. The little girl stood at the side of the queen-size bed and stared at her mother. When willing her mother to open her eyes didn't work, Janie leaned over and put her own face as close as she could to Eliza's without touching it. It was her daughter's soft breath that finally awakened Eliza.

"I didn't wake you up, did I, Mommy? I was quiet."

Eliza smiled and stretched. "No, honey, you didn't wake me up. Thank you."

"You're welcome." Janie climbed in beside Eliza. "We have to get up, Mom. Remember? We're going to Hannah and Hudson's this morning."

"That's right. We are," said Eliza, though the plan had completely slipped her mind. She looked at the clock. "We have to get up soon if we're going to make it to church first." But she made no move to get out of bed.

"I love Mrs. Hizdak's pancakes," Janie said happily as she snuggled closer to her mother.

"Me, too," said Eliza. "But you pronounce their name 'Vizdak,' honey."

"That doesn't make sense, Mommy. It starts with the letter *H*. I saw it on their mailbox. And *H* makes the 'huh' sound."

"I know, but their name is H-V-I-Z-D-A-K. The *H* is silent, and you pronounce the *V.* 'Vizdak.'"

Janie had a puzzled expression on her face.

"I know it's confusing, Janie, but there are some words that don't sound the way they're spelled. Hvizdak is one of them."

"I'm hungry, Mom." Janie had moved on.

Eliza sat up, swung her legs around the side of the bed, and stood. "Come on. Let's go downstairs and get you some fruit and me some coffee."

Downstairs in the kitchen, Eliza sliced some melon and turned on the coffeemaker. Much as she loved and depended on Mrs. Garcia, Eliza enjoyed having the house to herself and Janie as much as possible on the weekends. Mrs. Garcia had been looking forward to going to her daughter's house today to celebrate her grandson's birthday, and Eliza had planned to have the whole day alone to focus on Janie.

Waiting for the coffee to brew, Eliza picked up the remote for the kitchen television set and switched the channel to CNN. A picture of Constance Young's face popped onto the screen as a reporter recapped yesterday's events. Next, the image of a cream-colored carved unicorn appeared on the screen as the reporter announced that police had confirmed that an ivory unicorn, similar in appearance to the one Constance Young had been seen wearing, was missing from the Cloisters. The unicorn was touted as having been a gift from King Arthur to Lady Guinevere in the Middle Ages.

What in the world is going on? wondered Eliza. *How did Constance get that unicorn? Could she possibly have stolen it? Could she have been killed for it?*

Eliza picked up the phone and pushed a number on speed dial.

"Range? It's Eliza. I hope I didn't wake you."

"What? Are you kidding? I've been up for hours. In fact, I'm on my way in to the Broadcast Center."

"So B.J. heard right," said Eliza, pouring the black liquid into her mug. "Think we should have reported the missing unicorn last night as 'KEY News has learned . . . '?"

"Let's not second-guess ourselves, Eliza. We didn't have confirmation," said Range. "And in one way at least I'm glad we didn't. Linus Nazareth is on the warpath. He says we screwed Lauren on the air last night and made her look like an idiot. And that was just over your question to her about the dog. If you'd asked her about the ivory unicorn, too, I think Linus would have stroked out."

"Not to mention Lauren," Eliza observed. "I'm still wondering why B.J. called *me* about it but didn't tell *her*."

"I'm not sure why," said Range. "But B.J. is no longer assigned to *KTA*."

"So that's his punishment, huh?" asked Eliza.

"Yep. And Linus told me he's letting Annabelle Murphy go, too, because he figures she was either B.J.'s accomplice or an incompetent," said Range. "But I heard through the grapevine that he didn't fire her. Annabelle quit."

"Well, I don't know if she was in it with B.J. or not," answered Eliza. "But the last thing I would ever call Annabelle is an incompetent."

"Me, too," Range agreed. "That's why I already phoned her this morning and asked her to come work for *Evening Headlines*."

"And?"

"She said yes."

Eliza smiled. "Great. *KTA*'s loss is our gain. And what about B.J.?"

"I've already had him scheduled to work for us today. He's on his way out to that dump where Constance's pool boy told us he got rid of the dog."

"Good call," said Eliza. "Now that we've settled that, I was thinking I want to go up to the Cloisters today. Look around, see where the ivory unicorn had been stored, see if we can get anyone to talk to us." She paused to take a sip of coffee. "I'd like to do a piece for tonight."

"Someone else can go up and do that, Eliza. Mack McBride is going to get his shot at anchoring tonight. This was going to be your only day off this week. The story will still be around when you come in tomorrow."

"I know it will, Range. And I don't want to anchor the show, but I want to be a part of tonight's show. Constance Young's death carries a lot of weight, with us in the news division and with the public as well. I want to get a feel for the Cloisters. I've never been there. Why don't you put me in tonight's schedule as doing the unicorn angle?"

"All right, if that's what you want. I'd love to have you in the broadcast. But I hate cutting into your day with your daughter."

"You aren't cutting into it," Eliza replied. "I'm bringing Janie with me."

Chapter 31

Sipping a cup of coffee, Vinny Shays leaned on his elbows reading the newspaper that was spread out over the front counter. He looked up when the front door opened.

"Hello," he called. "Good to see you again."

"Thanks for opening up for me this morning, especially in all this rain."

"No problem. I wish there were more people like you. It's wonderful you're taking another dog. We have so many who need homes. Have you given any more thought to what kind you want?"

"I don't think I need something as big as a Dane this time. Just one that can keep Marco company."

"Let's take a look around and see what we've got," Vinny suggested.

They began to walk down the aisle. There were a boxer, a schnauzer, and a beagle-basset mix right near the front.

"Any of these warm your heart?"

"Let's keep going. Let me see what you have farther in the back."

At the rear of the room, they came to a cage that housed a black Labrador retriever.

"That one looks nice."

Vinny nodded. "She is. Very good-natured and gentle. We've started calling her 'Lucky' because Animal Control found her wandering the streets before she got hit by a car, or worse. And she's already been spayed and has all her shots."

"Would you mind taking her out of the cage?"

Vinny turned his attention to opening the cage, unaware that behind him a weapon was sliding from a jacket pocket.

"Okay, Lucky," said Vinny. "Let's get you out of there."

He reached in to guide the dog out of the cage, talking to her reassuringly. Vinny turned to look at the dog's prospective owner. The hopeful expression on Vinny's face turned to horror in the second it took for the hammer to come crashing down on his head.

Finishing the job with the hammer was always an option, but if the shelter stocked any sort of euthanasia solution, that would be a lot less work. And less bloody.

Among all the boxes and bottles and tools in the back room, the visitor found the sodium pentobarbital that was used to solve the problem of the animals nobody wanted to adopt. It didn't take long at all to prepare the lethal syringe. It took longer to find the vein in Vinny's arm. As the injected chemicals closed down the young man's central nervous system, Lucky started barking. And by the time the kind human being who took such good care of them died, every dog in the shelter was howling.

Chapter 32

B.J. sat in his car eating a jelly doughnut and calculating how much extra money he was making, because not only was he working on a Sunday, he had not gotten the hours of turnaround time since his shift the day before as stipulated by his union contract. It was going to make for a nice fat paycheck.

He looked out at the piles of debris, discarded furniture, and old appliances and wondered if he'd missed it. He checked his watch. Had the police already been here this morning and found the dog?

B.J. got out and walked around to the rear of the car. He took his camera gear from the trunk. As he closed the lid, he noticed a van pulling in through the entrance to the dump. The van, lettered on the side with the words PACHECO POOLS, drove up next to the KEY News crew car and parked. A young man got out and walked toward B.J.

"You waiting for the police?"

B.J. nodded. "What about you?"

"Yep. I told the cops I'd meet them out here and show them where I left a dog."

"Oh, so you're the guy who worked for Constance Young," said B.J. "Thanks for letting us know where you dumped the dog. As you can see, the police didn't announce it to any of the other news organizations, or else they'd be swarming all over this place. KEY News will air it exclusively."

"You're welcome. By the way, my name is Frank Pacheco." He extended his hand.

"B.J. D'Elia."

"How do you like working for the news?" asked Frank, gesturing to the camera.

"It's a living," said B.J.

"Must be really interesting."

"Sometimes, yeah," answered B.J. "But there can be a lot of hanging around and waiting." B.J. looked at his watch again. "I've been sitting out here for an hour and a half."

"So I guess you want to get some pictures of the dog, huh?"

"Yeah, if the cops will let me get close enough," said B.J. "Otherwise they can't stop me from taking video from a distance, of them searching."

"Maybe I could help you," said Frank. "I can show you where the dog is before the police get here."

"That would be great," B.J. said enthusiastically. "Thanks a lot."

Frank was staring purposefully at the top of B.J.'s head.

"You like this cap?" asked B.J.

"Yeah. I do."

B.J. popped open the trunk of the car again. He pulled out a new red baseball cap and a navy blue T-shirt, both emblazoned with the KEY News logo.

"They're yours," said B.J., handing over the loot.

Frank donned the cap and threw the T-shirt on the front seat of his van. "Come on," he said. "I'll show you."

They tramped across one of the paths that cut through the piles of rubbish, making their way toward the back of the dump.

"Why did you bother going all the way back here?" asked B.J.

"Because they have big fines if they catch you throwing anything in here but what they allow. Dead animals don't fit the bill."

"So you'll be fined for coming forward with the information about the dog?"

"They said they'd make an exception in this case"—Frank looked pleased—"since I'm helping them out with the Constance Young investigation and all."

When they got to the edge of the property, Frank pointed. "There it is," he said.

B.J. looked in the indicated direction. A dirty white blanket covered a motionless mound. As he approached, he lifted up the edge of the blanket and shrank back. "That's it, all right," he said, wincing. He raised his camera and made the necessary adjustments to begin recording. He took video of the shrouded dog from a variety of angles and sprayed the area with the camera lens to get shots that would give a good picture of the overall location.

"You want me to pull back the blanket all the way so you can get pictures of the dead dog?" asked Frank eagerly.

"Not really," said B.J. "But I better get them anyway."

The black Great Dane lay on its side, and B.J. had to consciously direct his thoughts to the mechanics of getting good video instead of allowing himself to think of how sad it was that the beautiful animal was now lying lifeless and discarded like trash.

"All right, that's enough," he said. "I hope we don't have to use them, but at least the editor will have the option to totally exploit this poor thing."

"What did you say?" asked the pool guy.

"Never mind," said B.J. as he capped his camera lens.

Chapter 33

Trying to keep the packages and newspapers balanced in his arms, Jason Vaughan fumbled for his keys and cursed the day he'd been forced to move into a building without a doorman. He held the door open with his hip, struggling to get the key out of the lock again, as the newspaper slipped from beneath his arm. He had to put the grocery bags down in order to gather up the pages of newsprint that had scattered over the vestibule floor. Another tenant in the building strode right by without stopping.

Jason hated living in this place.

He walked into his first-floor apartment, ever conscious of the iron bars on the windows that allegedly protected him from crime coming in from the outside world. Jason looked around the room. This was the richest city in the world. Why would a burglar even bother trying to get into this place? There was nothing worth taking. A sofa and a chair he'd bought on sale at a furniture store already known for its low prices and low quality. A television that at least worked, but had none of the bells and whistles that were so popular. A table and a couple of lamps he'd picked up at a secondhand store. Even the computer that sat on his card-table desk, the computer on which he'd written *Never Look Back,* was the one he'd had for years. It needed to be replaced. A new computer would be his first purchase when the money from the book started flowing in. A new computer and a better apartment, for sure.

Jason spread the newspaper on his kitchen table and studied every page. It looked as if the *Daily News* had assigned at least a dozen reporters to the Constance Young story, and Jason was reading details he hadn't gotten from the television news reports.

One that grabbed his attention was a sidebar story about a woman named Ursula Bales, the woman who discovered the body. The story said that Bales, a widow, worked as Constance's housekeeper and also gave knitting lessons to make ends meet. The *News* photographer had taken a picture of her as she walked into the Dropped Stitch Needlecraft Shop.

Ursula Bales was quoted as saying, "Please, leave me alone. I'm so nervous about this whole horrible thing. My sister talked to the police once, and when the media found out, she ended up dead. I don't want what happened to her to happen to me."

Jason sympathized with Ursula Bales. He knew what the media could do to a person. He had experienced it firsthand.

Chapter 34

The Hvizdak family lived in a thirteen-thousand-square-foot French château–style home that sat on four acres of property. Out front a graceful fountain greeted visitors, and limestone lions guarded the path to the imposing double doors. Hundreds of purple, yellow, and white irises bloomed from carefully tended beds.

After the breakfast of pancakes, bacon, yogurt, and some early strawberries from her own garden, Michele suggested that everyone go out to the backyard to enjoy the beautiful day.

"We can stay for a little while longer, Janie," Eliza warned.

"I just want to see the fish, Mommy," said Janie as she and Hannah ran to the pond at the back of the property.

"That's Wilbur, Copper, Lady, and Princess," Hannah said, pointing at the koi that traveled gracefully in the water.

Eliza turned to Michele. "Thanks so much for having us. This was fun."

"You're welcome, but it's fun for me, too," said Michele, her eyes on Hudson as he played with his plastic dinosaur. "Richard is away so much. It's great to have another adult around."

"I'm sorry to be eating and running," Eliza apologized.

"You know, you can certainly leave Janie with us," Michele offered. "It would probably be more fun for her than going with you."

Eliza looked at her daughter. "What do you want to do, Janie?"

"I want to go with you, Mommy."

"Good," said Eliza. "I want you to come with me, too."

"Who's going to watch Janie if you're working?" asked Michele.

"I'm only going to be there for a couple of hours, and Paige, my assistant, is meeting us there. She'll be able to keep an eye on Janie when I can't."

Suspecting that it might be cool by the Hudson River, Eliza and Janie stopped back at home to get sweaters.

Inside the house Eliza made a phone call to the KEY News assignment desk and asked to be connected to Boyd Irons.

"Boyd, this is Eliza Blake."

"Oh, hi, Eliza," said Boyd, sounding a bit surprised.

"I want to ask you about this unicorn that everybody's talking about. I saw it on Constance at the lunch. Do you know how she got it?"

Boyd hesitated. "I think it was a gift."

"Do you know who gave it to her?"

"I think it was from a man named Stuart Whitaker."

"Stuart Whitaker? The guy who made millions manufacturing those video games with the jousting knights and fire-breathing dragons?"

"That's the one," said Boyd. "Poor guy. He was smitten with Constance, but she wasn't giving him the time of day before . . . " His voice trailed off. "Anyway, he asked me if I could get the unicorn back for him."

"When did he ask you that?"

"Just as the luncheon was getting under way," said Boyd. "He was sitting at the bar waiting for Constance to arrive. I tried to tell him as tactfully as I could that he should leave and not cause any unpleasantness. He only agreed when I promised I would try to get the unicorn for him."

"And did you try to get it back from her?" Eliza asked.

"Are you kidding? I wasn't going to ask Constance for it! I never intended to get it for him," said Boyd. "I just wanted him to leave the restaurant."

Eliza reached for a pen. "Boyd, do you have Stuart Whitaker's phone number?"

Chapter 35

*O*nce the search-engine page was on the computer screen, "URSULA BALES" was typed in the box provided for the name of the subject to be researched. A moment after the search button was hit, several results appeared, most of them fresh newspaper articles regarding the death of Constance Young and the fact that the anchorwoman's body had been discovered by her housekeeper, Ursula Bales. There was only one other hit on the results page: a story that had appeared in the Journal News over two years ago. At first it seemed to have nothing to do with Ursula Bales.

Helga Lundstrom, 43, of Mount Kisco, died at Northern Westchester Hospital from injuries sustained in a suspicious car accident. Lundstrom was the key witness in a drug case and was scheduled to be called to the stand to testify in the trial. Her death is expected to be a major blow to the prosecution's case, now lacking an eyewitness to the crime.

The article went on to explain the details of the drug case, but a line near the end was more interesting.

She is survived by her husband, Hans, and a sister, Ursula Bales of Bedford.

In this morning's Daily News *article, Ursula Bales said she didn't want to end up like her sister. Why would she say that if she'd merely discovered Constance's body?*

Could she have witnessed the murder?

Chapter 36

Faith stole in through the garage door, hoping she wouldn't have to explain why she'd been out so long. But Todd was sitting in the kitchen wearing a baseball cap and cleats, waiting for her.

"Where were you?" he asked, scowling.

"Church," Faith replied, tossing the parish bulletin onto the counter.

"You left three hours ago, Faith."

Faith tried to keep her emotions in check as she answered. "I found out yesterday that my sister is dead, Todd. I wanted to take some extra time to sit and reflect and pray. I talked to the priest. Is that okay with you?"

"Yeah, it's okay with me, but you should have let me know you'd be gone so long."

"What's the difference, Todd? It's Sunday. The kids don't have games or lessons or anything they need to do."

"As a matter of fact, now that you're back, I'm going over to the field and play some ball with the guys."

Todd walked out of the kitchen, leaving Faith alone. She took a box of Mallomars from a cabinet, walked over to the picture window, and looked at the backyard. She couldn't help but admire the pink and white azalea flowers. She had always loved May. It was such a beautiful month. Good for weddings, good for funerals. Tears streamed down Faith's cheeks.

After eating a half dozen comforting cookies, Faith went down the hall to her mother's room. Mercifully, the old woman was sleeping. Mercifully for Mother at least, though probably not for Faith. Slumber during the day meant little sleep later, and Faith knew she would be hearing her name called repeatedly in the middle of the night.

She listened to her mother's thick snore, watched her chest slowly rise and fall. Her eyelids flickered but did not open.

Faith spoke to her. "What should we do now, Mom? Should we have Constance buried or cremated? I don't want to decide by myself."

There was no response from the old woman who lay asleep in the bed. And that was merciful, too, thought

Faith. No parent should have to endure the death of a child. It was a good thing, a mercy that Mother hadn't seemed to grasp the idea of Constance's death when Faith told her of it yesterday.

Faith inhaled the smell of medicine and disinfectant and old age, but she groaned as she recognized the other odor. She would need to give Mother a bath, getting her from the bed to the tub and then lifting her out after she'd washed her frail body. Faith would change the bed linens, do more laundry, get everything clean and fresh just to have the cycle repeat itself, over and over again.

She really didn't want her mother to die, but the fatigue and chronic worry of being a caretaker made Faith daydream about how long it would be before their mother went to join Constance in heaven.

If heaven was where Constance was.

Chapter 37

The assortment of news vans and crew cars that crowded the Cloisters' parking lot suggested that all the other media outlets were eager to pursue the angle of the missing unicorn as well. While the news organizations waited for the results of Constance Young's autopsy, they didn't know what they were dealing with. It could be a heart attack, an accidental drowning, a murder, or something else. But making a connection between Constance Young and the purloined medieval artifact was something concrete to pursue.

When Eliza and Janie arrived, Paige was there to greet them as they got out of the car.

"There's a children's program going on that I thought would be fun to take Janie to, if you don't mind me not being available to help you, Eliza."

"That sounds like a plan," said Eliza. "What's the program about?"

"Shoes," said Paige. She leaned down to Janie. "Would you like to learn how people dressed their feet in the Middle Ages?" she asked the little girl.

Janie stared back with a blank expression on her face.

"It's never too early to learn about shoes, Janie. And we can get some ice cream afterward."

As her daughter went off with her assistant, Eliza spotted Annabelle Murphy. "So you're working on the *Evening Headlines* now," said Eliza, giving her a hug. "I couldn't be more pleased."

Annabelle smiled and shook her head. "I can't believe how well all this is working out. Yesterday at this time, I was working for *KTA* and trying to keep Linus and Lauren happy."

"No mean feat," observed Eliza. "But don't worry. We'll do our best to drive you crazy as well."

The two women began to discuss their ideas on what they wanted to accomplish that afternoon.

"I called Boyd Irons, who told me that Constance received the ivory unicorn from Stuart Whitaker," said Eliza.

"Stuart Whitaker, the video-game wizard?" Annabelle asked.

"That's the one," said Eliza.

Annabelle whistled softly. "So we're thinking what? That Stuart Whitaker *stole* the unicorn?"

"Don't know what to think," said Eliza. "But I called him, and he's agreed to come up here and be interviewed this afternoon. He says he'll only talk to us."

"Nice. An exclusive." Annabelle nodded with appreciation. "You're doing my work for me, Eliza," she said. "I think I'm going to like this job."

"What about the curator, Rowena Quincy?" asked Eliza.

"We have to get in line for that one," said Annabelle. "We may be the only ones who know about Stuart Whitaker's involvement with Constance, but everybody now knows that the unicorn is missing. All our competitors will be interviewing Rowena Quincy, too."

Because the museum administration wanted the Cloisters to be cast in the best possible light, and because Stuart Whitaker was a major donor, Annabelle was able to obtain permission to have Eliza's interview taped on the West Terrace, overlooking the Hudson River. The area was cordoned off so the visitors who were touring the museum couldn't interrupt.

Stuart Whitaker arrived wearing a dark suit, a white shirt, and a green tie, fairly formal dress for a Sunday afternoon. He immediately came forward and took Eliza's hand. "May I?" he asked.

Before she could respond, Stuart leaned forward and lifted her hand to his lips. "It is an honor and pleasure to meet such a fine lady," he said.

"Thank you, Mr. Whitaker," said Eliza, withdrawing her hand and wondering what this guy's story was. "Won't you take a seat?"

Stuart did as she suggested. He looked out across the water to the New Jersey side of the river.

"It's such a glorious spot here, isn't it?" Eliza commented.

"Yes, it truly is," answered Stuart as a microphone was clipped to his jacket. "And we can thank John D. Rockefeller Jr. for funding this wonderful place and for buying all that land across the river and giving it to the state of New Jersey so that nothing would be built on it." He gestured widely. "The view may change with the weather and the seasons, but it will always be as magnificent as it is today."

"Yes, we can all be thankful that some people are as generous as they are, can't we?" said Eliza. "I understand that you, too, have been a major contributor to the Cloisters."

"I do what I can," said Stuart.

Eliza didn't want to go any further until the camera was recording. She waited while B.J. finished setting up and then gave the signal to begin. "Let's talk first about your affinity for the Cloisters, Mr. Whitaker."

"I could not begin to describe how much this place means to me." Stuart made another expansive gesture. "Look around. It is remarkable."

"So the Middle Ages interest you?" Eliza asked.

"That is putting it mildly," Stuart answered. "It was an absolutely fascinating period in the development of Western civilization, and its impact is felt these many centuries later, though we do not stop to think about it."

"Can you give me some examples?" prompted Eliza.

"Well, the heroes of the Middle Ages—King Arthur, Joan of Arc, and Robin Hood—are still heroes to twenty-first-century Americans. The dragons, giants, dwarfs, and witches—the supernatural villains of the Middle Ages—are in our fairy tales and fantasy novels and young people's video games. Even the castle standing in the center of a Disney theme park is based on modern notions of a medieval castle."

"Interesting," said Eliza.

Stuart continued, eager to express his feelings. "But what has always moved me the most is what the Middle Ages did for love."

"What do you mean?" asked Eliza.

"Medieval poets wrote about the heart as a symbol of passion. They came up with romantic metaphors that we now think of as clichés—the 'wounded' heart, the 'broken' heart, the 'stolen' heart, and so forth. The idea of courtly love developed in the Middle Ages. Knights would accomplish heroic deeds to win the hearts of the ladies they loved."

"Romantic," said Eliza. "But I suppose it could be dangerous, too."

"Sometimes it was," said Stuart. "But I bet if you asked them, those knights would say it was worth risking everything for the women they loved."

"Changing the subject for a moment, Mr. Whitaker, I understand you were a good friend of Constance Young's."

Stuart's demeanor grew solemn. "Yes. She was a remarkable lady, and I was privileged to know her. Her death is a great loss, to me and to the nation."

"Yes, it is a tragic thing," said Eliza. "And there are so many troubling aspects to it. Constance was an accomplished swimmer. For her to die in a pool doesn't make sense."

"For her to die at *all* does not make sense," Stuart said.

"Yes, you're certainly right," agreed Eliza. "But there's also this report of a carved unicorn missing from the Cloisters' collection here, along with the images we have of Constance wearing that same unicorn, or one remarkably similar, on the day she died."

Eliza paused, hoping that Stuart might volunteer some information. When he didn't, she decided to come out and ask him point-blank. "Did you give Constance Young the unicorn she was wearing, Mr. Whitaker?"

"As a matter of fact, I did."

"You *did*?"

"Yes. I did." Stuart sounded defiant. "She admired the one in the collection here when we visited one day. I had a reproduction made for her."

"So you're saying Constance was wearing a copy, while the authentic medieval unicorn is missing from the Cloisters' collection."

"Yes," Stuart said firmly. "That is what I am saying."

"But there's still a problem," said Eliza. "As far as we know, the police haven't found the unicorn that Constance was wearing. So that would mean both the genuine unicorn *and* the reproduction are missing. That seems like an unlikely coincidence, Mr. Whitaker, doesn't it?"

Stuart stared straight into Eliza's eyes. "It may seem like an unlikely coincidence, but I do not know how else to explain it. Strange things happen," he said, shrugging. "But I agreed to come up here to talk with you today because I wanted an opportunity to announce what I would like to do to honor Constance."

"And what would that be?" asked Eliza.

"I would like to donate twenty million dollars to the Cloisters, five million of which would go to create a Constance Young Memorial Garden here. If Constance's family agrees, and we get permission from the museum board of directors, I would hope to see Constance spend eternity in this perfect place."

KEY News had a chance to interview the Cloisters' curator after ABC and CBS did. To save time, Annabelle arranged for Rowena Quincy to come to the West Terrace as well, so B.J. wouldn't have to pack up his gear and then set up all over again.

In her hand Rowena held a large, glossy close-up photo of the missing ivory unicorn, which she handed to Eliza. The detail was so defined that the filigree engraving on the eight-pointed crown was clearly visible.

"First of all, let's straighten out some confusion," said Eliza once they started talking. "I thought King Arthur and Lady Guinevere were only fictional characters, that Camelot was a place that never existed."

"That's what many do believe," Rowena answered. "But there are other theories, and one of them is that Arthur was inspired by a fifth-century 'king' of the

Britons, named Riotamus. We think our ivory unicorn might have come from him."

"So you're not exactly sure?" asked Eliza.

"No," admitted Rowena, "and that is something we will make absolutely clear when we open the exhibit on Thursday."

"So the exhibit will open as scheduled?" Eliza asked.

"Yes," said Rowena. "Our unicorn was a star of the show, but we have many other wonderful things for the public to see. And let's hope we'll have some luck and get the unicorn back by then."

"Do you have any leads at all on what happened to it?" asked Eliza.

"The police are investigating. You'll have to ask them."

"Obviously, Ms. Quincy, there's more intense interest in this artifact because of the fact that Constance Young was seen wearing it." Eliza held up the photo. "Or something remarkably like it."

Rowena nodded.

"What's your opinion?" asked Eliza. "Do you think that Constance Young had in her possession your King Arthur unicorn?"

"Again, I wouldn't venture an opinion," said Rowena. "That's for the authorities to determine."

When their conversation ended and Rowena Quincy had left for her next interview, Eliza and Annabelle waited while B.J. packed up.

"She knows something she's not saying, doesn't she?" asked Annabelle.

"Yes. I was thinking exactly the same thing."

Chapter 38

Back at the Broadcast Center, Eliza went to her office to work on her script while Annabelle went downstairs to screen the tapes they'd shot at the Cloisters. As Eliza stared at her blank computer monitor, searching for inspiration on how to begin her narration, Janie galloped around the office on the unicorn-headed hobby horse purchased at the Cloisters gift shop.

Paige appeared at the door. "Want me to take Janie down to the cafeteria for something to eat?" she asked.

"She's really eaten enough junk this afternoon," said Eliza. "But I *would* really appreciate it if you found something else for her to do while I get this script written."

"Come on, Janie," said Paige, holding her hand out to the little girl. "Let's see if the director will let you sit in your mommy's chair and show you how you look on TV."

Twenty minutes later Eliza was more than halfway through her script when she heard a man clear his throat. She looked up to see Mack McBride standing in the doorway.

"May I come in?" he asked.

"Sure," she answered. "Take a seat. I'm just working on a script for your show tonight."

Mack sat in the chair on the other side of Eliza's desk, leaned back, crossed his legs, and smiled. "That has a nice ring, doesn't it? *You* doing a piece for *my* broadcast. I like that."

"Don't get too used to it, my friend." Eliza smiled back.

"*Am* I your friend, Eliza?"

Eliza looked away, picking up a paper clip from the tray on her desk. "Of course you're my friend," she said. "We're adults. What happened between us is ancient history."

"Not so ancient," said Mack. "And it's not what happened between us that I regret. What we had between us was one of the best things that ever happened to me. It's what happened when we were apart that I regret. You don't know how much I wish we could go back to the way things were, Eliza."

Eliza pulled at the metal clip, straightening it out, but she remained silent.

"I don't know how many times I can tell you how sorry I am, Eliza," he said. "Won't you please forgive me?"

"It's complicated, Mack," she said softly.

Mack leaned forward. "Not really, Eliza. It's not that complicated at all. I fell in love with you when we were here in New York together. When I got to London, I got drunk one night and slept with somebody else. It was a big mistake. I would do anything in the world to take it back, but I can't. I've lost you. End of story."

"I hate that story, Mack."

"I hate it, too, Eliza. But let's edit it. We can change the ending."

Mack rose from his chair, walked around the desk, took Eliza's hand, and guided her to her feet.

"Look, I know you don't want to trust me anymore," he said as he gazed into her eyes. "I know I've hurt you, and I hate myself for it. But I promise I will never do anything like that again."

Eliza's instincts told her that Mack meant everything he was saying, but her brain told her to beware. She didn't ever want to experience again the tearful, sleepless nights and excruciating disappointment and hurt she'd felt when she found out that Mack had been unfaithful. She couldn't afford to go through that again. She had a daughter who depended on her and a demanding job that required she be focused and mentally healthy and on top of things. She had to take care of herself. It would be stupid to risk getting involved with a man who was capable of hurting her the way Mack had.

Getting involved with Mack again had danger written all over it. Yet in the months he'd been gone, she'd missed him so. "I guess it wouldn't do any harm to just have dinner together," she said, surprised at her own words.

Mack's eyes lit up. "Great. Tonight?"

"No, I can't tonight," said Eliza. "I want to get Janie home."

"Well, I'm leaving to go back to London on Tuesday morning," said Mack.

"All right, then. Tomorrow night, after the broadcast," said Eliza, knowing she was taking a risk, past being able to resist anymore.

Chapter 39

While the roast beef sat in the oven and got drier by the minute, Faith waited for Todd to come home. The over-thirty baseball team had obviously stopped for a couple of beers after the game.

"When are we eating, Mom?" asked Ben.

"I'm hungry," whined Brendan.

"We're going to eat as soon as I mash the potatoes," she said.

Faith poured herself a glass of burgundy before turning on the electric mixer and running the rotating blades through the boiled potatoes. She fumed as she added warm milk and butter and muttered to herself as she scooped the creamy mixture out of the bowl and onto the boys' plates.

"What are you saying, Mom?" asked Brendan. "I can't hear you."

"She said a bad thing, Brendan," answered Ben. "How come you can say 'son of a bitch,' Mom, and we're not supposed to?"

"That's enough, Ben," said Faith. "Now, sit down and eat."

"Without Daddy?" asked Brendan.

"Yes, without Daddy," said Faith. "In fact, since Daddy isn't here, do you guys want to eat upstairs in your room and watch television?"

The boys looked at her with eyes wide. She was always nagging them about having to eat at the kitchen or dining room table, and now she was actually suggesting that they go eat in front of the TV. They weren't about to question the opportunity.

As soon as the boys were settled with their trays, Faith went back downstairs and snapped on the television set just in time to see Eliza Blake's report on *The KEY Evening Headlines.* She listened as Stuart Whitaker described the multimillion-dollar contribution he wanted to make to build a memorial garden for Constance at the Cloisters.

Even in death, fame would follow Constance.

Faith got up and went into the kitchen to pour herself another glass of wine. This Stuart Whitaker character could do whatever he wanted with his money, but only she could decide where Constance would be buried.

Chapter 40

After spending the better part of Sunday afternoon in the *KTA* studio rehearsing her debut on the next morning's show, Lauren Adams and Linus Nazareth sat on the sofa and watched *The KEY Evening Headlines* together in the executive producer's office.

"So Eliza Blake has another scoop," Linus growled when the broadcast was over. "Last night Eliza told the world about the dead dog. And now she's reporting about this boyfriend of Constance's donating a cool twenty million so he can have a pretty little resting place for her." Linus pounded the top of his thigh. "This should be *our* story. *KTA*'s story. Eliza's *Evening Headlines* is breaking the news, instead of us."

"Try to stay calm, Linus. If *you* lose it, *I'm* going to lose it." Lauren stroked his arm. "It's the weekend, honey.

Tomorrow morning is what really counts. Everyone will be watching the first broadcast without Constance."

"Yeah, I guess you're right. The ratings are going to be off the charts," Linus conceded. "But just the same, I want *KTA* to be out in front with this story."

"Me, too," said Lauren, "but we've just lost two of our best people and actually handed them on a silver platter to Eliza and the *Evening Headlines*. How smart was that?"

Linus looked at her, incredulous. "Last night you were crying about the miserable job Annabelle Murphy did for you and the fact that B.J. D'Elia gave important information to Eliza instead of you. You were practically raving about looking incompetent on the air."

"I know," said Lauren. "And I'm still furious at those two, but maybe I shouldn't have been so hard on them yesterday. Maybe I'd get better results if I wasn't such a bitch. You know the old saying, 'You can catch more flies with honey . . . ' "

"Tough," Linus hissed. "There is absolutely no excuse for either of them to have shown you anything but the loyalty and professionalism you deserve. Their job is to help gather all the elements to tell the story and to make you look good. They failed. They're out."

"All right, Linus. You're the boss. You've been at this a lot longer than I have, but I'm really worried." Lauren put her head on his shoulder.

"Hey," said Linus, stroking her hair. "Stop it. You have to be confident and sure of yourself. If you aren't, the audience will smell it."

"You're right." Lauren dabbed at her eyes. "The pressure and all."

"You just have to relax, be yourself, and trust me," said Linus. "I made Constance the star she was, and I can do it for you, too, baby."

"Please, Linus, don't call me 'baby.' And don't treat me like one. You can only do so much for me, and we both know it. At the end of the day—or rather the morning—I'm the one who's out there, I'm the one who'll be judged. The pressure is on *me*." Lauren hurled a cushion across the office.

"This is normal, Lauren. Good luck, even," said Linus. "I remember Constance freaking out the night before she took over for Eliza."

"Did you comfort Constance like this, too?" asked Lauren.

"Don't be ridiculous, Lauren. Of course not. There was nothing between Constance and me like there is between us. I reassured her, but I didn't take her in my arms."

Linus leaned over to kiss her, but Lauren pulled away, pouting. There was a knock at the office door. If the senior producer was surprised to see the executive producer and the new host sitting close together on the couch, or thought it inappropriate, Dominick O'Donnell didn't show it.

"What is it, Dom?" asked Linus.

"I just want to run this past you, even though I'm fairly certain what your response will be."

"Go ahead."

"We passed on it when his publicist pitched it a few weeks ago, but Jason Vaughan's publisher is putting a full-court press on getting him on television this week. Remember? He's the guy Constance exposed as a fraud?"

"Yeah, I remember," said Linus, stifling a yawn.

"Well, he takes some real swipes at Constance in this new book of his. Says Constance and the media ruined his life."

"And I would want to give him *publicity*? Why?" Linus asked, rising from the couch and fetching his jacket from the back of his chair.

"That's what I thought," said Dominick. He turned and closed the door behind him.

MONDAY
MAY 21

Chapter 41

Like more than 40 million other Americans, Eliza switched back and forth between *KEY to America* and *Daybreak* on Monday morning, eager to watch Lauren Adams's debut as *KTA* host and see how the team at *Daybreak* was reacting to the loss of the woman who'd been hired to lead their network to morning-television supremacy. Both programs, predictably, led with the Constance Young story. In fact, almost the entire first half hour was devoted to the subject. In case anyone had been living under a rock all weekend, every single bit of information that had been reported over the last two days was repeated, repackaged, and regurgitated.

To Eliza, Lauren Adams was visibly nervous. She made her share of mistakes, at times looking into the wrong camera, stumbling on a few words, missing a couple of cues. But Eliza suspected that none of the media critics were going to judge Lauren too harshly. After what had happened to Constance, it was understandable that Lauren would be rattled. It was a tough way to start a new job. Eliza found herself feeling sympathy for Lauren, and she thought the viewing public might, too. If Lauren handled herself well in these first days after Constance's death, if she could strike the right balance between authoritative newsperson and caring human being, she had the potential for attracting and establishing some loyal viewers.

"I want to watch SpongeBob SquarePants."

Janie's voice pulled Eliza back to the task at hand, getting her daughter out to school for the day. Janie sat at the kitchen table, halfheartedly eating the bowl of Cheerios that Mrs. Garcia had fixed for her.

"Mommy has to watch this for work, sweetheart. You know that. Now, eat your breakfast."

Janie just stared down at the cereal bowl.

"Janie, come on now." Eliza's voice was sterner.

With tears in her eyes and a protruding lower lip, the little girl looked up at her mother. Eliza snapped off the television set, bent down, and wrapped her arms around her child.

"Oh, sweetheart, what are you crying about? I wasn't yelling at you, Janie. I just want you to finish your breakfast so you can have a good day at school."

Janie sniffled. "I'm not crying about that."

"Then what's bothering you?"

Janie buried her face against her mother's chest. Eliza stroked the child's dark hair.

"What is it, Janie?"

"I don't like what's on TV. I don't like watching the lady who died. I don't want you to die, Mommy."

Eliza closed her eyes and pulled her daughter closer. What could she possibly have been thinking, having the television on with all the coverage of Constance's death? There were a half dozen other television sets in the house, and she certainly shouldn't be watching the one in the kitchen with Janie sitting right there. And what about dragging Janie with her to the Cloisters and back to the Broadcast Center yesterday while she worked on her story? That had been a thoughtless mistake, too.

Janie was bright, and her little eyes and ears missed nothing. To her this wasn't an impersonal, anonymous story on the news. Constance worked in the same building as her mommy. Constance Young was on television just like her mommy. Constance even had the job her mommy used to have. If something had happened to

Constance, something could happen to her mommy. Janie was already missing one parent. Of course she'd be terrified of losing the other one.

Eliza whispered, trying to soothe the child, "Oh, my sweet angel, don't worry. I'm not going anywhere. Nothing is going to happen to me."

"You promise?"

"I promise. How could I ever leave you? I love you more than anything in the whole wide world. You know that, don't you?"

Janie nodded. "I know, but you told me Daddy loved me, too—and he left me."

Here it was. The conversation that Eliza had known would come someday. The talk she'd tried to prepare herself for but had always dreaded. Janie had never known a world with her father in it. In her baby and toddler years, she had developed normally. The first word, the first step, the first birthday, the first day at nursery school, even the first day of kindergarten— Janie had marked all those milestones without any demonstrable sign that she felt the absence of a father. Yes, she remarked a few times that her playmates had daddies, but she'd always seemed to accept the fact that she didn't—and this was just the way life was. This morning was the first time that Janie had expressed, in her way, the confusion, loss, and sense of abandonment she must be experiencing as she came to understand that her father would never, ever be there, and the utter terror at the thought of losing her other parent and being left alone in the world.

"He didn't want to, Janie. He wanted to be with you very much. He tried as hard as he could to stay in this world, mostly because he wanted to see you. But I guess God had other plans for Daddy."

Janie wiped her nose against her mother's bathrobe. "What kind of plans?"

"I'm not really sure, sweetheart. I'm going to ask God that question when I see him. But I do know for certain that a big part of God's plan for Daddy while he was in this world was to be your father. That was the most important thing Daddy ever did, and I know he felt that way about it."

"You do?" Janie was hanging on every one of her mother's words.

"Mm-hmm." Eliza kissed Janie's forehead. "One of the last things he said to me was that he was so happy to know that you would be coming soon. He said it made him feel like he was really contributing something wonderful to the world."

"What's 'contributing'?" asked Janie.

"Giving. When you contribute something, you give it."

Janie considered the explanation. "Like a present?"

Eliza nodded enthusiastically. "Exactly. You are my and daddy's present to the world, Janie."

The child smiled up at her mother. Then Janie pulled away and turned her attention to the bowl of soggy Cheerios. Eliza watched her daughter eat, wondering if she'd said the right things, praying that she had, certain that this would not be the last time the subject would come up, knowing that she had the sacred responsibility of raising this child and making sure Janie was never an orphan.

Chapter 42

In, out, pull. In, out, pull.

The steel needle maneuvered its way through the canvas. One by one the tiny squares filled with yellow yarn. Ursula was trying to concentrate on the needlepoint canvas.

Ursula loved her needlepoint. It was so satisfying, so relaxing. It was such a pleasure watching the canvas come to life, painted by the different-colored wools she placed there. When she concentrated on her needlepoint, the worries of the world melted away.

But this morning even her beloved needlepoint did nothing to soothe Ursula. After what had happened over the weekend, she felt compelled to turn on KEY News and watch their morning broadcast. And while she tried to work on her needlepoint, all the news about

Constance and the fact that the results of her autopsy were expected to be released later today led Ursula to make a mistake on the canvas. She pulled out the errant strand, listening to Lauren Adams report on Constance's death. Ursula's stomach twisted at every word.

Ursula held the needlepoint canvas out in front of her and admired her handiwork. She had designed this piece as a tribute to Constance, and if something happened, it could help the police solve Constance's murder—as well as her own.

In block letters, the first stanza of the sonnet was outlined in black wool:

Lady of allure,
A lonely shining star,
Determined and so sure,
And worshipped from afar.

Ursula knew that it was her duty to go to the police and tell them what she'd seen. But she wasn't going to, at least not yet. Maybe the police could figure things out themselves. She hoped so, because she didn't want to end up like her sister. A good citizen who had come forward as a witness to a crime, but lying dead now, six feet under the ground.

Chapter 43

As soon as her twins were out the door and off to school, Annabelle jumped into the shower. She put on her makeup in the bathroom, listening to the raised volume of the bedroom television set, which was tuned to KEY.

Applying her mascara and listening to another report on Constance Young's death, Annabelle marveled: One weekend could change things so drastically. On Friday, *KEY to America* had said good-bye to Constance, and Annabelle had been scheduled to come in very early on Monday morning to be part of the production of Lauren Adams's first day as host. Today Constance was dead, and Annabelle no longer worked for *KTA*.

Annabelle finished in the bathroom and walked into the master bedroom, pausing at the television to turn the volume a bit lower. As she put on her clothes, all the attention to the Constance Young story was beginning to seem excessive to her. Yes, everyone at KEY News, perhaps even in the entire news business, was riveted by the story. And true, the American public was fascinated by the trials and tribulations of celebrities. But there were actually other things happening in the world, events of more importance than the death of Constance Young. You'd never know that from the coverage on *KTA* this morning, however.

Switching channels, Annabelle noted that *Daybreak* was joining in the Constance Young frenzy. She clicked the remote control again and again, finding that the other stations were doing their versions of the story as well. But then a face she recognized from the past appeared on the screen. Annabelle put the clicker down.

It was Jason Vaughan, a man Annabelle remembered from all the media coverage about two years ago. Vaughan was hawking his new book, and the interviewer was holding up a copy of *Never Look Back.*

Annabelle had heard that Vaughan was writing a book about the media and its ability to ruin someone's reputation and then move on to the next news cycle without a backward glance or any regard for the havoc wreaked in the subject's life. She'd also heard that Constance came in for quite a lambasting in the book. She'd done an interview with Vaughan after he was declared a hero for rescuing several people from a burning building. Under Constance's persistent and blistering questions, Vaughan had stuttered and contradicted himself and ended up looking like an impostor. Immediately following the interview, witnesses came forward and said that in the confusion and smoke of the fire, they weren't entirely certain it had been Vaughan who'd extricated them from danger. Other media got on the bandwagon, and Vaughan went from being heralded as courageous and noble to being derided as suspicious and untrustworthy.

"I still maintain that I rescued those people," Vaughan explained to the interviewer on the screen. "But after that interview with Constance Young, no one ever believed me. I ended up losing my job on Wall Street—no one wanted to trade with somebody they couldn't trust. I had to move out of the apartment I was living in. People who'd been hailing me as a hero began avoiding me in the elevator. Not to mention I couldn't afford the rent in a luxury building anymore. The strain of it all was too much, and my marriage ended as well."

"What are you doing now? How are you making a living?" asked the interviewer.

"I'm trying to make it as a writer," answered Vaughan. "But it hasn't been easy."

Annabelle studied the careworn face, the deep creases in the man's forehead, his earnest expression. She was relieved she hadn't had anything to do with the background research or production of the interview Constance had done with him. If it turned out Vaughan was telling the truth, his life *had* been ruined.

Slipping on her shoes, Annabelle recalled that the woman who produced the *KTA* book segments had mentioned that Vaughan's book had been dismissed by the major publishing houses as predictable sour grapes and that he'd garnered a pretty measly advance from what was considered a second-rate publisher. But from Jason Vaughan's perspective at least, with interest in Constance Young at an all-time high, the timing of the publication of *Never Look Back* couldn't have been better.

Chapter 44

Near the end of *KEY to America*, Harry Granger, with Lauren sitting beside him, introduced the last piece of the show.

"Our broadcast this morning has focused largely on the untimely death of our colleague Constance Young, whom so many of you have watched here every morning. We are all in shock, but, as you all know, Lauren Adams succeeds Constance at the anchor desk, and this is Lauren's first day. She's already familiar to you from the many stories she has contributed as *KTA* lifestyle correspondent, but we thought you'd like to get to know more about the woman we hope you'll be starting your day with every morning."

Harry disappeared from the screen, and a picture of a little girl on a pony appeared.

"Lauren was born in Frankfort, Kentucky, the daughter of a homemaker and a stable manager for one of the Blue Grass State's biggest horse farms. Even before she could walk, Lauren loved to ride."

Lauren appeared on-screen in an interview that had clearly been shot recently. "I remember waiting for the school bell to ring every afternoon, just so I could get out and get to the stables. I loved trailing my dad around and seeing him watch over the horses. I loved feeding them and brushing them and talking to them. I even didn't mind cleaning up after them. I adored them, and I still do."

Up came a picture of Lauren, in riding clothes and velvet helmet, jumping a fence on her Thoroughbred mount, followed by a shot of her wearing a sparkling tiara and holding an armful of roses.

Harry's narration continued. "Lauren rode competitively, winning many equestrian prizes, but when she was a senior in high school, she won the title of Miss Kentucky Reel, excelling in the talent competition with a mesmerizing display of baton twirling. From there she went to Kentucky State University, where she graduated with honors, earning a degree in communications."

The piece went on to include videotape of Lauren covering different stories over the years. When the piece was over, the camera came back to a two-shot of Harry and Lauren on the sofa.

"Miss Kentucky Reel, eh?" Harry smirked.

Lauren smiled as she protested. "Hey, don't knock beauty pageants. The lives of many prominent television journalists and personalities have been influenced by their participation in those competitions. As you know, Harry, Constance won the Miss Virginia title, Diane Sawyer was America's Junior Miss, Deborah Norville was a Georgia Junior Miss, Paula Zahn was a finalist in the Miss Teenage America Pageant, and Gretchen Carlson was Miss America. Even Oprah Winfrey was involved in a pageant. She won Nashville's Miss Fire Prevention title in 1973."

"Do tell," said Harry.

Lauren laughed. "All right, make fun if you want to. But I never learned more from any other single experience than I learned from that pageant."

Chapter 45

It was early, but already the bouquets of flowers were arriving from well-wishers eager to impress Lauren on her first day. Boyd made several trips back and forth from Lauren's office to the Broadcast Center lobby to pick up the lavish arrangements being dropped off by Manhattan's finest florists.

He shifted the bouquets around the office until he was sure they were displayed to their best advantage. Then he turned on the television monitors mounted to the walls, knowing that Lauren was obsessed with keeping track of the competition. Boyd set out some new magazines in a neat pile on Lauren's desk, made sure every pencil in the drawer was sharpened, and booted up her computer. He stood in the doorway and gave the office one more look, wanting to be certain that everything would be pleasing to Lauren when she came up from the studio. Satisfied, Boyd turned to go back to his desk in the outer office when the image on one of the televisions caught his eye.

Boyd felt his stomach tighten.

Jason Vaughan was being interviewed. Then a book cover flashed on the screen. *Never Look Back.*

Boyd sank down onto the sofa and aimed the remote at the television to turn up the volume. The more he listened to Jason Vaughan talk, the more worried Boyd felt.

Months ago it had seemed like a good idea to talk with the disgruntled author. Boyd had been so angry himself, so fed up, with Constance and the dismissive and disrespectful way she treated him. Vaughan had promised that he wouldn't reveal his source. Yet even as he'd answered Vaughan's probing questions, Boyd had a nagging feeling that he could be making a big mistake.

Now he knew for certain he had. Even if Vaughan kept his word, somebody might be able to read something in the book and deduce that the information had come from her personal assistant. And with Constance dead now, anyone who had expressed such awful things about her might be looked at as a person of interest in her death if the autopsy showed there'd been foul play.

Chapter 46

As she stepped into the elevator, Eliza didn't know how long Lauren would be staying around after her first show. Not wanting to miss her, Eliza bypassed the second floor and went up to the seventh.

The door to Lauren's office was closed, but Boyd Irons sat in the anteroom.

"I'll buzz her and let her know you're here," he said.

The door opened almost immediately. Linus Nazareth stood in the doorway.

"Eliza, Eliza," he said in a loud voice. "To what do we owe this honor?"

"I just wanted to come up and personally congratulate Lauren on surviving her first day," said Eliza as she walked into the office. Lauren was leaning against the edge of her desk.

"Well, thank you, Eliza. That's very sweet of you," she said. "And thank you for the flowers. They're gorgeous." Lauren pointed to the glass cylinder filled with two dozen long-stemmed white roses.

Eliza laughed. "It looks like a florist shop in here."

"People have been very kind." Lauren smiled.

"As well they should be," Linus said. "They know that Lauren is going to be the next queen of morning television."

Neither Eliza nor Lauren said anything.

"All right," said Linus. "Maybe, under the circumstances, that wasn't the most tactful thing to say. But the fact remains, Constance is dead, and that creates a vacuum. Lauren is going to do the filling." Linus smiled confidently. "Now I'll leave you two girls to it."

Both women watched as the executive producer walked out of the office.

"You've got to give credit where credit is due," said Eliza after he was out of earshot. "Linus is absolutely devoted to making *KTA* a ratings success. I bet his first waking thought is about *KTA* and he falls asleep thinking about *KTA*. No doubt he dreams about *KTA*, too."

"You're right. He does," said Lauren. "I don't know what I would have done without him. He's helped me every step of the way. I wouldn't be here without Linus."

Eliza searched Lauren's face. "It's a lot of pressure sitting in that chair, isn't it?" she asked.

"If only the two hours the viewers see was all of it," said Lauren as she walked around her desk and signaled for Eliza to take a seat opposite her. "It's the research and prep time and the time spent doing publicity interviews and trying on clothes and experimenting with makeup and hairstyles and knowing that everything you say and do on-screen is being analyzed. I never understood how important privacy is until I was named as Constance's successor."

"Yes," Eliza acknowledged. "It can be a lot, but let's not forget that if we don't want to do it, there are plenty of others who would jump at the chance. As far as the privacy is concerned, it's really important to have friends you can trust and to be able to carve out time that's all yours."

"I can tell already you're right about that," said Lauren, snapping her gum. "Thank God I have my riding. When I was a little girl, I could get so involved in the stable and in riding that I'd be lost for hours at a time. It's still pretty much the same way. Horses mean so much to me. When I'm riding, I'm in a zone."

"Do you have your own?" asked Eliza.

"Yes," answered Lauren. "I used to ride at the Claremont Riding Academy here in the city, but when

I signed my new contract, I decided I could afford my own horse. I keep him in upstate New York. I was up there Saturday morning when I got the call about Constance. That's how I got there so quickly."

"About Saturday," said Eliza tentatively. "I'm sorry about what happened in our two-way on the *Evening Headlines* that night. I truly had no idea that you didn't know about the stolen unicorn. I hope you believe me when I tell you I wasn't trying to make you look foolish."

"I realize that now, Eliza. But to tell you the truth, I was reeling mad then. I screamed blue murder to Linus about it, but I regret that now. I didn't treat Annabelle Murphy and B.J. D'Elia well enough. That's why B.J. went to you with the information instead of telling me. Because of that, we've lost two good people on *KTA*—and now the *Evening Headlines* has Annabelle and B.J. Our loss is your gain."

Chapter 47

P aige was waiting when Eliza reached her office.

"The Cloisters wants to know if you would consider being the mistress of ceremonies Wednesday night for the reception and preview of their Camelot exhibition. It's primarily for their major donors, but there will be a limited number of tickets available to the public. Constance was supposed to do it, but obviously that isn't going to happen now."

"Gee, Paige, I don't know," said Eliza, grimacing a bit. "I don't really know enough about the Middle Ages."

"They say they'll send down some research if you like, but they don't expect you to be anything approaching an expert. Basically they're looking for a charming, well-known personality who will bring some prestige to the evening—more of a hostess than a lecturer or teacher."

"Another night away from Janie? No," said Eliza. "Tell them I'm sorry, but I won't be able to do it."

"All right," said Paige, "but I really had to feel bad for the woman who called. Not only has she lost her emcee, but the focal point of her exhibition is missing. She sounded beside herself."

"Surely she could find someone else," said Eliza. "I bet Lauren would be happy to do it."

"I actually suggested Lauren to her," said Paige, "but she wasn't enthusiastic. She said Lauren isn't well known enough."

"Lauren would love to hear that," said Eliza. She thought for a moment. "All right, I'll do it. I know how it is to be organizing something like that and have things seem to fall apart right before the event. And since Constance was going to do it, it would be nice if KEY News came to the rescue. Call the woman up, tell her yes, and ask her to send me that information about the exhibit."

Chapter 48

Annabelle came into Eliza's office and held out the report.

"I thought you'd want to see this."

Eliza took the document and scanned the autopsy findings. She looked up at Annabelle. "Cardiac arrest was the cause of death?" she asked. "That makes even less sense than drowning. Constance was in amazing physical shape."

"Keep reading," answered Annabelle.

There'd been alcohol in Constance Young's system, but not an excessive amount. Her skin was rough, swollen, and wrinkled, consistent with being immersed in water. But there was no sign of the struggle usually associated with drowning, nor were her lungs or stomach filled with water. There were hemorrhages in her middle ear, sometimes seen in drowning cases, but the report noted that hemorrhages of this kind could also occur in cases of head trauma, mechanical asphyxiation, and electrocution.

The document went on to cite the police report finding that the lights and heater at Constance's pool had shorted out, suggesting a possible surge of electricity. Eliza knew that electrocution victims die of cardiac arrest when current flows through the heart, disrupting the normal coordination of the heart muscles. The muscles lose their rhythm and begin to fibrillate. Death soon follows. Death when the heart stops. Cardiac arrest.

Taken together, the findings suggested that Constance Young had been electrocuted. But the question was, had the electrocution been accidental? Or deliberate?

Just as Annabelle was about to leave, Boyd Irons arrived at Eliza's office.

"Constance's sister called," he announced. "She wants to have the funeral service tomorrow morning. At eleven."

"Tomorrow? Isn't that a bit quick? The autopsy was just released today," said Eliza. "That makes me think the body is only being released today as well."

"Yes, it's quick all right," Boyd agreed. "Faith told me she wants to get this over and done with. So I'm calling around like a crazy person, inviting people to come to the funeral home."

"What kind of response are you getting?" asked Eliza.

Boyd shrugged. "Too soon to tell. But I do know there'll be no lack of media. The press information department tells me the calls are coming in nonstop from every possible news and entertainment outlet."

"Entertainment, huh?" said Annabelle. "What does it say when funerals are featured on entertainment shows?"

"I don't know what it says," Boyd answered. "But their viewers want to see that stuff, and the producers are eager to give them what they want."

"Will cameras be allowed in the funeral parlor?" asked Eliza.

Boyd shook his head. "No, but they'll be swarming all over the place outside."

"Constance would have liked all the attention," Annabelle said quietly.

After Annabelle and Boyd had departed, Eliza turned to her assistant.

"Paige, will you please call and order flowers to be sent for Constance's funeral and order another arrangement and have it sent to Constance's sister in New

Jersey," Eliza instructed. "Boyd can give you the addresses. And see if you can track down Margo Gonzalez for me, will you please?"

Ten minutes later the intercom in Eliza's office buzzed. "Dr. Gonzalez is on line two, Eliza."

"Thanks." Eliza picked up the telephone receiver. "Hi, Margo. How are you?"

"Fine, Eliza. But I just got a phone call inviting me to Constance's funeral tomorrow morning."

"Will you go?"

"If I can move a few things around, I guess so," said Margo. "But to tell you the truth, I'm surprised I'm being invited. I haven't been working at KEY very long, and I didn't know Constance all that well—in fact, I never felt she cared to give me the time of day. If this funeral is by invitation only, I don't think I really qualify as one of the attendees."

"I'm going to let you in on something," said Eliza. "I gather that pretty much anyone who worked on *KTA* with Constance is receiving an invitation."

Margo laughed. "Ah, now I get it. They want to make sure there'll be enough people to fill the seats."

"Something like that, I think," said Eliza.

"Okay," said Margo. "I'm going to try to be there."

"That would be good of you," said Eliza. "But that's not really why I wanted to reach you, Margo."

"What is it?"

"Actually, it's about my little girl." Eliza described the conversation she'd had with Janie at the breakfast table that morning, Janie's fears, Eliza's reassurances.

"It sounds like you handled it very well," said Margo.

"I hope so," said Eliza. "You're never sure with kids."

"Here's what I've found over the years, Eliza, and what many studies have proved. Children don't need to have two parents to be emotionally healthy. And parents don't need to be perfect in their actions and responses, and that's a good thing, because none of us *are* perfect." Margo continued, "But they do have to be dependable and consistent for the child to feel on solid ground. I have the feeling from what I know of you, and what you've just told me, that Janie feels secure in your love and devotion to her. With that as a basis, it's likely she'll be able to handle whatever life hands her."

"God, you don't know how much I needed to hear that, Margo. Thank you."

"You're welcome," said Margo. "It's not easy being a single parent. I hope you'll call me anytime you want to talk."

Chapter 49

The Great Dane lay on the examining table. Before he began any cutting for the necropsy, the veterinarian waved a wand over the dog. The wandlike scanner emitted low-frequency radio waves that picked up on a tiny transponder, the size of a grain of uncooked rice, implanted under the loose skin on the Dane's shoulder.

The microchip supplied a number, displayed in the scanner readout window. The number would lead to the dog's owner, someone who had thought enough of the Great Dane that he'd gone to the trouble of having the microchip implanted so that he wouldn't lose the animal. How had that same animal, which had, at one time at least, clearly been prized, end up dead in Constance Young's swimming pool?

The veterinarian wrote down the number on his report sheet, then picked up a scalpel.

Chapter 50

The police called Constance Young's assistant, wanting to know if there was someone named Graham Welles in her Rolodex or her computer address book. Boyd checked.

"There's an Alexander Wells, W-E-L-L-S, at 79 Gleason Court in Westwood, New Jersey, " Boyd offered.

"No," said the detective. "W-E-L-L-*E*-S. Graham Welles, middle initial P. as in Peter. And the address is 527 East Thirty-seventh Street in Manhattan."

"Would it be all right if you told me why you wanted to know?" Boyd asked as he scribbled down the name and address and continued to search. He felt he and the detective were almost friends by now. They'd had so many conversations over the last few days, and Boyd had answered so many questions. Had Constance had any fights with anyone lately? Did Boyd know if she had any enemies? Who had she been dating? Was there anyone Boyd could think of who would want her dead? Boyd had answered at length, wanting to help as much as he could, hoping to stay on the good side of the police by cooperating.

"The dead dog that was found on the property was registered to this guy, but he's no longer at the address listed on the database," the detective said. "We're going to the postal service to see if he left a forwarding address, and there are things we can do beyond that to track him down, but I just thought I'd run it past you first."

"Sorry, Detective," said Boyd as he finished his search. "I wish I could be of more help."

Boyd hung up the phone, wondering if he should tell Linus or somebody from *KTA* about the conversation with the detective. But Boyd didn't trust Linus enough to be certain he wouldn't use the information in some way that would come back to haunt him. Besides, Boyd rationalized, the *Evening Headlines* would be the next broadcast to air. Any new information should be passed along to them, and Boyd felt that he could count on Eliza Blake to protect her source if it should come to that.

"**Back so** soon?" Eliza asked when Boyd walked into her office.

Boyd recounted his conversation with the detective and held out the piece of paper on which he'd written the name and address of the dog's owner. Eliza took it from him.

"I'm going to give this to Annabelle and see what she can find out," said Eliza. "Thanks so much for the tip, Boyd."

"No problem, Eliza," said Boyd. "But I hope I won't get into any trouble for telling you about this."

"You mean with the police?" asked Eliza.

Boyd nodded. "Or with Linus. I don't know which one scares me more."

Chapter 51

Mr. Welles? Mr. Graham Welles?"

"Speaking."

Yes. Annabelle pumped her free hand in the air in a fist as she held on to the telephone receiver with the other. She had found him.

"Hi, my name is Annabelle Murphy. I'm a producer with KEY News. I was hoping I could ask you a few questions."

"Yes?" Graham Welles answered cautiously.

"I was wondering if you owned a Great Dane," said Annabelle.

"Who is this, *really*?" asked Graham.

"I'm Annabelle Murphy, and I'm calling from KEY News in New York City. I understand you once lived in Manhattan?"

"What show do you work for?" the man asked, still unsure.

"*Key to Amer—*" Annabelle caught herself. "Excuse me, *KEY Evening Headlines* with Eliza Blake."

"Oh, I'm a big Eliza Blake fan," said Graham. "I watch her every night."

"She'll be glad to hear that, sir."

"That place of yours must be in quite an uproar, huh?"

"Yes, sir, it is."

"Constance Young. Such a terrible thing to happen to such a young woman," the man mused aloud. "Does anybody know exactly what happened yet?"

"No, not yet." Annabelle patiently answered the man's questions, wanting to build up as much connection as anyone could in a short, transcontinental phone call.

"I watched Constance Young all the time, too," said the man. "To tell you the truth, I was going to follow her over to *Daybreak.* But I guess I'll stay with *KEY to America* now."

"Mr. Welles," said Annabelle, "I'm hoping that you might be able to help us with a story we are doing on Constance's death."

"*Me?* How could *I* help you?"

It was obvious now to Annabelle that she had beaten the police in tracking down the Great Dane's owner.

Inwardly she congratulated herself on using the available technology and following through faster than law enforcement.

"There was a dog found on Ms. Young's property," said Annabelle. "A dog registered to you."

"Marco?" asked the man.

"A black Great Dane?" asked Annabelle.

"Yes," said Graham. "But how could that be? Did Constance Young adopt my Marco?"

"I don't understand what you mean," said Annabelle.

"I had to give Marco up when I moved out here to the West Coast to live with my daughter and her family. I put ads in the paper and called everyone I knew, but nobody would take him. He's such a big fella, you know."

Oh, crap. In her eagerness to follow the lead on the dog's owner, Annabelle hadn't given any thought to the fact that she was going to have to break the news that the Great Dane was dead.

"When I took Marco to the animal shelter, I was praying someone would adopt him." Graham Welles sounded relieved.

"What animal shelter was that, Mr. Welles?" asked Annabelle. As she wrote down the answer, Annabelle knew she was being careful to get the information she wanted before risking upsetting her interviewee.

"I'm so glad they found a home for Marco," said the man. He paused as a thought occurred to him. "But if Constance Young is dead, what will happen to Marco now?"

Annabelle braced herself. She could fib with some vague reference to the Westchester County animal authorities taking care of the dog, or she could avoid the question altogether and let Graham Welles hear from the police, when they inevitably contacted him, that his beloved Great Dane was dead. Either option wasn't really playing it straight.

"I'm afraid I have some very sad news, Mr. Welles. Marco is dead." No response came from the other end of the phone connection. "I'm so sorry, Mr. Welles. I really am." As gently as she could, when the man began to ask questions, she told him an abbreviated version of what she knew. The dog had been found in the woods near the pool. The veterinarian had found the identifying microchip while examining the dog, which had led her to call. She didn't mention that Marco's body had been thrown into the dump or that the vet was dissecting Marco's carcass to figure out how the dog had died.

"Again, Mr. Welles, I'm so very sorry," said Annabelle. "But thank you for talking with me. Now I know which animal shelter to check to see who claimed Marco."

"You mean, you don't think Constance Young adopted him?" Graham sounded puzzled.

"I'm not quite sure what to think," said Annabelle. "But if Constance had gotten a dog, I think her assistant would have known about it. As far as I know, he didn't."

"So you think Marco might have been with somebody else?" he asked. "Somebody else brought him to that house? Do you think that somebody might have *killed* Marco?"

"I'm afraid that's a possibility," answered Annabelle. "We are going to keep looking into this. But, Mr. Welles?"

"Yes?"

"Would you be willing to go on camera and talk to us for the story we're doing tonight? We could send a producer and camera crew from our Los Angeles bureau to your house."

Graham hesitated. "Oh, I don't know about that."

"It might help us find out what happened to Marco," urged Annabelle. "If somebody knows something that could be helpful and hears you talking about him, it might prompt them to come forward with their information." Annabelle took a deep breath, knowing how much she was asking.

"Well, all right," Graham Welles agreed. "I'll do it."

Chapter 52

O h, my God, you're not going to believe this, guys,"
said Annabelle, as she walked into the Fishbowl,
where Eliza, the senior producers, the director, and
production assistants were going over what would be
on the *Evening Headlines* that night.

"Try us," said Range Bullock.

"I just got off the phone with the animal shelter
that took in the Great Dane that was found dead on
Constance's property. One of the shelter attendants was
found murdered this morning."

Range emitted a low whistle.

"And what about the dog?" asked Eliza. "Did they
tell you anything about the Great Dane and who adopted him?"

"They're checking their records," answered Annabelle.

"We should go over there and get some pictures and see who'll talk with us," said Range.

"I've already asked for B.J.," said Annabelle. "He's loading up his gear now."

"I want to go with you, too," said Eliza.

There was yellow police tape blocking off the entrance to the animal shelter. B.J. leaned in to try the door. It was unlocked.

"After you," he said. Eliza and Annabelle bent down and slipped under the tape. Inside, there were cages of animals, some barking, some sleeping, some pacing back and forth, but no police in sight.

Eliza went up to the counter and introduced herself.

"I know who you are," said the woman who staffed the desk. "This day couldn't possibly get any more surreal."

"Well, this is Annabelle Murphy, our producer, and B.J. D'Elia, our cameraman," said Eliza. Hands were shaken all around.

"Can you tell me what happened?" said Eliza.

"I guess so. The police have already come and gone," said the woman. "It's probably just another New York City homicide to them, but Vinny was the world's nicest guy." Her eyes filled with tears.

"Would you be willing to talk with the camera rolling?" asked Eliza.

"All right," said the woman. "I suppose so."

B.J. looked around the room. "Maybe we could do the interview closer to the cages," he suggested. "It would make the shot more interesting to have the animals in the background."

After B.J. miked the two women and made all the necessary adjustments to his camera gear, the interview began.

"Okay, let's start with what happened," said Eliza. "What can you tell me?"

The woman took a deep breath. "Well, I came in this morning, and the minute I opened the door, I really had a feeling that something was wrong. The dogs were all staring at me and barking like crazy. It was like they were trying to tell me something."

Eliza nodded and waited for the woman to continue.

"So I put my stuff down on the counter, and then I started walking to each of the cages, talking to the dogs, trying to calm them down, you know?"

"Yes," said Eliza.

"But they didn't calm down. They went on barking and yelping, and I was getting a creepy feeling, but I kept on going. And then I got to the back." The woman pointed to the rear of the spacious area.

"Could we walk back there together?" Eliza asked.

"I suppose so," said the woman. "But I wouldn't want to go back there by myself. Not for a while anyway."

B.J. followed them with his camera. The woman stopped in front of a cage that housed a black Labrador retriever.

"This is where I found him," said the woman, her voice shaking. "This is where I found Vinny. He was just lying there. I could tell right away he was dead."

"So then you called the police?" asked Eliza.

"Well, I called 911. They sent an ambulance anyway, but that didn't do any good. They couldn't bring Vinny back. The police came and searched around. Look at the mess they've made."

"Did the police speculate on how Vinny was killed?" asked Eliza.

"Yes." The woman lowered her voice. "I overheard one of the detectives talking."

"What did they think?"

"Sodium pentobarbital. We keep some in the back to put down animals if we have to."

"And the police think that Vinny was injected with it?"

The woman nodded. "And some of the vials are missing, too—which is really scary." Her mood brightened a bit when she thought of her coworker. "As for Vinny, he was the loveliest, most sensitive guy you'd ever want to meet." She looked around the room. "He was so committed to finding homes for these animals. He didn't deserve what happened to him. Not at all."

"I'm so sorry," said Eliza.

"Thank you," the woman said with a sniffle.

"Let me ask you about something else," said Eliza.

"What is it?"

"Well, you've probably heard that one of our colleagues, Constance Young, was found dead at her county house over the weekend."

"Who *hasn't* heard?" the woman said with a sarcastic tone. "That's all that's been on the radio and television."

"And did you hear mention of a dead dog found on her property as well?" asked Eliza.

"I think I heard something about it, but to tell you the truth, I started not paying much attention after the first ten stories I listened to."

"Well, it turns out the dog was once here," said Eliza. "We know who brought it in, but we want to find out who took it out."

The woman hesitated. "Why haven't the police questioned me about this?" asked the woman.

"I don't know why," said Eliza. "But you can bet they will. Maybe the county police haven't been talking to the city police. Maybe they haven't made the connection with the dog and this shelter."

The woman's facial expression grew even graver. "So you think there's some connection with the dead dog, this shelter, and Vinny's murder?"

"That's what we want to find out," said Eliza. "We already have the name and New York City address of the man who owned the dog and brought it here before he moved out of town."

The woman considered Eliza's words. "All right," she said finally. "Let's go back up front to the computer."

A few strokes of the computer keys and the information came up.

"Here it is," said the woman. "Graham Welles. He brought in a male black Great Dane named Marco. I remember now. Vinny had been so worried that nobody would choose that dog. He was so excited when he found a home for it."

"Can you tell me who adopted the dog?" asked Eliza.

The woman squinted at the computer screen. "Yes. Ryan Banford," she said, pointing to the data. "And here's the address."

As Eliza, Annabelle, and B.J. drove back to the Broadcast Center in the crew car, B.J. speculated.

"How much you want to wager there's no Ryan Banford at that address?"

"I'm not going to take that bet," said Annabelle. "But can you believe we beat the police in making the connection between the dog and this animal shelter?"

"Nice work, Annabelle," said Eliza. "And let's hope they don't make that connection before airtime. Then we'll have an exclusive."

"And let's hope something else," said B.J. as he steered the car through midtown traffic. "Let's hope that missing sodium pentobarbital isn't used on anybody else."

Chapter 53

The detectives entered the office building of Whitaker Medieval Enterprises. The receptionist buzzed Mr. Whitaker's secretary, who escorted the investigators upstairs.

As they walked down a long hallway, the detectives observed the artwork hanging on the walls. Renderings of dragons, dungeons, armor, crossbows, and spiked-ball flails flanked the dimly lit corridor. The detectives shot looks at each other.

"Please, have a seat here in the conference room," the secretary said. "Mr. Whitaker will be right with you."

A huge circular table dominated the room. Its legs were carved with menacing gargoyles and human figures with angry faces. A reproduction of the table reputed to be that of King Arthur and his Knights of the

Round Table in the Great Hall of Winchester Castle in England, the table must have weighed a ton. The names of the knights were painted at each place, with a portrait of the great mythical king painted at the place farthest from the door. Neither of the detectives had the nerve to sit at King Arthur's place, choosing instead to sit in two of the other twenty-four chairs stationed around the table. As they waited, they took in the other medieval accoutrements in the room. At one corner, a full suit of armor stood with lance in hand, arranged like a knight going into battle. In another corner, hammered iron shackles hung from thick chains on the wall.

"Does this place creep you out, or is it just me?" one detective asked.

"This Whitaker guy is one strange customer," said the other, shaking his head and looking around the room. "God, and to think he's made millions with this stuff. We're doing something wrong, buddy. Why couldn't we have thought of making video games based on crap from the Middle Ages?"

"Probably because we couldn't even say when the Middle Ages were."

"You're right."

The conference room door opened. Stuart Whitaker entered, followed by another man.

"Hello, gentlemen," said Stuart, shaking both detectives' hands. "This is Philip Hill, my attorney."

The attorney nodded at the detectives.

"You'll notice there is no head to this table, gentlemen. Everyone is equal at a round table," said Stuart as he took a chair across from the detectives. "That's why King Arthur had his knights sit at a round table."

"Is that so?" asked one of the detectives. "You learn something new every day."

"Mr. Whitaker," said the other detective, "let's get to why we're here."

"Please, do," said Stuart, taking off his glasses and wiping the lenses with a snowy white handkerchief.

"We're here about the ivory unicorn and the death of Constance Young."

Stuart put his glasses back on and waited.

"The Cloisters' security staff has informed us that you and Ms. Young had access to the unicorn on a private tour you took there."

"Yes, that is correct," said Stuart.

"Well. Let me come right out and ask you, Mr. Whitaker. Did you take the unicorn?"

Stuart looked from detective to detective and then to his lawyer. Philip Hill nodded encouragement to his client.

"I *borrowed* the unicorn," said Stuart. "I intended to make a copy for Constance, who had admired it so. But then I could not wait to show it to her. She loved it and, when I placed it around her neck, it looked so beautiful on her. I couldn't bring myself to take it back. Constance was a true queen, and she deserved the real thing, not a fake." Stuart hung his head. "I realize that was not the right thing to do."

"Did Ms. Young know that the unicorn was the real thing, or did she think it was a copy?"

"At first she thought it was a copy. I did not tell her until last Friday that it was the authentic unicorn."

"Friday? The day she died?" asked a detective.

"Well, Friday, her last day on *KEY to America* anyway," said Stuart. "I do not know exactly when Constance died."

"So you saw Ms. Young on Friday?"

"No. I spoke with her on the phone that morning after I saw her wearing the unicorn on television. I called her to tell her that she was breaking her promise not to wear it in front of anyone but me, and that I was disappointed in her."

"So you were angry with Ms. Young," stated the same detective.

The attorney interjected. "Mr. Whitaker said he was disappointed in Ms. Young. He didn't say he was angry with her."

The detectives gave the lawyer a resigned look.

"Well, Mr. Whitaker," one detective asked, "*were* you angry?"

"You don't have to answer that, Stuart," said the attorney.

"That is all right, Philip," said Stuart quietly. "I have nothing to hide. In fact, I want to get this off my chest. I was, as I said, disappointed that Constance was wearing the unicorn amulet, even though she had promised me that she would wear it only when we were together. And, of course, I was worried as well."

"Worried about what?" continued the detective.

"Worried that someone would recognize the unicorn and realize that it had been stolen," said Stuart.

"And then figure out that you took it from the museum?"

Stuart nodded.

"So then what happened?" the other detective asked.

"I told her the unicorn I had given her was not a copy, that it was the real thing. I asked her to give it back to me," said Stuart.

"What was Ms. Young's response?"

"She said the unicorn had brought her good luck and she would not ever want to part with it." Stuart rubbed his hand over his bald head. "Then she rushed me off the phone."

"So she didn't care that you could be in trouble for taking the unicorn?" asked the detective.

"I do not know how she felt," said Stuart. "I loved Constance, and I cannot allow myself to think that she would be so callous."

The detectives watched closely for any expression, any hint of emotion on Stuart Whitaker's face. What they saw was a paunchy, pale-skinned, middle-aged man looking defeated and sad.

"So that was it, Mr. Whitaker?" asked a detective. "That was the last conversation you had with Constance Young?"

Stuart nodded.

"And you made no further attempt to get that unicorn back?"

Stuart looked quizzically at his attorney.

"It's all right, Stuart," said the lawyer. "Tell them."

Stuart nervously cleared his throat. "Well, I did try to get the unicorn back. At least that was my plan. I went to the restaurant, Barbetta, where the farewell luncheon for Constance was being held, in hopes of seeing her and asking her again to return the unicorn to me."

"And did she?"

"I never got to talk with her. I never even saw her," explained Stuart. "Her assistant was worried there would be a scene, and he thought I should leave."

"Was that Boyd Irons?"

"Yes. He told me he understood what it was like to have Constance give him a hard time. He said he would do his best to get the unicorn back for me."

"And what did you tell Mr. Irons?"

"I said that I would make it worth his time if he did. I asked him if he could get the unicorn for me. I didn't mean that he should kill her for it."

Whitaker's attorney interrupted again. "Detectives, it would seem you are investigating two separate things here—the theft of the ivory unicorn from the Cloisters and the death of Constance Young. On the first point, Mr. Whitaker has already admitted that he misguidedly borrowed the artifact from the museum with every intention of returning it. I have been in contact with people at the Cloisters, who have already agreed that this was all a gross misunderstanding. They understand that Mr. Whitaker, a longtime and generous patron of the museum, had only borrowed the unicorn amulet. And they have assured me that they will not be pressing charges against him. If the unicorn is not physically recovered, Mr. Whitaker will make financial restitution for it."

The detectives looked at each other knowingly. It was nice to have money.

"On the second point," the lawyer continued, "as to the death of Ms. Young, my client knows absolutely nothing about that horrible tragedy. He left the restaurant on Friday without ever seeing Ms. Young. In fact, he never saw her again."

The attorney rose from his seat and indicated that Stuart should follow suit.

"As Mr. Whitaker just informed you, he told Boyd Irons that he would pay him if he could reclaim the unicorn. I suggest you talk to Mr. Irons about how successful he was in that regard."

Chapter 54

Just after five o'clock, Jason pushed the buzzer and waited in the hallway until the apartment door opened. A boy with dark, tousled hair and a thin, serious face opened the door.

"Are you ready, buddy?"

"Yeah, Dad. I'll be right there. I got to get my stuff."

"Don't forget to bring everything you need for your homework," Jason called after his son. He walked through the door and stood in the small vestibule. He could hear Nell wrapping up a telephone conversation. When she hung up, she walked out to acknowledge him.

"Hi. How's it going?" she asked.

"Actually, Nell, it's going pretty well," Jason answered, happy to have the first positive thing to report to the mother of his son in a very long time. "Have you been following the news?"

"How could I not?" she asked. "It's everywhere you turn. And now this missing Lady Guinevere unicorn? That's fascinating. I'd love to see that Camelot Exhibit. But do you think Constance Young was really killed for that unicorn?"

Jason shrugged. "Who knows? But all this is turning out to be great for book sales."

"That's kind of sick, don't you think, Jason?"

Jason shrugged. "Maybe," he said. "But it's hard for me to feel too sorry for her after what she did to me."

"Well, do me a favor, will you please?" said Nell. "Don't say that in front of Ethan. He's a nine-year-old boy, and he doesn't need to be tainted by your personal problems any more than he already has."

"Don't worry, Nell. I won't say anything to him about my feelings toward Constance Young. But I would like to share with him the news about the book doing so well. Did you guys see me on television this morning?"

The uncomfortable expression on Nell's face told Jason that his call alerting his ex-wife and son to the cable news show interview hadn't induced them to make a point of watching it.

"That time of morning is always tough," said Nell. "Ethan is rushing around getting ready for school, and I'm trying to get to work."

Jason tried not to let his disappointment show. "Don't worry. There will be other interviews," he said. "So how *are* things in the real-estate business anyway?"

"All right, I guess."

"That doesn't sound very convincing."

"It can be tough working on commission," she said.

"Then why don't you get a salaried job?"

"Because this job gives me flexibility," said Nell. "I can plan my schedule somewhat and be here when Ethan gets home from school, at least a few afternoons a week. He's not a little kid anymore, but there's no less reason to keep track of where he is and what he's doing."

Jason nodded. "You're right. But I hate that our lives have been like this, Nell. Think how much better it would be if we were all together again. I hate seeing Ethan only a couple nights during the week and every other weekend. I could be with him all the time, and you wouldn't have to work unless you wanted to."

"That presupposes that you'd be making enough money to support us, Jason."

"If this book does as well as my agent thinks it will, there *will* be enough," he answered. "I already have an idea for the next one, and Larry feels confident he'll be able to sell it."

Nell sighed. "Finances aren't the only problem, Jason. We've grown apart. I don't feel like we know each other anymore."

Chapter 55

*T*he *KEY Evening Headlines* began precisely at
6:30 P.M. At the top of the broadcast, Eliza Blake
delivered the forensic findings.

"Constance Young died of cardiac arrest. There was
no sign of any struggle usually associated with drowning. Neither her stomach nor her lungs were filled with
water."

Eliza took a breath before continuing. "The fact
that the lights and heater at the pool had shorted out
suggests a possible surge of electricity. Therefore, authorities are working on the supposition that Constance
Young died of cardiac arrest when an electrical current
pulsed through her heart, stopping it.

"While the results of the autopsy answer some questions," she concluded, "there are still others left to be

answered. Chief among them: If Constance Young was electrocuted in her swimming pool, was it an accident? Or was she deliberately killed?"

Eliza turned to look in the direction of another camera.

"We already reported to you that a dog was found lying dead on Constance Young's property last Friday morning. That dog has been recovered, and while we don't know the results of the necropsy yet, KEY News has learned that its original owner had delivered the Great Dane to an animal shelter a few weeks ago. This is what Graham Welles, who now lives in California, had to say when he spoke with KEY News today."

An image of a distinguished elderly man appeared on the television screen.

"Marco was the best dog anyone could ever want," the man said. "I loved that dog from the moment I got him as a puppy. I treasured him. That's why I got that microchip implanted, so if he ever ran off or got lost, somebody could track Marco back to me. I could have gone with a tattoo, like a lot of folks do, but I thought the chip would hurt him less."

Eliza appeared on the screen again.

"Today we went to the animal shelter that took the dog when Graham Welles moved from New York to live with his daughter on the West Coast. We found out that the Great Dane had been adopted just last week, the day before the dog was found dead on Constance Young's property. And in an even more troubling twist, the shelter employee who facilitated the transfer of the dog to its new owner has been found murdered."

Images of the interior of the animal shelter popped up. The words KEY NEWS EXCLUSIVE appeared in the bottom-left-hand corner of the screen.

"The body of thirty-seven-year-old Vinny Shays was discovered when one of his coworkers opened the animal shelter this morning. It is suspected that Shays was injected with sodium pentobarbital, the product often used for the euthanasia of animals. Containers of the substance were found in disarray in a storeroom at the rear of the shelter."

The director switched back to a shot of Eliza at the anchor desk.

"So we have a dead animal found on Friday and Constance Young found dead the very next day. A coincidence? Perhaps. But the fact that the last person known to have seen the dog alive has now been murdered raises worrisome questions that all of this is somehow connected.

"In addition, we've traced the name and address that were given by the person who adopted the Great Dane from the animal shelter. There is no such person at that address. In fact," Eliza continued, "there is no such address at all."

Her luminous blue eyes looked directly into the camera lens.

"KEY News will continue investigating this story, and we will, of course, keep you informed of everything that develops."

Chapter 56

Watching and listening to Eliza Blake, Ursula knew what she should do. She should go to the police and tell them what she'd seen, but she just couldn't bring herself to do it. The police would say they would protect her, but they really wouldn't. They always promised they could ensure the safety of a witness, but the reality was that the witness was never totally safe. If the killer wanted to get to her, eventually it would happen.

Ursula looked around her modest living room and wondered if Constance might have left her anything in her will. Her small house wasn't much by the standards of the many wealthy people who lived nearby, but she loved her cozy little place. She worked hard, she paid her bills, she went to church, she taught the rich ladies how to knit and do needlepoint. She guessed most would judge it to be a small life, but it was a life she treasured. Ursula wanted it to last.

Willing to kill Constance, the killer would certainly be willing to murder her, too. But if the killer did figure out that Ursula had seen everything that night at the pool and decided to kill her, Ursula was determined that she leave behind some indication of her killer's identity.

She turned her attention to the needlepoint canvas that lay on her lap. Ursula picked up the canvas, but her hands trembled. Forcing herself to concentrate, she selected a strand of black wool and began weaving it through the holes, finally finishing the second verse of her tribute to Constance:

Men wooed her as a queen,
Sought after for her charms,
Known only on the screen,
If rarely in her arms.

A tribute to Constance and the key to the identity of a killer.

Chapter 57

A microchip in the Great Dane. Who could have anticipated that?

It had gotten to the point that technology had its invasive tentacles everywhere. There was no real privacy anymore. There were cameras trained to catch you running red lights and tapping devices that could record your most confidential conversations. And every single address you visited on the Internet could be tracked. You couldn't possibly anticipate each potential for detection.

There had been no thought at all to the chance that a tiny microchip transmitter had been implanted in the dog. And yet that unanticipated element could have ruined everything.

Thank God for good old-fashioned lying and deception! A fictitious name, a fake address, and a subtle disguise had, in the end, saved the day. Those, plus trusting one's instincts and taking the initiative to do what needed to be done with Vinny. It turned out that the poor do-gooder hadn't had a clue—but who knew what he might have recalled when the police came around and plumbed his memory of the morning the Great Dane was adopted by his new owner?

The idea that KEY News was all over this was somehow more worrisome than knowing that the police were investigating. Were there any other loose ends that had been left hanging?

The carved unicorn lay nestled in the pocket of a coat in the hall closet. It seemed as good a place as any to hide it. Maybe the unicorn's power lay not in possessing it but in making sure it got to where it could do the most good. Maybe it was time to transfer it from one pocket to another.

Chapter 58

It was a balmy evening, and Eliza and Mack walked the blocks from the Broadcast Center toward Columbus Circle.

"You said you wanted to go somewhere relaxed," said Mack. "I thought maybe we could go for a burger."

Eliza smiled, somewhat disappointed that Mack didn't exactly seem to be pulling out all the stops for this dinner date that he'd practically been begging her for. Passing by dozens of upscale shops as they cut through the curving arcade at the base of the Time Warner Center at the southwest corner of Central Park, Eliza considered that Mack might just want to surprise her. There were several wonderful, highly touted restaurants located in the newly constructed center. But when they walked straight through the arcade and exited onto West Sixtieth Street, Eliza had no idea where they were going.

"I'm staying here," said Mack as they entered through the glass doors of a skyscraper a few yards away.

"KEY News is obviously improving its selection of expense-account-approved hotels," Eliza commented as they got into an elevator.

"KEY News isn't paying for the night here," said Mack. "I am. I moved over from the regular hotel they put me up in the last few nights."

"Does that mean you think you might get lucky?" Eliza asked, with a twinkle in her eye.

Mack smiled, showing his even, white teeth. "A guy can hope, can't he?"

The elevator doors opened. Mack took Eliza's arm and led the way to the Lobby Lounge of the Mandarin Oriental hotel.

"So you're trying to impress me after all," said Eliza as the hostess escorted them to a sofa by the window. They were thirty-eight floors up and looking out at the most spectacular floor-to-ceiling views of Broadway and Central Park. The vistas changed almost by the minute as lights began to go on all over the majestic skyline.

They ordered drinks, curried crab quesadillas, and a selection of miniburgers described as bacon-cheddar, caramelized onion–Gruyère, and wild mushroom–blue cheese.

The ice-cold martinis arrived first.

Mack leaned closer. "To us," he said, touching his glass to hers. "I didn't know if we'd ever be sitting together again like this."

She looked into his eyes, then averted her gaze and turned her attention to her drink, taking a sip.

"Mmm. That's just right." Eliza leaned back into the sofa. "It feels good to relax. The last few days have been so intense. And I'm not looking forward to that funeral tomorrow morning."

"You know what, Eliza?" Mack put his martini glass down on the low table in front of the sofa. "This whole thing with Constance has really made me think. It's been a wake-up call. Life is short and very unpredictable."

"Don't I know it!" said Eliza. She took another sip of vodka as an image of John crossed her mind. How un-predictable all that had been. Her young, smart, virile husband cut down so unfairly and with such suffering. They'd been married for only a few years and thought they would have a whole lifetime together. The great cosmic joke had been on them. All that promise, all their dreams, gone.

As Eliza felt for the scar on her chin, she caught a whiff of her perfume on her wrist. A memory came rushing back. It was one of the last nights in the hospital with John. He was dozing as she entered the room. All the painful treatments had not worked. He was very thin, flushed with fever, and Eliza could see his chest laboring, slowly up and down, beneath the cotton hospital blanket.

When John opened his eyes, his gaunt face cracked into a weak smile as he saw her. She smiled back and leaned down to kiss him. She felt the heat coming from his emaciated body as he held on to her.

Then, in a wheezing voice, he'd whispered, "Oh, you smell so good."

Eliza had never forgotten it, could never forget it. John had known he was going to die. Yet, as sick as he was, he'd taken pleasure in something as simple as her perfume.

God, she'd loved him so. But more and more, Eliza found herself having to look at a photograph to reestablish his handsome face in her mind. It had been over six years now, and she thought she might be ready to love someone again.

Mack reached out, pulled her hand from her chin, and held it. "You deserve happiness, Eliza," he said, as if reading her mind.

"So do you, Mack," she said, looking intently into his eyes.

"Yeah, but I want us to have that happiness together," Mack said. He raised her hand to his lips. "I'm so sorry for what I did, Eliza. I truly am. I'm sorry that I hurt you, and I'm sorry that I ruined what we had together."

"Let's not go over it again, Mack. You've apologized and apologized. I believe you when you say you're sorry. Now it's just a question of whether I can let go of what happened."

"Do you think you can?" he asked earnestly.

"Oh, I don't know," she answered, "but I do know I *want* to. I'm going to be honest, Mack. No coyness or playing hard to get. I've missed you."

The server brought the food, and the conversation shifted. Mack asked about Janie and how she was doing in school.

"I miss that little character," he said.

Eliza told him about Janie's upset over the stories about Constance Young on television.

"You don't have to be a rocket scientist to understand that," said Mack. "The kid must be scared to death something could happen to you."

Eliza nodded. "I really should be home tonight, shouldn't I?"

Mack's face fell.

Eliza couldn't help but laugh a little at the expression on his face. "Don't worry," she said. "Janie is fine and very excited. She's staying over at the Hvizdaks' house tonight. That's a big deal, with it being a school night and all."

"And where are *you* staying tonight?" Mack asked.

"New Jersey. I told my driver to pick me up at ten o'clock," she said.

Mack looked at his watch. "That doesn't leave us much time," he said.

"Time for what?"

His eyes crinkled at the corners as he smiled. "Oh, I don't know. Maybe see what one of the rooms in this fancy hotel looks like?"

As Eliza regarded Mack, she knew she really loved him. She knew by the sleepless nights she'd spent after she broke it off with him, by the way her heart beat faster each time she viewed one of his reports from London, by the fact that there hadn't been a single day she failed to think of him or wonder how he was or what he was doing over these last months, by the agony she had put herself through, holding herself back from calling him and resisting his repeated attempts to make things right between them.

Mack had made a mistake. He had apologized again and again and pleaded for another chance. Though she was scared, something was telling her to go ahead and give it another try. Maybe she would end up regretting it, but she was willing to risk it now.

"I guess I could call the driver and ask him to come a little later," Eliza said quietly.

The check came. Mack signed the bill and stood up from the sofa. He held his hand out to Eliza and she took it.

TUESDAY
MAY 22

Chapter 59

The heavy rain fell steadily as the taxicabs and limousines let out their passengers in front of the Cameron Finlay Funeral Home on Manhattan's East Side. The invited mourners scurried past a dozen drenched camera crews set up on the wet pavement. Boyd joined the others, shaking their umbrellas and hanging up their raincoats on the racks provided in the vestibule off the main foyer. One by one the guests found their way to the chapel, took their seats, and filled up the rows until there was standing room only.

Boyd walked halfway up the side aisle and rested against the wall. He surveyed the room, thinking it could have been lunchtime at the KEY News cafeteria. He recognized almost every somber face. Eliza Blake was already there, flanked by Dr. Margo Gonzalez and

Range Bullock. Annabelle Murphy sat behind them. Linus Nazareth sat on the opposite side of the aisle, surrounded by most of the *KTA* staff. Boyd watched as Lauren Adams strode down the center aisle and took the seat that Linus had saved for her.

In the front row, Boyd spotted Constance's sister and deduced that the doltish-looking character sitting next to her must be her husband. There were two young boys seated on the other side of Faith. Those were probably the kids Constance commanded he go out and buy Christmas presents for last year. She hadn't offered the slightest hint of what might interest them, because she had no idea. Boyd wondered how wise it was for them to have been brought here today, considering that the brass box on the table contained the remains of their aunt.

He felt for the envelope containing the copy of Constance's will in the inside pocket of his suit jacket. *In a little while,* Boyd thought, *Faith is going to be absolutely miserable.*

There was a middle-aged woman he couldn't place, sitting near the back of the room. Boyd studied her lined, makeup-free face. Though he had never met her, Boyd guessed she might be Ursula Bales, Constance's housekeeper. She had said that she was going to come when he'd called her yesterday to let her know about the funeral.

There was Stuart Whitaker, looking like he'd lost his only friend. Boyd watched as Stuart took off his glasses and rubbed his red-rimmed eyes. Stuart must have felt he was being watched. He glanced up and nodded at Boyd. *You poor bastard,* thought Boyd, as he nodded back. *You really loved that woman, didn't you?*

Scattered around the room were several clean-shaven, somberly dressed men who Boyd speculated could be plainclothes police officers, there to study the crowd. Murderers had been known to come to the funerals of their victims—or at least that was what they always said on television crime dramas.

Leaning against the wall waiting for the service to begin, Boyd supposed it stood to reason that he'd be stuck standing for Constance's funeral. To the very end, he was being reminded of his place in her life. Expected to show up, but not considered important enough to have a seat.

From the corner of his eye, Boyd caught someone new entering the room. As he turned and recognized the man with the dark, windblown hair just finding a seat, Boyd felt a burst of adrenaline. He hadn't invited Jason Vaughan. What was *he* doing here?

Chapter 60

O God of grace and glory, we remember before you this day our sister Constance. We thank you for giving her to us, her family and friends, to know and to love as a companion on our earthly pilgrimage. In your boundless compassion, console us who mourn. Give us faith to see in death the gate of eternal life, so that in quiet confidence we may continue our course on earth, until, by your call, we are reunited with those who have gone before."

As the service wore on, one of the mourners started coughing and eventually got up and walked out to get a drink. On the way back from the water fountain, there was time to stop at the coatracks.

Boyd Irons had hung his trench coat on one of the front racks. A monogrammed handkerchief and crumpled credit-card receipt in the pocket confirmed ownership.

The killer took the unicorn out and went to wipe it thoroughly, determined not to leave any fingerprints on it. But in the rush to complete the task, the unicorn slipped, its pronged crown and horn slicing across the killer's palm.

With no time to waste, the killer finished wiping the unicorn clean before dropping it into the pocket of Boyd's trench coat.

Chapter 61

A candle burned in front of the brass box that held Constance's ashes, and Ursula tried to keep her eyes fixed on it. She concentrated on her breathing, struggling to calm herself. She had seen the killer leave the room and then return, walking right by her on the trips up and down the aisle.

Ursula didn't think the killer had noticed her, though. For once she was grateful that she was a middle-aged, basically nondescript woman who wore no makeup and didn't color her hair. She was a wren, not a swan, and people didn't notice her much. Ursula wanted it to stay that way.

At the conclusion of the service, Ursula stood and waited with respect as Constance's sister and her family filed out first, followed by each of the other people in the aisles from front to back. As the killer approached, Ursula felt a cold sweat break out across her brow. She steadied herself using the back of the chair in front of her. The killer came closer, and Ursula's heart beat faster until she felt her legs slide out from under her and everything went black.

"Give her some air, will you? Stand back and give her some air."

The small group that had gathered around the unconscious woman shifted position.

Ursula heard the voice calling.

"Wake up. Wake up."

Ursula felt somebody rubbing her forehead. Slowly, she was able to will her eyelids open. She stared blankly, unable to focus.

"Do you hear me?" asked the voice. "Can you hear me?"

Ursula's eyes widened as the image of the face above her became clearer. She pressed back against the floor, cringing beneath the figure kneeling over her.

"So we meet again."

"I won't tell," Ursula whimpered. "I won't tell. Please, don't hurt me. I won't tell."

"She's coming to, but she's making no sense," said someone in the crowd. "She's incoherent."

"What is she talking about?" asked another voice.

The killer stared directly into Ursula's eyes and, reading the abject fear there, knew with deadly certainty just what Ursula was talking about.

Chapter 62

Faith stood at the back of the funeral home, shaking hands and accepting condolences. The expression on her face was somber, but when Boyd Irons pressed the envelope containing a copy of her sister's will into her hands, Faith had to work hard not to break out in a smile.

"Mrs. Hansen? I hate to bother you at a time like this, but my name is Stuart Whitaker. I was a great admirer of your sister."

Faith glanced over at the brass box holding Constance's ashes, which had been placed on the table in the funeral home hall, and then extended her hand. "Thank you, Mr. Whitaker," she said. "I know who you are."

"You do?" asked Stuart. "Did Constance talk about me?" The downcast expression on his face brightened a bit.

"No," said Faith. "I saw you on television the other night talking about the memorial garden you want to create for Constance at the Cloisters."

Stuart's mouth turned down again. "Oh, yes. I am hoping that you and I will be able to talk about the garden at some time that might be convenient to you. I would like very much to have your input."

Faith thought the man looked and sounded sincere. Observing Stuart Whitaker's bald head, paunch, and bitten fingernails, Faith was confident that her sister had never gone for this guy, though *he* had so clearly gone for Constance. Faith felt sorry for him and wished she hadn't been so quick to let him know that Constance had never bothered to mention him.

"Thank you, Mr. Whitaker. That's very kind of you."

Stuart looked over at the brass box sitting on the table.

"Do you mind telling me what you are going to do with them?" he asked.

Faith followed his gaze. "Oh, the ashes?" she asked. "For now I'm taking them home with me until we decide what we'll do with them. Though, honestly, my boys just told me they don't want to ride in the car with them back to New Jersey."

Stuart looked longingly at the brass box. "Forgive me for being so presumptuous, Mrs. Hansen," he said, bowing slightly, "but it would be my honor to take care of Constance's remains until they can be transferred to the memorial garden."

"Pardon me, Mr. Whitaker, but we haven't even settled on the fact that Constance remains *will* be transferred to the garden."

"Oh, Mrs. Hansen, of course that is your decision entirely," said Stuart, flustered. "I just thought that Constance's family would like the idea of her having a peaceful and fitting resting place. Since Constance was so young, I guess I just assumed that there would not already be plans in place for where she would spend eternity."

At that, two young boys approached and began whining that they wanted to go home. Faith picked up the brass box.

"Mr. Whitaker, it's clear you cared deeply about Constance. Let's talk about the future of these ashes. Do you have a card?"

Stuart dug a business card out of his wallet.

"I'll call you," said Faith.

Stuart watched Faith walk away, carrying what was left of the woman he loved tucked under her arm.

Chapter 63

The rain had let up, but as the mourners filed out of the funeral home, they were barraged instead by a crowd of camera crews and reporters shouting their names.

Before getting into a waiting car, Eliza Blake stopped to give the obligatory comment on what a fine newswoman Constance Young was and how she would be missed. Linus Nazareth, always eager for his own face to appear on the screen, said something about the rich and wonderful years at *KEY to America* with Constance as host. Lauren Adams spoke about how she had such big shoes to fill and the obligation she felt to the country's viewers to do her best to follow in Constance's footsteps.

"Who are you?" called one reporter to the young, balding man who came out of the funeral home.

"Nobody important, pal. Just her assistant," said Boyd, reaching into the pocket of his trench coat. As he pulled out his handkerchief to blow his nose, something fell to the sidewalk.

The reporter glanced down to see what had fallen.

"Jesus, is that what I think it is?" he asked. Without waiting for a reply from the stunned man staring down at the sidewalk, the reporter yelled for his cameraman to get a close-up of the ivory unicorn with the emerald eye lying on the wet pavement.

The word spread like wildfire among the journalists on the sidewalk in front of the funeral home. Reporters, producers, and camera crews jostled and pushed one another in an effort to get closer to Boyd Irons. Boyd picked up the ivory unicorn from the pavement and held it in his open palm, staring at it with astonishment.

"That looks like the King Arthur unicorn," said a reporter, thrusting a microphone at Boyd. "What are *you* doing with it?"

"That's the ivory unicorn that police think Constance Young could have been killed for!" yelled another reporter. "Where did you *get* it?"

Unable to speak, Boyd shook his head.

"Hold up that unicorn so we can get a picture of it!" called a cameraman.

Stunned, Boyd was about to lift up the unicorn to allow it to be photographed when he felt a strong hand pull his arm down.

"Come on, Boyd," said B.J. D'Elia. "Let's get out of here."

B.J. guided Boyd forward and pushed slowly through the noisy mob. As they finally reached the KEY News crew car, two of the men Boyd had noticed at the funeral service approached, flashed their police identification, and read Boyd Irons his rights as they fastened cuffs around his wrists.

Chapter 64

What luck! It couldn't have worked out any better than this. Now there'd be no reason for an anonymous call to the police with the information that Boyd Irons had the stolen unicorn. Boyd Irons had tipped off the police himself by dropping the unicorn for all the world to see. Perfection.

Still, there was the unsettling matter of Constance Young's housekeeper, looking up from the floor, the color drained from her face, promising that she wouldn't tell anyone what she'd seen. Thinking back to the night of Constance's electrocution, recalling the noise that had come from up on the deck, the killer felt with a fatal certainty that the housekeeper had been watching from some unseen perch. The article in the newspaper had detailed that Ursula Bales's sister had been killed after cooperating with authorities on a drug case. That would explain why Ursula herself had not gone to the police after watching Constance's final moments.

Ursula Bales knew too much. Ursula Bales had the potential to ruin everything. Ursula Bales was going to have to be taken care of, quickly, before she changed her mind and went to the police after all.

Chapter 65

The windshield wipers flipped from side to side as Eliza stared straight ahead, girding herself for what was coming. Mack was here, sitting beside her in the backseat, but soon he would be flying over the Atlantic Ocean to London.

"What time do you have to be at the airport?" she asked.

"Not till later this afternoon," said Mack. "I have plenty of time to stop and get lunch."

"Well, I wish I did," she said. "I've got to get back to the office. The service took up the morning, so Paige had to schedule me pretty tightly this afternoon."

"A cup of coffee, then?" asked Mack.

"Okay," said Eliza. "A cup of coffee."

They had the driver drop them off at a coffee shop a few blocks from the Broadcast Center. As Eliza walked down the aisle to a booth at the rear, she felt a few customers look up at her. She knew they recognized her. She deliberately took a seat with her back to the room.

After the waitress had filled their cups and walked away, Mack reached across the table and took Eliza's hands. "Last night was great," he said. "I loved being with you, Eliza. I still can't really believe that we're together again."

"I don't want you to leave," said Eliza, her eyes glistening.

"I don't want to go, believe me." He gently squeezed her hands tighter.

Eliza looked into his eyes and read intensity and sincerity in them. "When will you be back?" she asked.

"That depends on you, Eliza," Mack answered. "Before yesterday I wasn't planning to come home again for another six months, but now I'd be happy to fly to New York every weekend."

Eliza laughed. "You know that's not going to happen," she said.

"Who says?"

"It's not practical, Mack."

"Screw practical."

Chapter 66

Eliza had been back in her office at the Broadcast Center for only a short time when she got a call from the assignment desk notifying her that Boyd Irons had been taken into police custody. She immediately phoned the KEY News attorney and asked him to look into the matter with the police.

"See what's going on, will you please, Andrew?" she asked. "Boyd Irons has always seemed to me to be a decent young guy. Maybe he has his own attorney already, but I tend to doubt it."

As Eliza replaced the phone in the cradle, she looked up to see Annabelle and B.J. standing in the office doorway. Their facial expressions were grim. Eliza beckoned to them to come in and sit down.

"What do you know about Boyd?" she asked.

B.J. spoke first. "It was the damnedest thing," he said, shaking his head. "One minute I'm recording you and all the other big shots coming out the funeral home, and then all of a sudden there was this surge crowding around Boyd."

"So you, of course, crowded around, too," said Annabelle.

B.J. nodded. "And as I got closer, I heard the guys in the crowd saying that Boyd had the unicorn. The ivory unicorn everybody's been looking for."

"*Did* he have it?" asked Eliza. "Did you see it?"

"I saw it, but just for a second," answered B.J. "The poor guy looked like a deer caught in the headlights. He seemed dumbstruck. I tried to steer him to the car before he could show off the unicorn to every freakin' cameraman standing there."

"Then what happened?" asked Eliza.

"Just as we were about to get into the car, a couple of plainclothes cops strong-armed him away." B.J. slumped down in his chair, stretched out his legs, and groaned. "I was able to catch a shot of the unmarked police car driving away, but, damn it, I didn't get video of Boyd or the unicorn."

"That's not the end of the world, B.J.," said Annabelle.

B.J. looked over at her and rolled his eyes. "Nice try. What are you, kidding me? Every other network and local station will have those pictures, and KEY News won't. I was assigned to cover that story, and instead I got involved and didn't get what I needed to get."

"You helped a colleague, a friend, B.J.," said Eliza. "No one is going to fault you for that."

"And you know what?" said Annabelle. "We can probably get the video from our local station. Of course, it won't be B.J. D'Elia caliber, but then what is?"

B.J. managed a crooked smile.

"All right, gang, let's look at the bigger picture here," said Eliza. "If Boyd did have the stolen unicorn, what do we think about that?"

"That he killed Constance Young to get it?" asked Annabelle. "I find that hard to believe. Boyd has always impressed me as such a decent guy. I've witnessed Constance beat up on him pretty badly, and he always just stood there and took it. But maybe he reached a breaking point."

"I wouldn't blame him if he did off her. That woman was a world-class bitch," said B.J., sitting up straight again. "I don't see it, though. If Boyd had killed Constance and stolen the unicorn from her, I don't think he'd be carrying it around in his pocket."

"Or forget that he'd put it there and reveal it to a crowd of media people," said Eliza. "No, this whole thing doesn't make any sense."

"Well, if Boyd didn't put the unicorn in his pocket, that means somebody else did," said Annabelle. "Why?"

"To implicate Boyd in Constance's death," said Eliza. "To throw suspicion on him and away from the real killer."

"But why pick Boyd?" asked Annabelle.

"Hey, maybe the killer hates gays," B.J. suggested.

"Maybe Boyd did something to anger the killer," Annabelle offered.

"Or maybe the killer thinks Boyd knows something and has effectively silenced him—since anything he says now will be suspect," said Eliza as she looked at her watch. "Annabelle, why don't you call your police source and see if you can find out what the cops are thinking."

Chapter 67

I'm telling you. I have no clue how it got there." Boyd clasped his hands on top of the table. "But I don't think it was there when I went into the funeral home. I remember stuffing a credit-card receipt in my pocket, and I didn't feel anything then."

On the other side of the table, the detective turned his chair backward and sat down, straddling the seat. "You were Constance Young's assistant at KEY News, is that right?"

"Yes," said Boyd.

"How would you characterize your relationship with her?"

Boyd nervously crossed his legs and wiped his clammy palm across his damp forehead. "I'm not going to lie to you," he said. "Constance could be difficult."

"She gave you a hard time, huh?" asked the detective.

"Sometimes, yes,"

"Did that make you mad?"

"Look, I can see where you're going with this," said Boyd. "But don't you understand? I'm being framed."

The detective shrugged. "I don't know about that. I see a guy who had a boss that really rubbed him the wrong way and gave him a hard time and made him angry, a boss who had lots of celebrity and money and all the things that could make a guy jealous and resentful enough to do something to even the score."

"I'm telling you," Boyd pleaded, his voice rising, "I had nothing to do with Constance's death."

"And tell me again how you got the unicorn that she was seen wearing?"

Boyd was uncomfortable with what he was about to say, hated that he was going to implicate somebody else to shift the spotlight away from himself. But he was struggling to survive here.

"Look," he said, trying to sound calm. "There was a man who Constance dated who asked me to see if I could get the unicorn for him. Maybe he was desperate enough to kill her for it. Maybe he planted the unicorn on me."

"And that man would be who?" asked the detective.

"Stuart Whitaker," answered Boyd. "You know, the gazillionaire who makes all those creepy video games."

"As a matter of fact, yes, I know who Stuart Whitaker is. We spoke with him yesterday, and he told us that you'd told him *you* would get the unicorn for *him*—if he paid you for it."

"Oh, God," Boyd groaned. "That's not how it happened. He wanted the unicorn back, and I said I would see what I could do. I just wanted him to leave and not create a scene at the lunch. He's the one who offered to make it worth my while. I didn't ask him for anything. And I certainly didn't get the unicorn for him."

The detective studied Boyd, saying nothing.

"You don't believe me, do you?" Boyd asked.

The detective stood up. "Well, buddy, all I know is you were caught red-handed with that unicorn—a unicorn last seen around Constance Young's neck. You'll have to tell your story to the judge."

Chapter 68

I talked to my police source," said Annabelle, plop-
ping down on the leather couch. "Their working
hypothesis is that there's a connection between the
unicorn amulet and Constance's death. They think
Constance may have been killed for the unicorn."

"Okay," said Eliza, turning away from the computer
where she was writing her daily blog for her KEY
News Web site. "We had been thinking along those
lines, too."

"But here's the interesting part," said Annabelle,
taking a bite of a Twizzler and looking at her notes.
"It seems that the police now know *how* the unicorn
went missing from the Cloisters. I got this part off the
record, so we can't report it yet, but Stuart Whitaker,
the video-game magnate, says he *borrowed* the unicorn

because he wanted to have a copy made for Constance. He told the police he never got around to making the copy and gave Constance the real thing instead."

"So he lied to us when we interviewed him up at the Cloisters on Sunday," Eliza mused. "Whitaker said he *had* made a reproduction for her and didn't know how to explain that the real unicorn was missing."

"Well, get this," said Annabelle. "Whitaker is a major donor, and the museum isn't going to press charges against him."

"How nice for him," said Eliza, turning back to her computer and hitting the SEND button. "I guess promising to donate twenty million dollars to create a Constance Young Memorial Garden wins you a 'Get Out of Jail Free' card."

"Are you surprised?" asked Annabelle.

"I guess not," said Eliza, sighing with resignation. "But getting back to the idea that Constance may have been murdered for the unicorn, who would do that? It wasn't a case of a robbery gone wrong, because nothing else was taken. The perpetrator was quite specific in what he took and who he killed."

"What kind of person would kill for a piece of jewelry—or even for a historic artifact?" asked Annabelle.

Eliza shrugged. "I don't think you and I can figure that one out. But I have an idea about who we should discuss all this with." Eliza reached for the telephone. "If I can get Dr. Margo Gonzalez to come in so we can pick her brain, will you be available?"

"Name the time and place," said Annabelle.

"Fine," said Eliza. "And let's get B.J. to be there, too."

Annabelle started to leave and then turned around again. "And how could I forget this? The necropsy results are out. That Great Dane was electrocuted, too."

Chapter 69

Before she left for the day, Lauren marched into Linus Nazareth's office. She tossed a newspaper onto his desk.

"Did you see this?" she demanded.

Linus read the small announcement in the Metro section that Lauren had circled in red ink.

> KEY News anchorwoman Eliza Blake will host the reception celebrating the opening of the Camelot Exhibit at the Cloisters on Wednesday night. Blake will be replacing Constance Young, former cohost of KEY to America, who died over the weekend at her country home in Westchester County.
>
> Central to the Camelot Exhibit is the planned unveiling of a carved ivory unicorn said to have

been a gift from King Arthur to the Lady Guinevere. The ancient unicorn was discovered missing from the museum over the weekend. A unicorn resembling the one from the museum's collection was seen being worn by Constance Young at her final public appearance last Friday.

Tickets are still available for the event.

"So?" said Linus.

"So now look at page five in the Arts section," said Lauren.

Linus opened the newspaper to a full-page ad trumpeting the event. He read aloud the line at the top: " 'American News Royalty Presents the Treasures of King Arthur's Court.' "

"Why wasn't I asked to fill in for Constance?" Lauren whined. "Why did they ask Eliza instead of me?"

"I don't know, baby. Relax, will you?"

"When will you stop calling me 'baby'? I hate that." Lauren plopped down in a chair. "And I can't relax. With what's happened to Constance, everyone will be ultra-interested in this event. It would have been great exposure for me."

Linus got up and walked around the desk. "How about this?" he asked. "How about we do a show from the Cloisters on Thursday morning?"

Lauren looked at him skeptically. "You mean broadcast from there?"

"Yeah," said Linus. "A split show. You'll be up there, Harry will be in the studio."

"We could set that up so quickly?"

"I don't think the permissions will be hard to get," answered Linus. "The museum will want the publicity, and, as for our end, if we can set up within minutes for a live broadcast from the chaos of a major fire or a plane crash, having a couple of days' notice to broadcast from a quiet museum is a piece of cake."

"You'd do that for me, Linus?"

"Of course, I would, baby." He rubbed his hand over her dark hair. "You're right. Everyone will be interested in that Camelot Exhibit opening. They'll be tuning in on Thursday morning, millions of them—while Eliza's audience at the preview and reception will only be a couple hundred muckety-mucks and society wannabes."

Lauren's smile expressed her satisfaction with the executive producer's solution.

"You know, though, Linus," she said. "I'd like to go to that preview, too. It would be a nice run-through for the next morning's show, and it would be fun to get all dressed up and mingle with the high rollers. Plus, I have to admit I could probably benefit from watching how Eliza conducts herself."

"Oh, God," Linus groaned. "Those things bore me to death."

Lauren's face clouded again. "I can go myself," she said.

"No way," said Linus. "I'm coming with you. I'm not leaving you alone with all those rich men. But here's a little suggestion, baby: You might want to lose the gum."

Chapter 70

Ethan had forgotten his calculator when he was over the night before. Returning it provided Jason with a great excuse to see Nell again. He stood with the electronic device in hand as the front door opened. Nell looked surprised to see him.

"He forgot this," said Jason.

Nell took the calculator from him. "He would have realized it was gone when he did his homework tonight."

"Can I see him for a minute?" asked Jason.

"He's at a friend's house," said Nell.

There was an awkward pause as each waited for the other to speak.

"Look, Nell. I was wondering if you'd like to go with me to the Cloisters tomorrow night for the event they're having to kick off the opening of the Camelot Exhibit."

"Oh, yeah. I read about that in the paper." She looked skeptical. "But those tickets are kind of pricey, aren't they?"

"Yes, a grand a ticket," he said. "But Larry is spotting me the money because he feels so confident about where things are going. And I can write it off as either a charitable contribution or a business expense."

"Business expense?" asked Nell. "I don't get it."

"Larry is already negotiating a contract with another publisher for a book on the Constance Young case."

"And Jason Vaughan, the man who hated her guts, is writing it," said Nell. "That should be good for lots of television interviews when it's published."

Jason ignored the remark. "Come on, Nell. You said yesterday that you'd love to see that exhibit. And it would be fun to go to something top-drawer again. It's been too long."

He could see she was tempted.

"I guess I could get somebody to stay with Ethan," she said. "And I probably have something from the old days in the closet that I could wear."

"Great," said Jason. "And would you try to remember to have Ethan watch *KEY to America* tomorrow morning? I want him to see his dad as a winner instead of a loser."

Chapter 71

Washing her supper dishes in the tiny kitchen, Ursula's hands shook. As she rinsed a plate, she knocked it against the faucet. The slippery porcelain slid from her grasp and shattered. Ursula cleaned up the mess on the worn linoleum floor, wondering how she was going to get through her knitting class tonight.

Maybe giving the class would be the best thing she could do right now. It might get her mind off what had happened at Constance's service. Ursula hadn't been able to erase the mental image of Constance's killer looking down at her as she lay helpless on the floor of the funeral home.

Ursula had felt chilled and shaky all afternoon, one minute thinking she would go the police, the next thinking maybe she didn't have to. If only she could remember what, if anything, she'd said as she came to from her fainting spell. Had she given herself away?

But what if she hadn't really said anything that would lead the killer to suspect that she was a witness? Then she'd be all right after all, and going to the police would only complicate things. She would be forced to testify, and more than anything she didn't want to do that.

Ursula wiped the kitchen counter, hung up the damp dish towel, and went into the living room. She turned on the TV to catch the evening news before it was time to leave for the needlecraft shop. Sitting on the old couch, Ursula took the piece of needlepoint she was working on from her sewing bag. She had already finished the third full stanza imprinted on the canvas.

Left lying in a pool,
Left sinking like a stone,
Ending up so cool,
Dying all alone.

There were only two lines left to fill in. Ursula began on those while keeping an eye on the television as well.

Eliza Blake was narrating the story about Constance Young's funeral. Image after image of the people who had come to pay their respects flashed on the screen, including an image of a young man who Eliza reported had been arrested because he'd had the ivory unicorn that everyone had been looking for since Constance's body had been found. Boyd Irons, Constance's assistant.

Ursula recognized the name. Boyd Irons had been so nice, so courteous when he'd called to invite her to the service. Now, because he had the unicorn, the police were looking at him in connection with Constance's death. Ursula knew better.

It was one thing not to come forward and let a killer get away with a murder that had already been committed. Ursula couldn't alter the fact that Constance was dead, and it wasn't her responsibility to bring the killer to justice. But knowing that a young man was being implicated in a murder he had nothing to do with and not coming forward to clear him was absolutely wrong. She wouldn't be able to live with herself if that nice young man's life was ruined. She had to tell the police.

All the same, watching in terror as an image of the killer appeared on the television screen, Ursula wanted to sleep on her decision for one more night.

Chapter 72

Two men stood outside on the New York City courthouse steps, shaking each other's hand.

"Don't think I don't appreciate the fact that KEY News and you held sway here, Andrew," said Boyd. "You got me before a judge faster than I'd ever have been able to if I'd hired the kind of lawyer I could afford—cheap and no clout whatsoever. And thanks for talking the judge into letting me out of there."

"You're welcome," said the attorney. "We were lucky that the judge seemed to listen to my argument that if you'd really stolen the unicorn, you wouldn't be dumb enough to drop it in front of the national media. Plus, it didn't hurt that you have friends in high places, my man."

Boyd looked at him quizzically. "What do you mean?"

"Eliza Blake and Lauren Adams both called me about you."

Boyd tilted his head, baffled. "Wow. That does make me feel good. I wouldn't have expected that."

"KEY News takes care of its own, Boyd. But this thing isn't over yet, not by a long shot. Even though you've been released on bond, you're still looking at serious charges. Not only was the stolen unicorn found in your possession, it also connects you to the death of Constance Young. You better keep your nose clean between now and when we return to court."

"I will, Andrew," said Boyd. "I promise. I will."

The attorney looked at his watch. "No point in going back to the office now. Can I give you a lift anywhere?"

"No thanks," said Boyd, taking a deep breath of fresh air. "It'll feel good to walk for a while, and I have lots to do."

Chapter 73

The minute the broadcast was off the air and the director had good-nighted the crew, Eliza picked up the telephone at the anchor desk and called home. Janie answered.

"Hi, Mommy," she chirped.

"How's my sweetheart?"

"Good. Mrs. Garcia made me tacos for dinner."

"Oh, that sounds yummy. You love those."

"Yes, I do," said Janie. "When will you be home?"

"Well, I'm going to be just a little late, honey."

"Why?"

"Because something is happening here that I have to work on."

"But you were out last night, too, Mommy."

"I know, Janie," said Eliza as she thought of Mack somewhere over the Atlantic Ocean right now. "I'm sorry, but I shouldn't be too long. You take your bath and have Mrs. Garcia read you your stories. When I get home, I'll come right upstairs and give you a great big kiss."

"But I'll be asleep."

"That's all right. A kiss still counts when you're asleep, doesn't it?"

"I guess so." Janie didn't sound convinced.

Eliza hung up the phone, vowing that tomorrow night she would race right out of the studio the minute the broadcast finished. More and more she found herself wishing she were home after school and in the early evening to be with her daughter.

When Eliza arrived at her upstairs office, Margo Gonzalez was waiting for her, along with Annabelle and B.J.

"Thanks for coming in tonight, Margo," said Eliza.

"I'm sorry I couldn't make it in earlier," said Margo. "I hate to have made you all stay here late on my account, but I had patients."

"No problem," said Eliza. "You're doing us the favor. Why don't we help ourselves to the dinner that Paige has arranged for us and get down to business."

The group heaped food on their plastic plates and settled themselves in the chairs and on the sofa. Eliza filled Margo in on what had happened so far.

"So here's what we need to figure out," Eliza continued. "What kind of person kills for a single artifact, a single piece of jewelry?"

Margo swallowed the cheese and cracker she'd been eating as she listened to Eliza's recap. "First of all, we shouldn't forget that it looks like we have someone here who also killed a dog, as a dry run for the next day's murder."

"Well, what kind of person would kill an innocent animal?" asked Annabelle. "That's just sick."

"Only a monster would do something like that," said B.J.

"It's funny, isn't it?" Margo asked. "People seem to be able to stomach the idea that people kill other people. I guess we've become almost desensitized to that reality. But the thought of an animal being deliberately killed horrifies us."

"You're right," said Eliza.

"Well, the thing that comes immediately to my mind," Margo continued, "is that there are three major personality traits in children that are said to be warning signs for the tendency to become a serial killer. One of them is cruelty to animals. Many otherwise-normal children can be cruel to animals, such as pulling off the legs of spiders or grasshoppers, but future serial killers often kill larger animals, like dogs and cats, frequently for their own solitary enjoyment rather than just to impress their peers."

"So you think we might be dealing with a serial killer here?" Eliza asked skeptically.

"Not necessarily," said Margo. "But at the very least I think we're dealing with someone who has a warped sense of reality, someone who's used to death. Someone who's willing to commit unspeakable acts to get what they want, which, it would seem in this case, was making certain that electrocuting Constance Young was going to be successful. Choosing a Great Dane, a dog with approximately the same weight as Constance, was a very calculated, even—if you'll forgive me—a very clever decision."

"Aren't most killers like that?" asked Annabelle.

"People kill for different reasons," Margo replied. "And you might be surprised how many people who commit premeditated murders aren't anywhere near as smart as our killer appears to be."

"Not so smart that he didn't realize that the dog could be traced back to him," said Eliza.

"But smart enough to get to the animal shelter and kill the poor attendant who could help law enforcement find the dog's killer," said B.J., popping a grape into his mouth.

"Now that you bring it up, something has been troubling me about that," said Eliza. "Do you think the killer came to the shelter knowing that there'd be sodium pentobarbital available in the back and planning to kill the attendant with it?"

314 • MARY JANE CLARK

"Good question," said Margo.

"Well, that poor guy, Vinny, had been hit in the head, too, hadn't he?" B.J. reminded them. "It looks like the killer might have come with something to knock the guy out but decided he wanted to finish the job with the euthanasia drug. Who knows if he made that decision before or after he got to the shelter?" B.J. sat back in his chair and crossed one leg over the other. "And while we're at it, as the only male in the room, I have to ask: Why are we always calling the killer 'he'? The killer could be a female, right?"

"Right," said Margo.

Eliza wiped the corner of her mouth with a paper napkin. "I hate to bring this up, but I think we must consider something, as much as we don't even want to think it."

The others waited for her to continue.

"I think we can't completely rule out Boyd."

"But Boyd loves animals," Annabelle protested. "He's always taking care of Constance's cat. In fact, he told me he offered to adopt her cat permanently when her sister didn't want it. I can't see Boyd killing that Great Dane. No way."

"What about Constance's sister?" offered B.J. "She didn't look all that upset when she walked into the funeral home today. If you ask me, that one is already planning what she's going to do with the money that must be coming to her from Constance's estate."

"Well, we can't leave out Stuart Whitaker either," Annabelle stated matter-of-factly. "I've read articles about that guy. He's obsessed with the Middle Ages, collects medieval weapons, even had an antique torture rack in the basement of his office building, which he's had converted to look like a dungeon. That guy is strange, and if his obsession with Constance was strong enough for him to take a priceless unicorn from a museum to please her, that obsession could turn to a murderous rage if she spurned him."

"Look," said B.J. "Constance made some real enemies during her stay here on planet Earth." He turned to Annabelle. "Every time I turn around, I'm seeing the guy who wrote that book on television, talking about how she ruined his life. And there are people who work in this very building who couldn't stand her and were thrilled when they heard she was leaving."

"Don't count Linus Nazareth in that number," said Annabelle. "He was enraged that Constance had the gall to leave him and, worse yet, compete against him on another network."

"She never got the chance to do that, did she?" Eliza noted.

The four of them sat in silence for a minute, all with their own thoughts, until Eliza spoke again.

"All right. For now let's assume that Boyd has nothing to do with Constance's death. Let's assume that the unicorn was planted on him, that the killer wanted to throw suspicion on him and discredit him. Maybe Boyd had done something to anger the killer. Or the killer might even just have wanted to get rid of the unicorn because it would incriminate him or her. Whatever the case, we have someone out there who electrocuted a dog *and* Constance Young—and murdered an innocent guy who was just trying to do something good for poor, unwanted animals. If that's not a monster, I don't know what is."

Chapter 74

A call ahead of time to the Dropped Stitch Needle-craft Shop ascertained that Ursula Bales's knitting class met from 7:30 to 8:30 P.M. Just after eight a car pulled in to a parking space down the block from the shop. The killer got out and walked past the store, deliberately staying on the other side of the street.

Through the plate-glass window, ten women could be seen sitting in a circle, some with their heads down, concentrating on their needles. Others seemed to be doing more talking, laughing, and socializing than knitting. Shelves containing skeins of multicolored yarn lined the rear wall, providing a vivid backdrop for the scene. All was right with the world at the Dropped Stitch Needlecraft Shop.

Just then another woman came walking into the room from the back of the store. It was Ursula Bales, carrying a tray that she deposited on a table at the side of the room. It appeared the women were all too happy to put down their knitting projects and head for the refreshments.

The killer went back to the car and waited. At 8:35 the first woman came walking out, followed by another nine walking alone or in pairs. Getting out of the car again, the killer proceeded, hands in pockets, feeling for the syringe.

The lights still blazed through the shop's window, but there was no one in the front room. Trying not to make a sound, the killer opened the entrance door but was met with a tinkling bell meant to announce a customer's arrival.

"Did you forget something?" Ursula called from the back room. "I'm just cleaning up in here. I'll be right out."

When no one responded, Ursula came to the front. The room was empty, but she shivered, sensing she wasn't alone. Wiping her hands on her smock, her heart beating faster, she went to the front door and locked it from the inside. She looked out the window but saw nothing amiss, nobody walking away.

"Everything's all right," she said aloud to reassure herself. "It's all right." She snapped off the lights and started to return to the rear of the store. Her car was parked behind the shop, and she was eager now to let herself out the back door.

As she parted the curtain that separated the two rooms, Ursula heard a noise. She looked in the direction of the sound as two arms reached out and pushed her through to the back room.

"Oh, my God!" Ursula cried as she stumbled. Regaining her footing, she turned to face her attacker. Her eyes widened with fear as she saw the syringe approaching her.

"Please, please, don't hurt me! I beg you! Leave me alone!" she pleaded. Ursula backed away, feeling for the door behind her, knowing that it was the only possible path to safety.

"This will be easier for you if you stay calm and stay still."

As Ursula looked into the killer's face, she realized what Constance must have felt in the instant before the toaster hit the water, knowing what would happen, unable to do anything to stop it, terrified. But Constance had been in the pool, defenseless, while Ursula was close enough to see the beads of perspiration on her attacker's brow. She had to fight back. If she did nothing, she would die.

Ursula cast about, looking for something that could help her, something she could use to fight off her attacker.

Suddenly she realized that a deadly weapon was close at hand. She pulled the large knitting needle from the deep pocket of her smock and, using all her strength, thrust it outward. But the needle missed its mark as Ursula lunged forward. Losing her balance, she plunged through the open door at the top of the stairs leading to the basement. The awful thudding sound of her body tumbling down the wooden steps signaled a potentially deadly fall.

The killer went down the stairs and found Ursula, her body twisted, her bloodied face pressed against the cement floor. Turning the body over revealed the knitting needle impaled in the left side of the woman's chest. A check of the carotid artery indicated that Ursula still had a weak pulse.

The killer looked around the basement and grabbed an old towel from a pile of rags in the corner. By holding the towel over Ursula's face, the job was finished as, finally, the woman's breathing stopped.

There was no need to use the sodium pentobarbital. That could be saved for another time.

WEDNESDAY
MAY 23

Chapter 75

After a nearly sleepless night, Faith got out of bed, being careful not to wake Todd. They'd fought bitterly after the funeral service yesterday, had gone to bed angry with each other, and Faith didn't want to have anything to do with him. She would have insisted he sleep on the couch in the den, but he was already asleep when she got home from the car ride she took to see to some errands and clear her head. She thought of sleeping on the couch herself, but she didn't want the boys to worry that there was something really wrong between their parents.

In a way Faith didn't blame Todd for the horrible things he'd said after they read Constance's will. She was beyond furious with Constance herself, but even though *she* had a right to bad-mouth Constance, Faith didn't like it when anyone else did.

After going downstairs and checking on her mother, Faith filled a kettle with water and put it on the stove to boil. The will was on the dining room table, right where she'd thrown it after reading it. She picked it up and went into the living room, sat down in the comfortable wing chair, and studied the document again. The provisions were very clear. A trust established for the care of their mother, an amount for Ben and Brendan stipulated to go into an account set up as a college fund and expressly forbidden to be invaded for any other reason, a similar fund to be put in place for the children of Annabelle Murphy, and a nice monetary gift to her housekeeper, Ursula Bales, for her devotion and loyalty. The bulk of Constance's estate, $30 million, to create a school of journalism, plus an endowed chair in journalistic ethics, at Dominion State College outside Yorktown, Virginia.

"A major regret of mine was that I did not finish college. After winning the Miss Virginia title, I was offered and accepted my first job in television. I was eager to get started in the real world and did not understand then that I would never find the time to finish my formal education. I left Dominion State before graduating, but I would still like to leave a lasting contribution to the school."

Faith read her sister's words and remembered that she'd thrown the fact that Constance hadn't graduated at her during their angry encounter at the farewell luncheon. Just a few days ago, but a world away. The ugly fact was that Faith, having so little else with which to hurt her sister, had used that weapon against Constance before. Low blows.

Faith pulled the front of her bathrobe closed and continued reading.

"To my sister, Faith, I leave my pearls. Every time she saw them on me, she never failed to tell me how beautiful they were. They're yours now, Faith. Remember me when you wear them."

That was it. The pearl necklace. Nothing else.

Constance's message was clear. She had provided for Mother, provided for the boys, provided even for her housekeeper and the children of her friend. While it was certainly a financial relief knowing that Ben and Brendan would be able to attend college without the burden of student loans, Constance had set herself up as a philanthropist and snubbed Faith, deliberately and finally.

The kettle's whistle screeched. As she got up from the chair to go to the kitchen, Faith looked with rage at the brass box sitting on the fireplace mantel. She fought the urge to pick it up and hurl Constance's remains out into the street.

Chapter 76

Stuart felt for his glasses on the nightstand and put them on. He lay in bed staring at the ceiling and thinking about what had happened yesterday. The thought of Constance's ashes kept pushing to the front of his mind. He had to get Faith to part with them. But he also had to make sure that the ashes would find themselves in a resting place befitting a queen.

He got out of bed with more energy than he'd felt in the past several days. Stuart was eager to get to his computer and concentrate on the early stages of planning for the Constance Young Memorial Garden.

He already imagined a garden walk, a reflecting pool, and meditation benches for visitors to sit and relax under shade trees, surrounded by flowers. Of course there would be a columbarium to contain the urn of

Constance's ashes, and perhaps even an eternal flame like the one that marked John F. Kennedy's grave at Arlington National Cemetery. But the pièce de résistance Stuart dreamed of would be six newly created stained-glass panels set in stone frames, based on the Lady and the Unicorn tapestries housed in the Musée de Cluny in Paris and using Constance's face as the model for the maiden. Those tapestries imaginatively represented the six senses—hearing, sight, touch, smell, taste, and, Stuart's favorite, love.

After paying architects to design and contractors to construct the garden—as well as paying for the Cloisters' own experts to design and make the stained-glass panels—Stuart figured there should be some of the $5 million left over to be used as an endowment for the garden's upkeep.

Now if he could just get Faith to part with Constance's ashes. If Faith didn't decide on her own that it would be absolutely the best thing to preserve her sister's remains in such a glorious spot, Stuart hoped he might be able to persuade her with a financial inducement, but one had to be very careful about broaching something like that.

Even in death Constance was his exalted queen and he was her loyal liege. He would always and forever be in her service.

Chapter 77

In her dream Eliza felt the warmth of another body press against her. She sensed that it was Mack. Eliza turned over in bed, smiling as she opened her lids. She was met by two round blue eyes staring into her own.

"Hi, Mommy."

"Hi, sweetheart," Eliza whispered, closing her eyes again and realizing that Mack was back in London, probably eating lunch now. "Did you have a good sleep?"

"Uh-huh. But I missed you last night, Mommy."

"I missed you, too," said Eliza.

"Did you come in and kiss me when you got home?"

"Yep. Just as I said I would."

Janie snuggled in closer to Eliza. "You're coming home tonight, right?"

Eliza's eyes snapped open. The event at the Cloisters. It had completely slipped her mind.

"Oh, Janie, I forgot all about something I have to do tonight." Eliza reached out to hug the child. But Janie pulled away.

"You promised you were coming home tonight, Mommy," Janie protested. "That's not fair."

"I know I promised, and you're right. It's not fair. I'm sorry, Janie. But it's work, and there isn't really anything I can do about it."

"I hate your work." Janie pulled the blanket over her head.

Eliza gently rolled the cover back. "Janie, you have to try to understand, honey. Work is what people do to earn money to pay for their food and their house and their car."

"And toys?"

"Yes, and sometimes to pay for toys for their children. Work is very important, because without it people couldn't pay for the things they need in their lives." Eliza gathered the little girl in her arms. "But you know, Janie, if you're lucky, you don't work just for money. You work because you love what you do. I'm a very lucky person, sweetheart, because I'm fortunate enough to really love what I do."

"Do you love it more than me?" Janie looked as if she were going to break out in tears.

"No. Absolutely not, Janie. I couldn't ever love anything more than I love you. You are the most important thing in my life."

"Then why are you going to be working tonight when I want you to be with me?"

Eliza kissed the top of her daughter's head, glad that Janie's logic was so strong but also trying to think of an appropriate explanation to answer her question.

"Because I have a responsibility to do what I've been hired to do. If you tell someone you're going to do something, then you should do it."

"But you told *me* you were going to come home tonight," said Janie. "That means you should do it."

Eliza realized that Janie was not going to allow herself to be talked out of her position. She decided to try another tack.

"Here's the deal, Janie. I fouled up. I made a mistake. I hope you'll forgive me and let me make it up to you."

Janie was quiet for a few moments while she considered what her mother had said. Finally she delivered her absolution.

"Everyone makes mistakes sometimes," Janie answered with generosity. "It's all right, Mommy. I love you."

Chapter 78

Painfully early in the morning, Boyd found himself waiting in the chair on the *KTA* "living room" set, trying to wrap his mind around how fast everything was happening.

Lauren Adams herself had been on Boyd's answering machine when he got home the night before. It was fair to say she'd begged him to come and be interviewed on *KTA* Wednesday. "You've got to do this for us, Boyd," Lauren had said. "You'd be exclusive to us, and it would really help the show, not to mention the fact that you'd be able to tell the country your side of the story. You could explain that you're the victim here."

At the commercial break, Lauren walked across the studio from the anchor desk to take a seat in the upholstered chair facing Boyd's.

"All set?" she asked softly.

Boyd nodded.

"Are you doing okay?" she asked.

"I guess so," said Boyd. "And I want to thank you for everything you did to help me."

Lauren waved him away. "I didn't do anything except call our attorney. I couldn't very well leave my own assistant hanging, could I?"

Before Boyd could answer, the deep voice of the stage manager boomed through the studio. "Five seconds."

Lauren smoothed out her skirt, looked directly into the camera with the red light shining on top, and smiled.

"We're back. And with us is KEY News employee Boyd Irons, who—in the interest of fairness, I must tell you—is my administrative assistant, and until a few days ago he was also Constance Young's assistant. Boyd was arrested yesterday after the funeral service for Constance because he was in possession of the ivory unicorn stolen from the Cloisters museum collection. The same unicorn Constance Young wore right here on this broadcast last Friday." Lauren turned from the camera and looked at Boyd. "Good morning, Boyd. Thanks for coming in."

"Good morning, Lauren."

"I know that your attorney has told you to limit what you talk about here today, but can you tell us what happened?"

"Basically, I came out of the funeral home after the service for Constance Young yesterday morning and went into my raincoat pocket to get a handkerchief to blow my nose. But when I pulled it out, the unicorn came out with it."

"How did it get there?" asked Lauren.

"I have no idea," said Boyd. "My theory is that someone put it in my trench coat, which was hung in the vestibule, when I was inside the main room at the service."

"So you maintain that the unicorn was planted on you?"

"Yes, ma'am. I do." Boyd looked earnestly at Lauren.

"Do you have any idea who would do that?"

Boyd shrugged. "I guess it could have been anyone at the service."

At that point, videotape taken outside the funeral home began to run on the television screen. Lauren talked over it, describing what viewers were seeing.

"There I am with *KTA* executive producer Linus Nazareth. There's Eliza Blake with Mack McBride, our London correspondent. Can you identify some of the other people for us, Boyd?"

"A lot of the people who attended the funeral work behind the scenes here at KEY News," said Boyd as the pictures continued to roll. "And there's Faith Hansen with her family. Faith is Constance's only sister. And there's the video-game king Stuart Whitaker, and that's the author Jason Vaughan coming out."

"Jason Vaughan being the man who has just published a book about the recklessness of the news media in general and Constance Young in particular?" Lauren tried to clarify.

"Yes."

The camera came back to the pair on the set.

"If Jason Vaughan was so critical of Constance Young, why do you think he came to her funeral service?" asked Lauren.

"I'd only be guessing," said Boyd. "I have no idea."

"Well, Jason Vaughan is waiting in the green room now, and we'll see if we can get him to answer that question, right after this break." Lauren looked at the camera until the red light went out.

"Thanks so much, Boyd," she said. "That went well. And I'm so glad we had you on and nobody else did."

"You're welcome," he answered. Boyd unclipped the microphone, eager to get out of the studio. But as he reached the double doors to exit, Boyd came face-to-face with Jason Vaughan entering.

"**Thank you** for coming, Mr. Vaughan."

"Thank you for having me."

"How are sales?"

Jason smiled and held his thumb up. "Strong. In fact, we find out later today whether or not *Never Look Back* will be on the *New York Times Book Review* Best Sellers list. My agent feels confident we will be."

"Congratulations," said Lauren as she tucked a strand of dark hair behind her ear. "I'm going to be honest with you, though. There was quite a debate around here as to whether we should have you on today. Not because your book, *Never Look Back,* attacks the media but because it portrays Constance Young in a very unflattering light."

"Well, I'm glad you all came to the decision to invite me," said Jason.

Lauren continued. "Before the break we looked at footage shot yesterday in which we saw you attending the funeral service for Constance Young."

"Yes, that's right."

"I'm wondering why you would attend the funeral service for someone you so clearly detest."

"Maybe I needed to see things come full circle," said Jason.

"You mean going to the funeral of the person you say ruined your life gave you some sort of satisfaction?"

"It sounds horrible to hear you put it that way," said Jason.

"But accurate?" Lauren pressed.

"Somewhat, I guess," Jason answered. "Look, let's get it out there. I couldn't stand Constance Young for what I maintain was her cavalier treatment of my reputation. But if you read the book, you'll see that Constance Young treated many people badly."

"Well, let's get to the book, Mr. Vaughan, shall we?" Lauren flipped through the pages of the volume on her lap. "Here, on page forty-three, you describe a tantrum you say Constance threw over a ratings spike last year for her competition over at *Daybreak*, the broadcast she was about to join when she died. Yet you also say she was alone in her office at the time. If there was nobody in the office, how do you know that Constance threw this alleged tantrum?"

"A confidential source told me," said Jason.

"It would have to be someone who works here at KEY News, wouldn't it? Someone who had extremely close access to Constance Young?"

"As I said, I promised my source anonymity."

"All right," said Lauren. "Let's look at another passage. On page one hundred fourteen, you say that Constance made a deliberate show of being an animal lover when she was on the air but that she frequently mistreated her own cat, forgetting about it and leaving it alone for long stretches."

"Yes, that's right."

"Again, how would you know this?" asked Lauren. "Did the same confidential source tell you?"

"As a matter of fact, yes. He did."

"I'm skeptical, Mr. Vaughan," said Lauren. "You describe a tantrum when no one was present to see it and an abandoned cat who obviously can't corroborate the story of its alleged mistreatment. You could be making all this up."

Jason could feel his face redden. "Oh, no you don't," he said. "Not again. I'm not going to have you people discredit me and ruin my reputation again. People close to Constance Young showed no compunction about sharing details with me. A man who used to come in and make sure the cat was all right told me that story. I won't give you his name, but the story is absolutely true."

Chapter 79

The owner of the Dropped Stitch Needlecraft Shop parked her Volvo in one of the spaces behind the store. She was surprised to see Ursula's old car in the adjoining spot. Ursula wasn't scheduled to give classes today. She soon discovered that the rear door of the shop was unlocked as well.

"Ursula?" she called as she entered. "Ursula, it's me."

The owner's curiosity turned to concern when there was no response. She walked into the front room and spotted Ursula's needlecraft bag sitting on the table. She looked through the picture window to the sidewalk out front, hoping that Ursula was tending to the pots of annuals she had planted a few days ago. But nobody was there, and the front door was still locked.

"Ursula?" she called out again.

Should she phone the police? she wondered. Would they think she was overreacting? There were several possible explanations as to where Ursula might be. She could have gone to get a cup of coffee or a newspaper. She might have run over to the bank. Maybe she had to drop something off at the dry cleaners.

The shop owner went about her business, unpacking a shipment of wool and arranging it on the shelves. She attended to the first customer of the morning, helping her pick out some sock-knitting yarn. Then another customer came in to match some wool for the background of a needlepoint canvas she was finishing. After the third customer had purchased several skeins for an afghan throw she was starting, the owner went to the back of the store, ready to call the police.

As she reached for the phone, she realized that the police would ask her if she'd checked everywhere. She hadn't checked the cellar.

Chapter 80

When Eliza arrived at the Broadcast Center, she met up with Lauren Adams as they waited for the elevator. The two women walked together into the empty car.

"How's it going?" asked Eliza.

"Well, for starters, I just fired Boyd Irons," Lauren announced.

Eliza looked startled. "You're kidding. Why? Just yesterday you were speaking up for him with our legal department."

"No, I'm not kidding," Lauren said vehemently. "There's no way I want him to work for me anymore. I'd never be able to trust him. Did you see the show this morning?"

"Just a little bit," Eliza answered, thinking the time had been better spent paying attention to her daughter.

"The interviews with Boyd and Jason Vaughan, the writer?"

Eliza shook her head. "No."

"In a nutshell, Jason Vaughan pretty well told me that Boyd was the one who gave him the dirt on Constance. If he could do it to Constance, Boyd could do it to me."

The elevator doors opened on Eliza's floor. She pushed the button to stop them from closing again.

"You aren't certain that Boyd was the one, Lauren."

"Oh, yes I am," said Lauren. "I confronted him, and he admitted it. I'm sorry now that I tried to help him. Maybe he did kill Constance and stole the unicorn from her. If he helped Jason Vaughan spread his invective, maybe he hated Constance enough to kill her. I'm washing my hands of him, and you should, too."

"I'm sorry to hear that, Lauren." Eliza let go of the button and started to exit the elevator.

"You might want to think about how trustworthy Paige is. You know, Eliza, in our positions we can't be too careful," Lauren said as the elevator doors slid closed again.

"Oh, wait a minute," said Paige. "Eliza just walked in." Putting the call on hold, she whispered to Eliza, "It's Mack McBride."

Eliza smiled. "It's all right, Paige. You can say his name out loud." She walked through the outer office. "I'll take it in here."

Closing the office door, Eliza went to her desk and picked up the receiver. "You made it in one piece," she said brightly. "How was your flight?"

"The flight was okay, but every time I looked at that electronic map they keep flashing to show you where you are, I was bummed, because it reminded me I was getting farther and farther away from you."

"I knew there was a reason they say you're one of the best writers and correspondents at KEY News," Eliza answered. "You have a way with words and know exactly what to say."

"What do you mean *one* of the best writers and correspondents?"

"That's all you'll get from me," said Eliza. "That ego of yours is big enough."

They chatted for a while. Mack mentioned that he was leaving again in a few hours to do a story in Rome. The Vatican had issued a statement on the Middle East that was causing quite a stir in diplomatic circles. "I'm tired, though," said Mack.

"Don't ask me to feel sorry for you," said Eliza. "I adore Rome."

"Let's meet there this weekend, then," he said eagerly.

Eliza laughed. "Did you forget I have a six-year-old waiting for me at home?"

"Bring Janie with you," said Mack. "We'll show her how beautiful Rome is in the springtime."

Did he have any idea how many points he scored with her by suggesting they include Janie in their time together? "Sorry, Mack. Janie has a sleepover at the Hvizdaks' house this weekend. I'm afraid that trumps a trip to the Colosseum as far as she's concerned."

"All right," said Mack. "But I don't want to have to wait too long until I see you again."

Eliza was about to talk to Mack about the Constance Young story when he was interrupted.

"I'm sorry, honey, but I've got to go now," he said. "Call you tomorrow?"

"Even before that, if you want," she said.

Chapter 81

The Associated Press local wire broke the story first, and it quickly moved to the national wires. The body of Constance Young's housekeeper had been found at a needlecraft shop in Bedford, New York. Police were not certain if Ursula Bales's death was an accident or murder.

Eliza was reading the details of the account when Annabelle Murphy knocked on the door.

"You've seen it, huh?" Annabelle asked as she walked into the office.

Eliza nodded as she finished the article.

"It would seem to be a pretty strange coincidence that the housekeeper just happens to die in the middle of all this," said Annabelle.

"Stranger things have happened," observed Eliza, "but yes, I have a gut feeling that we're not dealing with an accident here."

"I'm having the tape pulled of the interview we did with Ursula Bales on Saturday after she came from Constance's house," said Annabelle. "God, she was nervous that day."

"Good," said Eliza. "We'll be able to use excerpts of that interview in our piece tonight. Are you going up to Bedford to see what's going on up there?"

"I'm on my way now, with B.J.," said Annabelle. "Want to come?"

"I wish I could," said Eliza, "but I have things to deal with here. You two go and be my eyes and ears."

Chapter 82

Waiting in the lobby for B.J. to bring the car around, Annabelle spotted Boyd carrying a large cardboard box. He saw her, too, and walked over.

"I guess you've heard," he said, resting the box on the floor.

"Yes, I did," said Annabelle. "You know how word travels around this place. I'm so sorry, Boyd."

"Yeah. It sucks," said Boyd. "But when you play with fire, you're gonna get burned. I was taking a big chance telling Jason Vaughan those things for his book. But when he called me, I was just so damned fed up with Constance that I let loose. I guess I don't really blame Lauren for canning me. She wouldn't be able to trust me."

Annabelle saw the downcast expression on Boyd's face. "You've had a rough few days, haven't you, kiddo?"

"I've had better," said Boyd.

"What's going on with the legal stuff?"

"Thank God, they released me late yesterday, but there's a court date next month," said Boyd. "I don't know how I'm going to get out of that. I was caught red-handed with the stolen unicorn. They even have it on tape, courtesy of several different media outlets. Unless the KEY attorney can convince a jury that the unicorn was planted on me, I'll be screwed. I might be screwed already," he reflected. "The KEY News attorney probably won't even represent me anymore, since I'll no longer be a KEY News employee."

"I don't think the KEY attorney was representing you because you were an employee as much as because Eliza personally asked him to get involved," said Annabelle. "But even if he does dump you, there are lots of other good attorneys out there."

"Try paying for them, " said Boyd.

"I hear you," Annabelle commiserated. She glanced away for a moment to see if B.J. had pulled up yet.

"Where are you off to?" Boyd asked.

"Upstate," said Annabelle. "Get this: Constance's housekeeper is dead."

"Ursula Bales?"

"You got it," said Annabelle as she looked out the lobby window. "There's B.J. now. I've got to run, but good luck, Boyd. Why don't you go up and say good-bye to Eliza before you leave?"

Boyd picked up the cardboard box. "I don't think so, Annabelle. I just want to get out of here." He turned away and then turned back again as he remembered something. "Hey, Annabelle, I wanted to tell you. Constance Young listed you in her will."

"What?"

"Yeah," said Boyd. "You're going to be hearing about it anyway from her probate lawyer now that she's dead, so I'm not breaking any confidence. Constance left money for a college fund for your twins."

The KEY News crew car traveled up the Hutchinson River Parkway.

"I'm stunned," Annabelle said to her companion. "Absolutely stunned."

"That's pretty cool," said B.J. "I guess it goes to show that everybody has at least some good in them."

Annabelle wiped away a tear from the corner of her eye.

B.J. pretended not to notice.

Chapter 83

Rowena Quincy was on the phone in her office at the Cloisters, pleading with the law-enforcement official on the other end of the line.

"Look, the unicorn is our property," she said firmly. "We want it returned. The exhibit opens tomorrow, and that unicorn is supposed to be at the center of it."

"I understand, but the unicorn is evidence now, ma'am. We aren't releasing it."

"But we aren't pressing charges for the theft," said Rowena.

"The unicorn is potential evidence in a homicide, ma'am."

"You don't know where or when Constance Young last wore that unicorn," said Rowena. "You don't know that she had it with her when she died or that she was

killed for it. Can't you take a picture of it or something?" asked Rowena.

"It's evidence, ma'am."

"Never mind," said Rowena angrily. "You will be
hearing from our lawyers."

Chapter 84

*T*here were no more loose ends.

Taking care of Ursula Bales meant that the eyewitness to Constance's electrocution would never tell anyone what she'd seen.

Taking care of the guy in the animal shelter meant that no one would ever be able to trace the person who had adopted the Great Dane only to turn around and electrocute it.

A dog.

A television news anchorwoman.

An animal lover.

A housekeeper.

Four executions, one death sentence following another. The first two had been planned; the next two were necessary to stay safe. That, hopefully, should *be it now. Murder wasn't enjoyable. It was hard work, nerve-racking and exhausting.*

It should be possible to go forward now with confidence. There were other problems that still needed to be addressed, but the murders were taken care of now, unless someone else got in the way.

Eliza Blake had to be watched—very carefully watched.

Chapter 85

KEY News wasn't the first on the scene at the Dropped Stitch Needlecraft Shop. The police were wrapping up, having searched and dusted for fingerprints, questioned the owner, and canvassed the neighboring stores in hopes that someone had noticed something. Camera and audio crews, reporters and producers from CBS, NBC, ABC, and CNN were out in front of the shop, as well as crews from local stations and print-media reporters. Ursula's body had already been taken away.

"Crap," cursed B.J. "We missed the money shot."

"I'll check to see if a police spokesperson or the owner is going to come out and make a statement," said Annabelle.

"You missed it," said the cameraman from CBS. "The police chief spoke already, and the owner sent out word she wasn't going to. Sorry, guys."

While the crews from the other news organizations packed their gear and drove away, B.J. walked across the street to get a long shot of the store's exterior. He muttered to himself as he crossed again and took a closer shot of the front door and the sign identifying the place.

"I'm just wondering," said B.J. "Why did we get such a late start on this?"

"You win some, you lose some, Beej," said Annabelle. "It would have been great to get here first, but we didn't. Now we have to see what we can salvage."

Annabelle approached the last police car remaining.

"Hi, Officer. My name is Annabelle Murphy. I'm a producer for KEY News. Would you be willing to answer a few questions for us?"

"On camera?"

"That would be great," answered Annabelle.

The policeman shook his head. "No, I don't think so. My boss already talked to the press, and I don't think he'd appreciate me being on the news instead of him."

"But we missed your boss," Annabelle implored.

The officer shrugged. "Sorry."

Annabelle walked back to B.J. as the police car drove away.

"That's good, Annabelle. Real good. No sound bites for our piece tonight. Everybody else's piece will have sound from a police spokesman, but not us."

Annabelle ignored him. She walked up to the front door of the shop and tried to open it. The door was locked. She knocked, and no one answered.

"Let's go around back," she said.

A woman was sitting on the rear stoop, her arms wrapped around herself. Annabelle introduced herself and B.J.

"This is a terrible thing," said Annabelle. "It truly is. We interviewed Ms. Bales this past weekend at Constance Young's house."

"She told me about it," said the owner. "Poor Ursula. She was always so worried about any kind of attention from the police. Her sister was killed because she was an eyewitness to a crime. Ursula was paranoid it would happen to her one day."

"Maybe it did happen to her," said Annabelle. "Maybe Ursula was killed because she saw something that the killer didn't want her to see."

"The police said they aren't sure that Ursula was killed or if she fell down the stairs accidentally," said the owner.

"Well, let's just assume that she was murdered," said Annabelle gently. "We'd all want to do anything we could to catch her killer, wouldn't we?"

"Of course," said the owner.

"It could be beneficial to let us into the store and take video inside," said Annabelle. "Quite honestly, the better the video we have, the more interesting the piece. And the more interesting the piece, the more people pay attention and talk about it afterward and, sometimes, come forward with information they have that could help."

The owner considered the logic of Annabelle's words.

"All right," she said. "Come in."

As fast as he could, lest the owner change her mind, B.J. recorded video of the back room, the door to the basement, and the steep stairs that Ursula had fallen down. There were chalk markings on the floor indicating where the body had been.

"Ursula gave a knitting lesson here last night?" asked Annabelle.

"Yes," the owner answered. "Her classes were always full. Everybody loved her." The owner led the way into the front room. "To think that Ursula was just going about her business, doing her job, not knowing that last night's class would really be her last." She caressed a canvas satchel sitting on the table. "This is Ursula's needlecraft bag," she said, her voice breaking.

B.J. aimed his camera at the bag. "Any chance we can shoot what's in it?" he asked. "It would be a nice element for our piece—it would humanize Ursula for our audience."

The owner opened the bag and took out a partially completed needlepoint canvas. "She had designed this. She was very excited about it. I never saw her work on another piece the way she did on this one. She wrote the poem as a tribute to Constance Young. Ursula worshipped that woman."

B.J.'s camera took a full shot of the canvas, and then he panned from the top to the bottom of the piece. He held the camera steady for a long time at the two final lines, the words outlined in black wool.

Careful not to tell,
Yet I was there as well.

After they walked out of the shop, Annabelle turned to B.J.

"It seems to me that Ursula Bales was saying that she knew who killed Constance because she was there and saw it happen," said Annabelle. "Are you getting that, too?"

"Yeah, I'd say so," said B.J. "But can you believe how Constance had that woman so completely snowed? All the junk about 'lady of allure' and 'lonely shining star' at the start of the poem. Give me a break."

"I couldn't care less if Constance had Ursula Bales fooled, " said Annabelle. "We're the only ones who have her poem. We'll be exclusive tonight." Annabelle pumped her fist in the air. "The early bird doesn't always catch the worm, does it, B.J.?" she asked as they got into the car to drive back to Manhattan.

Chapter 86

Her head ached as she pushed the vacuum cleaner around the living room, but Faith kept at it. She needed to work out some of her anger at Constance over stiffing her in the will. The physical exertion helped. The sound of the vacuum also made it impossible to hear her mother if she called out. That, too, was a good thing, at least for a little while.

Finished with the living room, she switched off the vacuum and pulled the plug out of the wall socket. As she moved the machine into the den, the phone rang.

"Mrs. Hansen?"

"Speaking."

"This is Stuart Whitaker calling."

Faith rolled her eyes. *Not now.* "Yes, Mr. Whitaker. How are you?"

"Holding together pretty well, I think. How, if I may ask, are you?"

"I've been better," said Faith.

"Of course, of course," said Stuart. "This must be such a difficult time for you. Again, I am so sorry for your loss."

"Thank you," said Faith.

"Mrs. Hansen, I hope you will not think I am too forward or inappropriate, but is there any possibility whatsoever that you might consider joining me tonight at the Cloisters? If you could get away for the evening, there will be a lovely reception for the new Camelot exhibit. I would be able to give you a tour of where I foresee the memorial garden I have been planning—the final and lasting tribute to your sister. After you have a better idea of where Constance will rest for all eternity, I think you will feel better about giving her remains to me."

Faith sank down onto the leather couch. Why this guy wanted Constance's remains so badly baffled her. And Stuart Whitaker's suggestion to go with him to the Cloisters was the last possible thing, save sex with Todd, that she wanted to do tonight. But as she thought more about it, it didn't sound like such a bad idea. It would be good to get away from Todd. And away from Mother and the kids, too.

"You know what, Mr. Whitaker?" she asked. "Thank you for asking me. I *would* like to go with you."

"Ah, wonderful," said Stuart. "I will send a car for you."

Again Faith's first instinct was to decline the offer. She was used to driving herself. But she thought better of it. Constance would never say no to a chauffeur, would she? Constance had taken care of herself, which is something Faith knew she had to start doing, too.

As soon as she and Stuart finished their conversation, Faith called her husband's office. She informed Todd of her plans and listened to his protestations, along with his complaints about Constance's will.

"Look, Todd. I'm sorry you're disappointed that Constance didn't leave me more. I am, too. But at least she provided for our boys. And I'm sorry that you were planning on playing twilight golf. But I need you to come home right after work so you can stay with the kids. I'm going out for a change."

Chapter 87

As soon as they got back to the Broadcast Center, Annabelle and B.J. rushed to Eliza's office. But Eliza was at a meeting with some KEY affiliate news directors who had come to town, and she would be out of the office for another hour or so.

"Call me on my cell when Eliza gets back, will you please, Paige?" Annabelle asked.

Annabelle and B.J. went downstairs to an editing room and looked at the tape they'd gotten at the needle-craft shop. When they reached the portion showing the needlepoint with Ursula's poem, Annabelle wrote down all the words.

Careful not to tell,
Yet I was there as well.

"What else could that mean, Beej?" asked Annabelle. "It comes right after

'Left lying in the pool,
Left sinking like a stone,
Ending up so cool,
Dying all alone.'

"She has to be referring to Constance drowning there," said Annabelle excitedly. "And then in that last couplet Ursula is saying she's been careful not tell—because she was there when it happened."

Next they screened the videotaped interview with Ursula that had been taken Saturday on the street outside Constance's country home. The poor woman looked so uncomfortable and nervous. Her voice trembled in spots, and in one scene it was clearly visible that her hand was shaking.

"See?" Annabelle pointed at the screen. "I think she knew damned well who'd killed Constance when she talked to us."

"You can't say that for certain," said B.J.

"No," said Annabelle, "but it would explain why she was so incredibly shaken."

"You'd be shaken, too, if somebody you cared about had just died."

"I guess you're right," said Annabelle. "But based on the videotape and now the poem, I think it's a very good bet Ursula knew more than she let on that day."

Chapter 88

"This is *The KEY Evening Headlines* with Eliza Blake," the announcer's voice boomed.

Dressed in a navy jacket over a pale blue sleeveless dress, Eliza appeared on the television screen.

"Good evening, everyone," she said. "What happened to Constance Young? Questions about her death, most likely by electrocution, have dominated the news this week."

A still picture of a plain-faced, middle-aged woman popped up behind Eliza's shoulder as she continued speaking.

"Today the story took another tragic turn. Fifty-two-year-old Ursula Bales, Young's housekeeper, was found dead in the cellar of a needlecraft shop in Bedford, New York."

Video of the Dropped Stitch Needlecraft Shop popped up on the screen, followed by video from the interior of the shop, including the stairs that led to the basement.

"Bales gave a knitting class last night—it was the last time she was seen alive. This morning the owner of the shop found Bales's body at the bottom of the stairs to the building's basement, a knitting needle impaled in her chest. Police are not yet sure if Bales's death was an accident or murder."

The video of the needlepoint canvas came up on the screen with the words KEY NEWS EXCLUSIVE superimposed in the upper-left-hand corner of the image.

"This exclusive video, shot today, shows a needlepoint canvas that Ursula Bales was working on when she died. It features a poem, entitled 'Constance,' which starts out as a tribute to Constance Young but ends with a startling admission."

Eliza read the words of the sonnet that Ursula had composed.

" 'Lady of allure, a lonely shining star, determined and so sure, and worshipped from afar. Men wooed her as a queen, sought after for her charms, known only on the screen, if rarely in her arms. Left lying in a pool, left sinking like a stone, ending up so cool, dying all alone. Careful not to tell, yet I was there as well.' "

Up on the screen, the last couplet was highlighted.

" 'Careful not to tell, yet I was there as well,' " Eliza repeated. "With those words it seems that Ursula Bales may have been revealing that she indeed witnessed the death of Constance Young. Bales's hesitancy to come forward could have stemmed from the fact that her own sister was killed several years ago, after she volunteered as a witness in a drug case."

Now the footage ran of Ursula being interviewed outside Constance's house.

"Ursula Bales, who told police she found Young's body when she came to work on Saturday morning, gave no indication that she had witnessed a murder the night before."

Ursula was shown speaking, her cheeks wet with tears.

"I saw something dark under the water. At first I didn't recognize it. And then I realized what it was. It was Miss Young in her black bathing suit, lying on the bottom of the pool."

Ursula bowed her head and cried, and then Eliza appeared back on screen, looking directly into the camera.

"Earlier this week it was discovered that a Great Dane, approximately the same weight as Constance Young, had been electrocuted in her pool the day before the anchorwoman died, giving rise to speculation that the dog was killed as a practice run for the electrocution of a human being. The dog, it turns out, had been claimed from a New York City animal shelter, but any chance of identifying the person who adopted the dog was squashed when the shelter worker, thirty-seven-year-old Vinny Shays, was found murdered by a lethal dose of sodium pentobarbital, taken from the supply room of the shelter. Sodium pentobarbital is the chemical compound used in animal euthanasia."

Now the director ordered a switch from the shot of Eliza at the anchor desk to a still photo of the purloined unicorn.

"Police had been working under the hypothesis that Young might have been killed for a priceless ivory unicorn, missing from the Cloisters, a museum specializing in medieval art—a unicorn she was seen wearing in public the day before she was found murdered."

Now video rolled of the people coming out of the funeral home after Constance's service, leading to a shot of Boyd being escorted into a police vehicle.

"A KEY News employee and Constance Young's administrative assistant, Boyd Irons, was discovered to be in possession of the unicorn, and though Stuart Whitaker, benefactor of the museum and former companion of Young, has admitted that he took the unicorn from the museum, police are still looking at Irons because his possession of the stolen object puts him in contact with Young on the day of her death."

The story finished with Eliza again looking into the camera.

"It all adds up to a story with more questions than answers. The major question: Who killed Constance and why? We here at KEY News, where Constance worked for so many years, are committed to getting to the truth, and we will continue to keep you informed of each new development in the case."

Chapter 89

The car pulled up to the entrance of the Cloisters. Flashbulbs popped as Eliza stepped out, dressed in a champagne-colored silk chiffon cocktail dress. Rowena Quincy was waiting for her.

"It's good to see you again," said Rowena, reaching out with a firm handshake. "You didn't really get a chance to do much exploring when you were here on Sunday. Let me show you around a bit."

"Thank you. I'd love that," said Eliza.

They walked into the Romanesque Hall, with its arched doors showing the evolution of medieval architecture.

"So the rounded arch is the Romanesque and the pointed one is the Gothic," said Eliza.

"Yes, that's right," said Rowena, nodding approval.

Eliza admired the carvings, frescoes, and pair of limestone lions that flanked the doorway to the next area.

"Lion sculptures often guarded the entrances to churches in medieval times," Rowena explained. "Lions were said to sleep with their eyes open, so they represented Christian watchfulness."

As they went through the halls, rooms, and chapels, Eliza nodded to the guests strolling through the museum, people who had contributed generously for the privilege of attending the private event. The most populated area was the room where the Hunt of the Unicorn tapestries hung.

"I've read about these," said Eliza as she gazed at the weavings. "But they're so much more impressive when you see the real thing."

"It's a miracle that they survived," said Rowena. "During the French Revolution, they were taken down from the walls of a wealthy family's château and were used for a generation or so to protect peasants' vegetables and fruit trees from freezing."

"Fascinating," said Eliza. "And I suppose that what's been happening with the *ivory* unicorn this past week will now become part of its lore. From Lady Guinevere to Constance Young. That's an amazing journey."

"Yes," agreed Rowena. "Our unicorn has quite a story to tell. I can't express how relieved I am that our lawyers were able to get the police to release it to us in time for our opening. It simply *makes* the exhibit."

Chapter 90

Some doctors took Wednesdays off, but Margo Gonzalez worked all day at the New York Psychiatric Institute and then had evening office hours for her private patients. After the last patient left the office, Margo kicked off her shoes and settled in at her desk to answer the slew of e-mails that had piled up during the day. Halfway through, she logged in to the KEY News Web site and clicked the appropriate icons to view the *Evening Headlines*. She hadn't heard any news all day.

Margo was shocked and saddened by the lead story. She listened as Eliza described how Ursula Bales had been found dead. Margo was touched as she saw the final needlepoint Ursula had worked on and the poem she'd written honoring Constance but also revealing that she had witnessed the murder. It was eerie to watch the video of the woman, taken just four days before, talking about discovering Constance Young's body at the bottom of the swimming pool.

When the story was finished, Margo watched it again, and then over again after that. After each viewing, Margo felt more uneasy.

Chapter 91

During the cocktail hour, many people came up and introduced themselves to Eliza. She shook hands and made small talk, trying to be as gracious as possible. As each person turned and walked away, Eliza found another waiting, all of them wanting to meet the anchorwoman.

"Hello, Eliza."

"Boyd," she said with surprise. "I didn't expect to see you here."

"I read about your hosting in the paper and thought I'd give it a shot. When Constance was scheduled to emcee tonight, the museum sent over a couple of complimentary tickets. I helped myself to one." Boyd's expression became more serious. "Security won't let me in the Broadcast Center anymore, so I can't come up to your office, but I wanted to thank you personally for your kindness and support. That was really very nice of you to call the legal department to help me."

"You're welcome," said Eliza. "I'm glad I could help. But I was so sorry when I heard that Lauren let you go, Boyd. Do you have any idea what you're going to do now?"

"It was stupid of me to talk to Jason Vaughan for his book. I can't say that I blame Lauren for firing me. I wouldn't trust me either, if I were her."

A waiter with a tray stopped beside them. Boyd took a Bellini and held it out to Eliza. "Want one?" he asked.

"Thanks, but better not," she said. "I have to speak in a little while."

Boyd swallowed some of the drink. "Anyway," he said, "I can find another job, as long as I get cleared legally. No employer is going to want to hire somebody being brought up on murder charges."

"Do you really think it will come to that, Boyd?"

"God, I hope not," he said, frowning. "I think having that unicorn in my pocket was a bad sign, but they can't prove I took it from Constance the night she died, because they can't say for certain that Constance had it with her then. They'll need more evidence against me." He paused for just a moment. "But if someone is trying to frame me, who knows what will happen?"

Chapter 92

Annabelle had just scooped out some frozen yogurt for the twins when the phone rang. It was Margo Gonzalez.

"I tried the Broadcast Center, but Eliza had left for the day. I don't want to call her at home with this, so I asked the assignment desk to connect to you at home. Let me run something past you."

Annabelle put her index finger up to her mouth, signaling to the kids to be quiet, as she walked from the kitchen into the bedroom. She shut the door and sat down on the edge of the bed.

"Okay. Now I can talk. What is it?" asked Annabelle.

Margo described what she had noticed in the news piece.

Annabelle thought back to when the videotape was shot on Sunday. "I don't know, Margo," she said. "I was right there. Ursula Bales just seemed nervous to me. That's understandable."

"There's a difference between nervousness and sheer terror," said Margo. "The pupils of the eyes actually dilate when confronted with something terrifying."

"I know," said Annabelle. "I did a story about that once. The pupils can also dilate when you have a migraine headache or when you lie. And besides, Margo, Ursula Bales had only a short time before watched as Constance's body was pulled out of the pool. That's a pretty terrifying thing to see."

Chapter 93

Eliza escaped to a secluded corner, pulled the cell phone from her evening bag, and called home.

"Janie? It's Mommy."

"Hi, Mommy."

"I just wanted to call and say good night, sweetheart."

"I'm not going to bed yet, Mommy. Mrs. Garcia says I can stay up till we finish the game."

"What game are you playing, Janie?"

"Candy Land."

"That sounds like fun," said Eliza.

" 'Bye, Mommy."

Click.

Eliza stood with the phone in her hand. This morning she had felt that Janie was aching for attention. Now Janie couldn't get off the phone fast enough.

Never overestimate your own importance, thought Eliza, smiling to herself. Satisfied that Janie was just fine, and not wanting it to interrupt her once she got up to speak to the audience, Eliza turned off her phone.

Chapter 94

It was growing dark as Stuart Whitaker walked with Faith Hansen on the hilltop overlooking the Hudson River. Just to the south, the lights on the George Washington Bridge came on. In the distance a strand of lights delineated the Tappan Zee Bridge.

"This is where I envision it," said Stuart as the museum's outdoor lights came on, illuminating the area. "This is where the Constance Young Memorial Garden will be built."

"It's a beautiful spot, Mr. Whitaker," said Faith, looking around at the blooming azaleas and rhododendron. "It truly is."

Stuart's arm swept through the air, indicating the spots where the highlights of the garden would go.

"The reflecting pool will be here, the memorial walk will be there, and the six stained-glass panels based on the Lady and the Unicorn tapestries in Paris will stand over there, each of them with an image of Constance's face as the maiden."

Faith was impressed. "You've given this a lot of thought, haven't you, Mr. Whitaker?"

"I find myself thinking about it all the time," Stuart said earnestly. "But it's been a great diversion for me. If I spent all my time thinking about Constance being gone, I wouldn't be able to function."

"You really loved her, didn't you?"

Stuart looked down at the ground. "With all my heart," he said. "I want to have an eternal flame burning here to symbolize forever how much your sister meant to me."

What a strange little creature he was, Faith thought as she looked at the man in the beautifully tailored suit. She felt sorry for him. He was alone in the world. He had no children, no one who depended on him emotionally, no one to shower with love. As much as caring for Mother was trying and exhausting, Faith could take satisfaction in the devotion she showed her parent. And though her marriage was a disappointment on so many levels, the children of that union were everything to her. The boys loved their father, and she wasn't going to rob them of his daily presence in their lives.

Faith looked at Stuart Whitaker, knowing that although he was exceedingly wealthy and successful, what he really wanted couldn't be bought. Stuart, God help him, had wanted to have Constance. Now, failing that, he wanted what was left of her.

Chapter 95

Eliza checked her watch. It was almost time for the program to begin. As she glanced around to see if she could spot Rowena Quincy, she was approached by a man accompanied by a woman wearing a simple sleeveless black cocktail dress.

"Ms. Blake, my name is Jason Vaughan."

Eliza recognized the name immediately.

"Hello, Mr. Vaughan," she said warily. "I've been hearing a lot about you and your book lately, though I haven't caught you being interviewed about it on TV myself."

"I'm flattered you know who I am," said Jason. "This is my wife . . . uh, former wife, Nell."

"Nice to meet you," said Eliza as she offered her hand to the woman.

"My pleasure," said Nell, smiling.

"Lovely event, isn't it?" asked Eliza politely.

"Yes, it is. I can't wait to see the unicorn," said Nell.

Eliza turned to Jason. "I hear your book is doing quite well," she said.

"Knock on wood, yes, it is," said Jason. "In fact, I received the happy news this afternoon that *Never Look Back* is debuting at number three on the *New York Times Book Review* Best Sellers list."

"Congratulations," said Eliza. "What brings you here tonight?"

"Mixing a little business with pleasure," answered Jason. "I wanted Nell to have the chance to see the exhibit, but honestly, I have another motive."

"What would that be?" asked Eliza.

"I'm beginning work on another book," said Jason. "This one will be about the death of Constance Young. It seemed natural to come tonight to see the unicorn returned to the Cloisters after Constance was killed for it."

"I see," said Eliza, wanting to get away.

"Would it be all right if I called you? Would you be willing to answer some questions for me in an interview?"

"What kinds of questions?" asked Eliza.

"I'd be asking how you, as a colleague and anchor-woman, view Constance's death. Do you think in some way Constance was only getting what she deserved?"

"No one deserves to be murdered, Mr. Vaughan."

Eliza turned, said good-bye to Nell, and began to walk away.

Jason called after her, "What goes around comes around, Ms. Blake."

Chapter 96

With the twins finally settled into bed and Mike at the firehouse, Annabelle brewed herself a cup of herbal tea. She sat down on the sofa and picked up a magazine, but the call from Margo Gonzalez nagged at her.

What if Ursula Bales had been truly terrified when she was interviewed in front of Constance Young's country house? What could that mean?

Annabelle went over to the desk and switched on the laptop. She did a Google search on Ursula Bales, reading the recent articles where her name appeared in conjunction with Constance Young's death, the ones from today announcing that Ursula herself had been found dead, and the article from a few years ago when Ursula was listed as the sister of a woman suspected to have been murdered because she came forward as an eyewitness to a crime.

The needlepoint poem indicated that Ursula had witnessed Constance's murder. After what had happened to her sister, it was understandable she'd be afraid to come forward. But in their excitement at determining that Ursula had been a witness, maybe they'd overlooked something. What if there was something else in the poem? Some clue they had missed.

Rifling through her tote bag, Annabelle found the notebook in which she'd written down the words of the poem.

Lady of allure, a lonely shining star, determined and so sure, and worshipped from afar. Men wooed her as a queen, sought after for her charms, known only on the screen, if rarely in her arms. Left lying in a pool, left sinking like a stone, ending up so cool, dying all alone. Careful not to tell, yet I was there as well.

She read the lines several times, gleaning nothing from them. Then Annabelle pulled out her cell phone.

"B.J., it's me, Annabelle. I think there's something in that poem, but I can't for the life of me figure out what it is. Will you take a look at it? Two heads are better than one."

Chapter 97

It was almost nine o'clock when Eliza took the podium. Large video screens at the four corners of the vast room had close-ups of her face, allowing those at a distance from the podium to feel as close to Eliza Blake as those who were fortunate enough to be seated in front.

"Good evening and thank you for coming to celebrate the opening of the new Camelot Exhibit here at the historic and beautiful Cloisters. I'm Eliza Blake, and it's an honor and a pleasure to be with you tonight."

Enthusiastic applause reverberated off the stone walls. Eliza looked out at the assembled audience. Among the many faces staring up at her, she spotted Linus and Lauren, Boyd, Faith Hansen, Jason and Nell Vaughan, and Stuart Whitaker.

Eliza looked at her notes and then back to the crowd.

"As everyone here undoubtedly knows, the past days have been especially difficult ones—for the family and friends of Constance Young, for her colleagues at KEY News, for her admirers around the country, and for the staff here at the Cloisters, who until just this afternoon weren't sure if they would have the centerpiece of their new exhibit available to be unveiled tonight."

Eliza gestured to the draped box that stood at the side of the room.

"The ivory unicorn, rumored to be a gift from King Arthur to his Lady Guinevere, has had an intriguing history. It has traveled through the ages, through sometimes romantic, sometimes tragic, and always complicated circumstances until, ultimately, it found its way to us."

Eliza paused deliberately before continuing.

"How fortunate we are to be among the first people to view this wonderful exhibit. And to have the opportunity to behold Lady Guinevere's ivory unicorn."

With that, all eyes turned from Eliza to the side of the room, where a royal blue velvet cloth was whisked off the glass box, revealing the ivory unicorn standing proudly inside. Cameras trained on the case zoomed in so that the large video screens around the room revealed the tiniest detail.

Chapter 98

B.J. finished his beer, paid the bill for his dinner, and walked the few blocks back to the Broadcast Center. The lobby was empty, save for the receptionist at the front desk and a security guard. B.J. swiped his ID across the glass panel on the security turnstile, and the gates slid open.

The halls were quiet. B.J. went directly to the editing booth and found the video he'd recorded up in Bedford earlier in the day. He slid the disk into a viewing deck and shuttled down until he located the shots he'd taken of the needlepoint Ursula Bales had been working on when she died. He read across the lines but gleaned nothing new from them.

He froze the video at the point where the full poem appeared on screen and studied it.

Lady of allure,
A lonely shining star,
Determined and so sure,
And worshipped from afar.

Men wooed her as a queen,
Sought after for her charms,
Known only on the screen,
If rarely in her arms.

Left lying in a pool,
Left sinking like a stone,
Ending up so cool,
Dying all alone.

Careful not to tell,
Yet I was there as well.

Chapter 99

Eliza stood with Rowena Quincy next to the unicorn's display case while photographers and videographers took pictures.

"Let's get a few shots with Lauren in there, too," said Linus as he nudged her forward.

The women posed behind the case, looking down at the unicorn.

"Look at how that emerald eye sparkles," said Lauren.

"Fabulous," said Eliza. "The lighting is trained on it just perfectly."

"That thing sparkles even in the dark, but you have to watch out for that crown—those points are deadly," said Lauren. She tapped the glass with her finger. "It looks like it should be safe this time," she said.

When the flashbulbs had ceased popping, Eliza turned to Rowena. "I'm going to be leaving soon," she said.

"Thank you so much for helping us," said Rowena. "You saved our evening."

"My pleasure," said Eliza. "Truly."

Chapter 100

B.J. stared at the screen studying Ursula's poem until he remembered the exercise he'd done in second grade as a Mother's Day gift. His mom still had it in a little frame in her kitchen.

Makes me happy.
Outstanding cook.
Tucks me in.
Hugs and kisses.
Excellent helper.
Really nice.

Now B.J. understood that Ursula Bales had done more than tell the world she'd been a witness to murder. She had also revealed who the murderer was.

He pulled out his cell phone and called Annabelle.

Chapter 101

Eliza tried to leave the reception, but she was stopped along the way by many guests wanting to have just a few words with her. Stuart Whitaker was one of them. On his face was a blissful smile.

"Miss Blake," he said excitedly. "I have the most exciting news. Mrs. Hansen has agreed to have Constance's ashes rest in the memorial garden. Is that not wonderful news?"

Eliza tried to summon up polite enthusiasm. "You must be very pleased," she said.

"I am over the moon," said Stuart. "I want all the world to know about it. I thought you might be able to help me with that."

"In what way?" asked Eliza.

"Put it on the news, of course," said Stuart.

"I'm afraid it's not enough to do a whole story on the *Evening Headlines*," Eliza explained. "But I'm sure the information will make its way on air at some point as part of a bigger story."

Stuart's face fell.

"Tell you what," said Eliza. "*KEY to America* is doing their broadcast from here tomorrow morning. Why don't we find Linus Nazareth, the executive producer, and see if he has any interest?"

Chapter 102

Annabelle went in to check on the twins. They were sleeping soundly. She tucked the blanket around Tara and stuck Thomas's foot back under the covers. Then she returned to the desk in the living room to study the poem again. She looked at it for a while but came up with no new revelation.

Beyond the fact that Ursula had witnessed a murder, what else could have contributed to her being as terror-filled as Margo Gonzalez claimed she appeared in the video? Annabelle wondered.

She thought back to that afternoon. B.J. had miked Ursula and pointed the camera to shoot the pictures. Lauren had held out the microphone and asked the questions. Annabelle herself had stood to the side, out of camera range, taking notes.

Ursula would have no reason to be afraid of any of us, Annabelle thought.

On impulse she went to the computer and did another Google search. When the name was entered, hundreds of hits appeared on the search results page. Annabelle narrowed the search by adding the word "death." She was engrossed in what she was reading when B.J. called.

"You aren't going to believe this," he said.

"Oh, yes, I will," said Annabelle.

Chapter 103

Eliza found Linus and introduced him to Stuart Whitaker. Then she explained that it had just been decided that Constance Young's ashes would be kept at the Cloisters.

"Do you have any interest in talking with Mr. Whitaker about it?" asked Eliza.

The executive producer considered the offer. "All right," said Linus. "That sounds like something we can use on the show in the morning. Lauren could take a little walk around the grounds, showing where the memorial garden would be built." Linus turned to Stuart. "Would you be able to come back up here in the morning and have Lauren interview you?"

Stuart bit his bottom lip. "Oh, I am afraid that will be problematic," he said. "I have to go out of town early in the morning. Is there any possibility we can do the interview tonight?"

"I suppose so," said Linus. "Let me check with Lauren first."

Linus walked over to confer with the *KTA* cohost. "Fine," he said when he came back, accompanied by Lauren. "I'll leave you all to it. I'm going home. I have to be back here way too early tomorrow."

"But how will I get home if you take the car?" asked Lauren.

Linus said nothing.

"Look," said Eliza. "I'm going to be here for a little while. I really should talk to some more of these people. If you can do the interview with Stuart right away, I'll drop you off on my way home."

Chapter 104

And listen to this," said Annabelle. Over the phone she read the short article aloud to B.J.

"It's an article from the *Louisville Courier-Journal,*" said Annabelle. " 'Lauren Lee Adams of Frankfort was named Miss Kentucky Reel at a ceremony in Louisville. Ms. Adams, who originally was first runner-up in the pageant, takes the place of Missy Goodwin. Ms. Goodwin died last month.' And get this, B.J.: 'At autopsy, sodium pentobarbital was found in Ms. Goodwin's system.' That's the same substance that killed Vinny Shays, the animal-shelter worker."

B.J. was about to respond, but Annabelle interrupted him.

"Hang up, B.J. I have to call Eliza."

Chapter 105

By the time Eliza finished speaking to all the people who'd lined up to talk to her, the crowd had thinned out considerably. She pulled her cell phone from her evening purse and called home.

"Janie is sound asleep," said Mrs. Garcia. "Everything is fine here."

"That's great," said Eliza. "I should be home in about an hour, maybe a little more. I have someone to drop off downtown first."

As she went to close the phone, Eliza noticed she had some messages. She would check them as soon as she and Lauren were in the car. All she wanted to do now was find Lauren and get going.

She looked around for Lauren, Stuart, and a cameraman, wishing that she'd thought to ask where they were going to do the interview, or that she and Lauren had set up a place to meet. Finally Eliza saw one of the *KTA* production assistants, who told her that she'd seen Lauren outside, walking toward the river with a nerdy-looking guy.

Pulling her wrap around her against the cool night air, Eliza walked out of the Cloisters and turned west. She walked several hundred feet before bumping into Stuart Whitaker.

"All done?" Eliza asked.

"Yes," Stuart answered, "and I think it went very well. Miss Adams said she very much appreciated that I gave her a personal tour and described for her what the memorial garden will look like. I showed her just where I think Constance's remains will be kept."

"I'm so glad you're happy, Mr. Whitaker," said Eliza. "Where is Lauren now?"

Stuart indicated over his shoulder. "She wanted to go over something with her cameraman. She's still back there."

Chapter 106

After repeatedly calling Eliza's cell phone and getting no response, Annabelle called B.J. back.

"Eliza doesn't answer," she said, her voice close to frantic. "She must have turned off the phone. I'll call 911 and keep trying to reach her."

"All right," said B.J. "And I'm going to head up to the Cloisters myself."

"Should I call Cloisters security?" asked Annabelle.

"It couldn't hurt," he said as he sprinted out of the editing room.

Chapter 107

Wow. It's beautiful up here," said Eliza as she stood at the top of the cliff, looking south at the George Washington Bridge and the lights of Manhattan.

"Not a bad place to spend eternity, huh?" asked Lauren as she joined Eliza in admiring the view. "I've always been a sucker for a sparkling skyline."

The two women stood together, gazing out over the Hudson below, enjoying the magnificence, but feeling the cool night breeze blowing off the river.

"Ready to go?" Eliza finally asked.

"Just about," said Lauren. "But would you mind terribly if I paced out the area that I'll be showing the audience in the morning one more time? I know you want to get going, but I'd feel more secure if I do it now, and then I'll be able to sleep better tonight."

"I remember what it was like doing your shift," said Eliza, trying to be understanding though wanting to leave in the worst way. "It was so hard to get a good night's sleep. Go ahead."

"Thanks so much, Eliza," said Lauren. She turned to the cameraman, who was packing up his lighting gear. "It's all right, Bob," said Lauren. "You can leave now."

Chapter 108

The Cloisters security guards combed the museum looking for Eliza Blake.

"She left a while ago," Rowena Quincy said after one of the guards informed her of the distressed call from Annabelle Murphy. "Let's check outside."

Rowena and the guards hurried out to the front of the building. A dark blue sedan was waiting at the door. Rowena signaled for the driver to roll down his window.

"Have you seen Eliza Blake?" Rowena asked hurriedly. "About five foot seven, brown hair, pretty. She was wearing a light-colored chiffon dress?"

"You don't have to describe her for me, ma'am," said the driver. "She's my boss. But I haven't seen her yet. I just got here to pick her up."

Chapter 109

The skirt of Eliza's dress rustled in the evening breeze as she waited. Under the spotlights Lauren practiced how she was going to walk and what she was going to say when the camera followed her around the site of the memorial park in the morning. Eliza had to give it to Lauren. The new cohost of *KEY to America* didn't want to leave anything to chance.

Finally Lauren was satisfied. She walked over to Eliza.

"Okay. Ready now," Lauren said. She bent down to pick up her purse from the ground. As she stood up again, a gust of river air blew her hair in her face. Lauren raised her arm and brushed back the errant hair with the back of her hand. On the pale skin of Lauren's palm, Eliza noticed the five angry-looking cuts.

"Those are just like the scratches that Cons—" Eliza stopped herself as she looked into the killer's eyes.

Chapter 110

The car sped up the West Side Highway. B.J. wove in and out of the relatively sparse traffic. Once under the George Washington Bridge, he started looking for the exit for Fort Tryon Park and the Cloisters.

As he steered the car off the highway and began the climb up the steep drive to the Cloisters grounds, he passed a few cars coming out. But when he rounded the turn that led to the museum, he could see the flashing lights of police cars up ahead.

Chapter 111

Lauren looked down at the wounds on her open palm.

"You don't know how sorry I am that you saw this," she said.

"My God, Lauren," said Eliza, aghast. "What have you done?"

"You're our illustrious KEY News anchor," said Lauren. "You figure it out."

"You killed Constance. You took the unicorn, and you planted it on Boyd," Eliza said, incredulous and slightly dazed as her mind began to put the pieces together. "Why? Why ever would you do it?"

"Constance was my competition," said Lauren.

"You're not serious," said Eliza.

"Oh, yes, I am," said Lauren. "I'm *very* serious. If Constance actually went over to *Daybreak*, do you think anyone would watch me? Our ratings were poised to plummet. And I would be blamed. And replaced."

"I don't believe what I'm hearing," said Eliza.

"My career and reputation are everything to me, Eliza."

"Well, your career and reputation are going to be worth absolutely nothing now," said Eliza.

Lauren opened her purse. Eliza backed away as she pulled out a syringe.

"You are crazy, absolutely crazy, Lauren."

"It won't hurt too much, if you stay calm, Eliza," said Lauren, edging closer. "I've watched many animals put down, and as long as you keep them calm, the end comes pretty peacefully."

Eliza considered her options. Her back was to the cliff. She considered running forward, but to get past Lauren she would have to run close enough to be jabbed by the needle.

"So you killed the poor guy who worked in the animal shelter," Eliza said, buying time, trying to come up with a plan.

Lauren didn't answer.

"And Ursula Bales?"

"They got in the way, Eliza. They could have identified me." Lauren stepped closer, causing Eliza to back up farther, trying to calculate how many more feet there were behind her before the ground dropped off.

"Lauren, put that needle down," Eliza pleaded. "Please, Lauren. We can get you help."

Lauren laughed. "I don't need any help. Things are still going to work out just fine."

"If you kill me, Lauren, everyone will know you did it. My driver is waiting for me by now, the camera guy knows he left us up here alone—even Stuart Whitaker knows I was on the way to find you."

"I'll figure something out. I'm an awfully good liar," said Lauren. "I'll tell them you slipped and fell off the cliff. It was all a terrible accident. A terrible, terrible accident." Lauren's lips curled in a sarcastic smile. "Just think what those ratings will be tomorrow morning."

Chapter 112

By now B.J. had joined the search.

"Hey, Bob!" he called to the man loading some camera gear into the back of a KEY News car. "Have you seen Eliza?"

"Yeah, I saw her," said the cameraman. "I just left her and Lauren a little while ago."

"Where?" asked B.J.

The cameraman pointed. "Up there, where that character wants to build the shrine to Constance."

Chapter 113

Lauren closed in, the syringe in her hand.

"Don't fight me, Eliza," she said. "This is working out better than I could have planned. I didn't know we'd end up here alone together tonight. I'd only brought the syringe with me as a precaution. But now I can use it, then roll you over the cliff. It will be better that way, Eliza. You'll be dead for certain instead of risking the possibility that you'd survive the fall, paralyzed but still alive. You would have hated that."

Eliza tried to stay calm. "But if you inject me with that stuff, an autopsy will show what killed me," she said. "Everyone will know you were up here with me. Everyone will know you are responsible."

Lauren considered Eliza's words. "You're right," she said. "You're absolutely right. I guess we'll just have to take a risk. I'll risk that the fall from a couple hundred feet onto the rocks won't kill you, and you'll risk spending the rest of your life in a wheelchair or worse."

At that, Eliza took her chance and lunged forward. She aimed for Lauren's midsection, hoping to knock her down. As she made contact, the syringe went flying out of Lauren's hand, up into the air, while Lauren stumbled backward.

Eliza cringed, fearful that the needle would land on her. In that instant, Lauren regained her footing and reached out, not wanting Eliza to have the opportunity to get it first, certain she'd be able to catch it. The syringe came down, point first, jabbing Lauren in the palm before bouncing off and tumbling to the ground.

Eliza got up but was pushed down again. Lauren jumped onto her chest. The women wrestled on the grass, rolling over, each time getting closer to the cliff's edge. Lauren smashed her elbow down as hard as she could into Eliza's side, causing her to cry out in pain.

Using all her strength, Eliza brought her knee up, jamming it into Lauren's stomach. Lauren loosened her grasp just enough that Eliza was able to wriggle free. Eliza scrambled to an upright position and began to run. But she was disoriented. Eliza thought she was running toward safety. Instead she was running toward the edge of the cliff.

Lauren struggled to get up and follow, holding her stomach, running clumsily, focused on Eliza and nothing else. Suddenly Eliza stopped and turned to face her attacker. At the last moment, she stepped to the side, dodging Lauren as she lunged at Eliza again. Lauren didn't know that Eliza had realized they were at the cliff's edge until she found herself falling through the air, tumbling over and over again, her body battered by boulders, rocks, and vegetation, on the trip to the ground below.

THURSDAY
MAY 24

Epilogue

G ood morning," Eliza Blake's voice welcomed the television audience. "It's Thursday, May twenty-fourth, and this is *KEY to America,* coming to you this morning from the Cloisters in New York City."

Eliza stood before the camera, still wearing, at Linus's insistence, the chiffon cocktail dress she'd worn the night before.

"It will be like Jackie Kennedy wearing the pink suit with the dried blood on it from Dallas back to Washington," he'd said. "It'll bring the horror home to the audience."

The fact that Lauren Adams, badly injured, had been taken away by ambulance, the fact that the woman Linus supposedly loved would, if she recovered, be tried for three murders, the fact that the cohost of his broadcast was clearly not the idol he'd been building her up to be for the American public— none of that seemed to be terribly important to him as he barked his orders to the *KTA* staff. For Linus the overriding fact was that virtually every television in the country was tuned to *KTA* this morning. Though the sweeps period, when ratings determined advertising rates, had ended just the day before, this was still a rare opportunity. Linus was determined to give the audience one helluva show and, in the process, steal viewers away from the other morning programs, hopefully forever.

Eliza recapped the events of the night before, voicing over the video of where she and Lauren had confronted one another, the future resting place of Constance Young. Eliza narrated the shots taken of the spot where Lauren had tumbled over the cliff—not a sheer drop, and broken by yards of brush and saplings, but brutally punishing just the same—and pictures of the police cars with flashing lights that had swarmed over the Cloisters' grounds.

Knowing that she would definitely be a witness in any future legal proceedings, Eliza was careful about describing what had happened between herself and Lauren. As a journalist she wanted to be truthful and thorough, but as part of the story herself Eliza did not want to say anything that could jeopardize a fair trial.

"KEY News reported yesterday that Ursula Bales, who worked for Constance Young and who was also murdered, had left behind a needlepoint canvas she was working on," said Eliza.

The entire needlecraft appeared on screen, while Eliza read the poem aloud.

Lady of allure,
A lonely shining star,
Determined and so sure,
And worshipped from afar.
Men wooed her as a queen,
Sought after for her charms,
Known only on the screen,
If rarely in her arms.
Left lying in a pool,
Left sinking like a stone,
Ending up so cool,
Dying all alone.
Careful not to tell,
Yet I was there as well.

"Ursula Bales will never be able to testify at any trial, but her testimony, in the form of an acrostic poem, speaks volumes. Take the first letter of each line and read them in sequence—they spell out 'L. Adams Killed CY.' ' "

"Here you go, Kimba, my love."

Boyd put a saucer of fresh milk out for the cat and turned his attention back to the television. He sighed with relief as he listened to Eliza Blake tell the world that he'd been falsely accused.

The telephone rang, and Boyd reached for it, hoping it was his mother. She'd been so worried.

"Hiya, Boyd," said the male voice. "Congratulations, brother."

"Who is this?" asked Boyd.

"It's Jason. Jason Vaughan."

"I don't have anything to say to you. You cost me my job, you know."

"Hold on a minute. I have something that you might be interested in."

"I doubt that," said Boyd.

"Just listen to me. I'm writing a new book about Constance Young's murder, and you were looking like a prime suspect, weren't you? I'd like to give you the chance to tell your side of the story, and I'll certainly make it worth your while."

Boyd didn't skip a beat. "No way. I'm hoping I might still be able to resurrect what's left of my career at KEY News."

At the end of the first half hour, during the break for affiliates to report their local news and traffic conditions, Eliza signaled to a production assistant to bring her a phone.

"Is Janie up yet, Mrs. Garcia?"

Eliza listened to the answer.

"All right," she said. "That's good. Don't wake her. But when she does get up, tell her she doesn't have to go to school this morning. Tell her that Mommy will be coming home as soon as I finish here, and we'll spend the rest of the morning together. She can go in to school after lunch for the afternoon session."

Eliza nodded as she heard the housekeeper's response.

"Yes, Mrs. Garcia. I'm fine. But whatever you do, keep Janie away from the television this morning. I want to explain things to her myself."

As she handed the phone back to the production assistant, Eliza wondered just how she was going to do that.

"I'm not answering that," said Faith aloud to herself. "If one more reporter calls, I'm going to scream."

She watched in resignation as her son picked up the phone anyway.

"Mom!" he called out. "It's a man!"

Faith shook her head and took the receiver from Ben. "Hello?"

"Mrs. Hansen, this is Stuart Whitaker. I heard the news on the television and wanted to call you. This must be so distressing for you. I know *I* was hoping it had been an accident, and I am sure you must have been as well."

"Can you hold a minute, please, Mr. Whitaker?" Faith put her hand over the mouthpiece. "Brendan, you're going to miss the bus. Hurry up."

Faith sat at the kitchen table and uncovered the phone. "My sister is dead, Mr. Whitaker," she said dully. "I guess it doesn't much matter how it happened. But I do want to thank you again for last night. I appreciate that you want to give Constance such a lovely final resting place."

"Well, it is I who need to thank you, Mrs. Hansen, for allowing Constance to spend eternity like the queen she was."

Linus walked over and signaled to Eliza to take off her microphone. She complied.

"I want you to consider coming back to *KTA*," he said.

Eliza marveled at the machinations of the executive producer's mind. Constance Young had been dead less than a week, Lauren Adams had been hauled off just hours before, and already Linus was looking ahead, plotting who would be the best replacement.

Though not surprised, Eliza didn't want to dismiss the offer out of hand. There were lots of reasons that going back to the morning show could be good for her. She would actually be able to be waiting most days when Janie got home after school, have dinner with her daughter, and supervise homework at night. Getting up so painfully early wasn't any fun, but the rewards of having a routine more conducive to motherhood had their appeal.

While she got tremendous satisfaction from anchoring the *Evening Headlines*, and while the position arguably carried more prestige, Eliza had loved her previous stint on *KTA* and the wide range of stories and interviews she'd been able to do. *Evening Headlines* was so grave all the time, while *KEY to America* provided a balance of fun sprinkled among the serious news stories.

"Is that something you would consider?" Linus asked.

"I'll think about it at least," said Eliza. "But even if I decided that I did want to switch, my contract isn't up for a while."

"Look," said Linus, "I'm sure something could be worked out with the powers that be—*if* you decide you actually want to make the change."

"I don't know, Linus. I really like the people I work with on the *Evening Headlines.* They would be tough to leave."

"Well, bring 'em with you," said Linus. "I'll do everything possible to get Range to release the ones you want."

"Starting with Annabelle and B.J.?" asked Eliza.

Linus shrugged. "If that's what you want. I didn't want to fire them anyway. Lauren insisted."

Eliza smiled wryly as she noticed the stage manager gesturing frantically for her to reattach her microphone. "I've known you long enough to know that you don't do anything you don't want to do, Linus."

"To get you, believe me, I'd hire them back."

At the end of the program, Eliza interviewed Dr. Margo Gonzalez about the kind of person who could commit such crimes, speaking in generalities, careful not to mention Lauren by name. When the interview was done, Margo reached over to Eliza.

"Are you all right?" she asked.

"I think so." Eliza nodded. "I just want to go home, hug my child, and take a hot bath."

B.J. stood out of camera range with Annabelle Murphy, who had come up to the Cloisters the minute her husband got home from his night shift at the firehouse. As soon as the program went off the air, they joined Eliza and Margo.

"If only we'd figured things out earlier, Eliza, you would never have had to go through that nightmare with that monster," said Annabelle. "I should have done research on Lauren sooner."

"Well, I certainly should have taken note of the look in Ursula's eyes the first time I saw that video, back on Saturday," said Margo. I should have realized she was scared to death because Constance's killer was right there, interviewing her.

"Yeah, and any six-year-old could have figured out that poem," said B.J. "But I was looking for something much more complicated."

Eliza shook her head. "We were all looking for something more complicated. Don't you dare beat up on yourselves," she said. "We figured this out together. You all are the best, and there's nobody I'd rather have on my team." She glanced around to see where Linus was. Not finding him, she whispered, "Linus just suggested that I come back to *KTA*."

"That man has no shame," said Annabelle. "He's jettisoned Lauren like yesterday's trash."

"Well?" said B.J. "Are you tempted?"

"Maybe," said Eliza. "But if I do decide to go back to *KTA*, I'd want you guys to come with me."

"That would go over real well with Linus," said Annabelle sarcastically.

"He already agreed," Eliza said with a smirk. "So with you two doing the investigative legwork and Margo here to help us understand how the human mind ticks, we should be able to handle anything that comes our way in the early-morning hours."

Annabelle laughed. "Our own little Sunrise Suspense Society."

The blue sedan sped over the George Washington Bridge. Eliza leaned back against the leather seat and closed her eyes. She was dozing when she felt her cell phone vibrate.

"I just heard. Are you all right?"

"Yes, Mack. I'm fine. Really fine."

"God, Eliza. If anything ever happened to you . . . "

"It's over now, Mack, and everything is all right."

"I never liked Lauren, but I can't believe that she killed Constance—and the others," said Mack. "I don't get it."

"She said she killed Constance because she was the competition. That everyone would watch Constance on *Daybreak* and no one would watch her. The other murders were committed to cover the first."

"Sick."

Eliza was tired, and she ached to stop thinking for a while about all the ugliness of the past week. But she didn't want to get off the phone with Mack.

"How's the weather over there?" she asked.

"Glorious," he answered. "Perfect Rome weather."

Eliza looked out the window. The sun was shining, a few wispy clouds punctuating the bright blue sky.

"It's beautiful here, too," she said.

"Great," he said, "because I'm coming back to New York next weekend."